I0779230

JANE DALY

Her Forever Home

Jane Daly

ISBN-13: 978-1-962168-51-9

Chapter 1

Lizzy Greene braked to a stop in front of her new home, silently thanking God and her new landlady, Mrs. Carmichael. After bouncing from a rented room in someone else's house, to run down apartment after apartment, she finally had a real home.

"This is it, Ladybug." Lizzy spoke over her shoulder to her daughter, Abby, sitting in the back.

"It's blue," Abby said, pointing to the front door with a grimace.

Lizzy laughed. "Yes, it is. Deep, indigo blue." Thank goodness old Mrs. Carmichael hadn't gone color crazy like one of her neighbors after her husband died. The house boasted eggplant purple shutters and lilac-colored stucco. Lizzy shuddered at the affront. Lilac and eggplant belonged inside the house, not outside. She started at the juxtaposition of colors, lost in thought at how the deep purple might look as decorative pillows on a soft mauve sofa. Perhaps a splash of pale yellow or even a light shade of orange to break up the purple. She'd have to grab her sketch pad. As soon as she could find it in the unpacked boxes piled inside.

Her thoughts swung to the house with the blue door.

This could be her forever home. After Mrs. Carmichael decided to move in with her son-in-law and daughter in Albany, she'd offered to rent her house to Lizzy at a huge reduction in the going rates.

"Earth to Mom. Can I get out?" Abby asked, reaching for the car door handle. Without waiting for Lizzy's answer, Abby jumped out of their ancient Honda and sprinted along the side of the house toward a swing set in the back yard.

Lizzy climbed out and stretched her tired back. Even with help from church friends, moving had not been an easy task. Grateful the incessant Oregon rain had let up, she leaned against the car, fingering the keys to the house.

"Thank you, Lord," she whispered. Her life was finally going in the right direction.

-*-

Roman didn't believe in love at first sight. Seriously, how could you love someone you didn't know? The whole concept seemed borne from a sappy Hallmark movie, one of which he'd never admit to watching. He was familiar with the concept; boy meets girl, lightning strikes, then circumstances evolve to keep them apart. Finally, they ride into the sunset together while harp music swells.

That isn't how Roman expected it to happen. Love should grow from mutual admiration and respect. Progressing in a logical forward trajectory.

From his vantage point, Roman could see through the yard adjoining his to the street beyond. He watched as four men, three women, two pickup trucks and two sedans pulled up to the house behind his. Since Mr. Carmichael died last year, Mrs. Carmichael struggled to take care of herself. When she broke her hip six weeks ago, her daughter had swept in and moved her to Albany to live with her.

Roman hadn't known the Carmichaels well, despite their adjoining back yards. No fence separated the two properties.

Which one of the people unloading furniture and boxes would be his new neighbor? Would it be the gray-haired matronly looking woman? The middle-aged guy with the paunch? The thirty-something guy in skinny jeans?

Squinting, he recognized a couple of faces from his church. Why hadn't he been asked to help?

Because you never talk to anybody at church, his inner geek said.

I talk to kids, Roman answered.

His inner geek laughed.

A couple of hours later Roman looked up from his laptop on the kitchen table to see a faded red sedan pull up to the Carmichael home.

A tiny girl leaped out of the car and stood hands on her hips. Her dark hair foamed around her head, and she looked every bit like a pixie straight out of a medieval forest.

She glanced around like a princess surveying her realm, then sprinted past the house he'd been watching, and across the expanse of lawn between the two.

Some time ago, he didn't know how long, someone left a metal swing set in his back yard. The pixie ran straight for the swing, plopped onto the splintery seat, and began to pump her legs. Her pink lips pressed together in concentration as she rose higher and higher.

Roman's spirits, which had been feeling gloomy over being left out of the moving party, rose with every pendulum swing.

He slid open the glass door from his dining room-slash-office and stepped onto the concrete slab he called the patio.

"Hello," Roman called.

The girl's face registered shock. She dug her feet in when the swing reached the bottom of the motion. "I'm-I'm sorry. Is this yours?" She thrust out a hand toward the structure.

"Yes, it is. But it's okay. You can use it any time you want." He took a step closer. "My name's Roman."

She jumped off the swing. "I'm Abby."

A dark-haired woman poked her head out of the door of the house behind his. Several things hit Roman at once. One, his new neighbor was beautiful. Two, she was totally out of his league. And three, he had to meet her.

"Abby, get over here!"

"Gotta go," Abby said with a mischievous grin.

Roman waved at the woman. "Hey!" She didn't answer. As soon as Abby disappeared into the house, the woman slid the door shut with a bang and pulled the curtains closed.

Roman looked up at the gathering clouds. "Wow."

Don't even think about it, his inner geek said.

-*-

Lizzy spied Abby talking to a man. On his property. She'd told her daughter a thousand times not to talk to strangers.

"Abby," she yelled. "Come over here." Lizzy hoped her glare would squelch her daughter's natural friendliness and discourage any kind of inappropriate behavior on the part of the neighbor.

Abby skipped across the lawns and scampered into the house. "Sorry, Mom."

"Sorry nothing, young lady. No talking to strangers, remember?"

"His name is Roman, and he's our neighbor. Not a stranger anymore."

Lizzy sighed. Neighbor or not, she wouldn't let her daughter near an unfamiliar man. Too many stories in the news of creeps who couldn't keep their hands off little girls. Lizzy shuddered.

"Come on, Ladybug. Let's get the rest of your stuff unpacked and your bed made."

Later in the evening after a dinner of frozen waffles and orange juice, Lizzy unpacked the final box of kitchen stuff. Thank goodness she didn't have much. Her former kitchen hadn't allowed much in the way of storage. By comparison, this two-bedroom bungalow felt like a mansion.

Lizzy made herself a cup of coffee and carried it to the back patio. The owners of the house had made a comfortable outdoor living space. The patio cover protected the furniture, graciously left behind by Mrs. Carmichael, from sun and rain. Potted plants lined the edges of the concrete pad. Lizzy itched for her sketch book but was too tired to go into the house and search for it. The sweet smell of blooming roses permeated the area. Lizzy imagined capturing the pinks and yellows of the flowers on her ever-present pad of paper.

Her head swept up at the sound of a sliding glass door opening. In the gathering dusk, Lizzy saw the man Abby had been talking to step out of his house.

He was of average height with medium brown hair falling across his forehead, giving him a boyish look. From what she could discern, he was in pretty good physical shape. The sleeves of his casual plaid cotton shirt stretched across tight biceps. Not that she cared.

"Hello, neighbor," he called.

Lizzy considered ignoring him and scuttling back into the house. She was a hot mess, with her hair falling out of the ponytail she'd gathered in the morning. Her tee shirt was dirty, and she'd torn her jeans. Not the fashionable kind of torn.

"Hello," Lizzy answered, without enthusiasm.

Unfortunately, it didn't discourage him. He walked across their two lawns and stood at the edge of her patio.

"I'm Roman."

"I know. My daughter told me."

"Abby." He nodded. "You have a cute daughter."

"Thanks. I'm Lizzy."

So far, on a scale of zero to ten, this

conversation hovered at about a one. But Lizzy was too tired to make nice.

Roman stepped closer and perched on the edge one of the chairs. In the porch light, she could see his eyes were a shade of blue she'd call 'ocean' or 'azure.' Now her fingers really itched for her sketch pad and pencils. She'd love to draw him. Unless he was creepy. Then not.

"Do I have something on my face?" Roman asked.

Lizzy inhaled sharply. She'd been staring. Again. "No, sorry. Sometimes I do that. Stare."

His mouth tilted up. "Okay. Anyway, welcome to the neighborhood. I was sorry to hear Mrs. Carmichael had to leave her home. But I'm glad she found someone to buy it."

Lizzy shook her head and set down her mug of coffee. "I'm not buying. I'm renting. One of my church ladies found out Mrs. Carmichael was moving and talked her into renting to me."

Roman swept his hair out of his face with one hand. It fell back over his forehead. "Church ladies?"

Lizzy felt her face grow hot. "Yeah, that's what I call my two mentors. They're a lot older, and they took me under their wing when I was going through a . . . a difficult time." Like when she was hugely pregnant, broke, and Abby's dad had disappeared.

"They pretty much saved my life." And her soul. Well, not them exactly. But they'd helped point her to Jesus, who *did* save her soul.

Roman nodded, then stood. "Welcome to the

neighborhood. If you need anything, I'm over there." He pointed to his house. "Obviously. Because I came from there." He spun and walked away without another word.

Lizzy covered her mouth to keep from laughing. She had him pegged. Computer nerd. Uncomfortable around the opposite sex. More comfortable with a laptop in front of him.

And no creepy vibe.

Lizzy sighed and sipped her now lukewarm coffee. Things were finally looking up. A real house instead of a rented room or dumpy apartment. Everything Lizzy had ever wanted for her daughter.

Plus, a nice neighbor who was easy on the eyes. Not that she cared.

-*-

Roman muttered to himself from the moment he stepped off the concrete patio and headed toward his house. Could he have sounded any dumber?

"Uh, yeah, I live, like, over there," he said, mentally smacking his forehead. His beautiful neighbor probably thought he was an idiot.

Double duh, Einstein, his inner geek said.

At least he'd learned her name. Lizzy. He rolled it around in his mind. What was it short for? Elizabeth, most likely. Not Beth, not even Liz, but Lizzy. A fun-sounding name. What if her personality matched. He hoped so.

She was gorgeous to boot. Time to get to know her. But how? His fumbling attempt at a smooth introduction was an epic fail.

Quit while you're ahead, loser, his inner geek said. Where was his inner angel when he needed him?

Roman paced the length of his living room along the familiar worn path in the carpet.

"I can do all things through Christ who strengthens me."

"God has not given us a spirit of fear, but of love, power, and a strong mind."

"Be strong in the Lord and the power of his might."

With each turn, he quoted a new Bible verse, repeating them exactly three times. When all three were exhausted, Roman breathed in, counting four counts in and four counts out.

There. He could do this. He could talk to her. With a nod of his head, Roman made himself a cup of gourmet coffee and carried it into the living room. He paused to pet Millie, his calico kitty, stretched out on the sofa.

Later, as he scrolled through the Main, Oregon Community Facebook page, he came across a new announcement:

Main, Oregon announces the First Ever House Lottery! Entrants must have lived in Main for at least six months. Details are as follows:

1. One entry per person

2. $25 per entry

3. Entrants must write a 1,000 - 2,500-word essay on what it means to live in a small town

4. Five finalists will be drawn. Of the five, one lucky winner will be drawn by lottery

5. The winner must live in the house for one year and pay all back property taxes

Roman read and reread the announcement, scrolling down to all the legal jargon in tiny print at the bottom. He pushed the hair off his forehead and opened a new Word document on his laptop. After copying and pasting the information onto a blank page, he printed it.

He'd take it to Lizzy tomorrow. She might love the opportunity to own her own home instead of renting Mrs. Carmichael's little two-bedroom bungalow.

-*-

Thank goodness for the church ladies. If they hadn't helped unpack Abby's clothes yesterday, Lizzy never would have gotten her to school on time. As it was, Lizzy pulled into the parking lot of the drugstore where she worked with exactly ninety seconds to spare.

No fault but her own for lingering over a second cup of coffee while staring out her kitchen window at her neighbor, Roman's house. Something stirred inside her she'd locked away since Abby's birth. Probably even before, when she and Dylan James had hung out in high school before he took off when he found out she was pregnant. Lizzy still carried the weight of once considering terminating the pregnancy. Her mind knew God had forgiven her, but sometimes her heart condemned. When she'd decided to trust Jesus with her life, Lizzy accepted the consequences of her sin and decided to carry Abby to full term. As difficult as it was being a single mom, Abby was the light of her life.

After Abby was born and Lizzy was forced to

grow up at seventeen, she vowed to do everything in her power to give Abby the mothering she'd not had. And to atone for even considering having an abortion.

Since then, Lizzy hadn't even looked at a man as a potential friend. It could too easily lead down a path she didn't want to travel again. She'd been on a couple of dates, usually at the urging of her friend Simone. Never a second date. No one wanted a woman with the baggage of a small child.

Putting Roman out of her mind, Lizzy rushed into the drug store while shrugging into her work smock.

"Good morning, Boss," she called out to Josiah.

Josiah frowned and tapped his watch. "You're late."

Lizzy scurried into the break room to log into the time clock. "Not yet," she said with a cheeky grin.

"You need better time management."

"You say the same thing every day," Lizzy said.

"Because every day you're late."

"Am not."

One of the other employees was already at the computer. Lizzy tapped her foot impatiently as Ada took her time logging in.

"Do you need some help? Looks like you're having some difficulty."

Ada turned, her wrinkled face filled with concern. "These computer thingies hate me. Why can't we go back to the regular time clock?"

Lizzy had guessed Ada's age to be around seventy, but she couldn't be sure. "Let me see," she said. A few keystrokes later, Ada was logged in and Lizzy was too. Josiah was right. Now she *was* late.

Lizzy returned to the break room for her lunch hour. She sank onto one of the hard plastic chairs with a groan. Slipping her feet out of hot athletic shoes, she pulled out her phone and sent a quick text to her best friend, Simone.

Lizzy: **Thanks for your help yesterday**
Simone: **Anything for you, girlfriend**
Lizzy: **I met the neighbor**
Simone: **Man, woman, child, or ???**
Lizzy: **:-) Man**
Simone: **Cute?**
Lizzy: **Maybe**

That would drive Simone crazy. Lizzy smiled, waiting for the little bubbles to turn into Simone's text.

Simone: **When do we order wedding invitations?**

This was followed by several hearts and smileys.

Lizzy: **Not that cute. Kind of a geek**
Simone: **They make the best husbands. Grateful for any woman's attention**

Lizzy shook her head. Simone was hilarious.

Lizzy: **Just because you're in a committed relationship doesn't mean the entire world should be too**
Simone: **(shrugging emoji)**

Lizzy ate her peanut butter and jelly sandwich,

scrolled through Instagram and Twitter, then went back to work.

Later in the evening after a dinner of tomato soup and grilled cheese sandwiches, a knock sounded on the back sliding glass door.

Abby jumped up off the couch and dashed through the kitchen. "Mom, it's Roman. You know, from the house behind us. Can I let him in?"

Lizzy did a quick sweep of her hair, tightening the ponytail which had gradually loosened throughout the day. Too late to change out of the tomato soup-stained tee. "Okay."

Lizzy stood from where she was seated on the couch and took a few steps into the kitchen. Abby opened the door and moved aside for Roman to enter. He glanced inside, eyeing her up and down before coming in. Lizzy put a hand over the soup stain.

"Hi. I hope you don't mind, but I printed something out for you."

"What is it?" Abby asked. "Can I see?" She grabbed Roman's arm and pulled it down to her eye level. "It's just words," she said with an exaggerated sigh.

Lizzy met Roman's amused eyes and smiled. He glanced away.

She motioned him in. "Come on in. Want some coffee?"

Roman's face lit up. Now Lizzy could see him in the light, his eyes appeared robin's egg blue. She'd bet they changed with the color of the shirt he wore, which today was a light blue polo. Interesting.

As Lizzy filled the coffee maker, Roman took a seat at the table. "I don't know if you're on Facebook, but I found something you might be interested in."

Lizzy reached into the cupboard and pulled out a package of generic Oreos. She couldn't afford the name brand, and these were almost as good. If she slid them onto a plate, Roman wouldn't notice they weren't the real thing.

"I'm not on Facebook much," Lizzy said, setting the plate in front of him. "I'm more of an Instagram and Twitter kind of girl." She rested her hip against the counter, waiting for the coffee to finish brewing.

"Thanks," Roman said, biting into a cookie. He crunched for a moment, then said, "I printed this out. It's a house lottery."

Lizzy poured two cups of coffee and set one down next to the cookies. "Do you take anything in your coffee?"

Roman shook his head. "Black."

"Same. What's this house lottery thing?" Lizzy asked, sitting across the table.

"Here, take a look." Roman slid the paper to her. "The City of Main is having a lottery to give away the house next to yours. The one up the little rise."

"Seriously?" Lizzy perused the information while sipping her hot brew.

"It's a community involvement thing. Something to get the city excited." Roman shrugged. "I'm thinking about entering."

Lizzy read the article again. A frisson of hope

blossomed inside before reality smacked her.

"I'd never win anything like that."

Why try? Nothing had gone her way in since, well, forever. Mountains of bad decisions followed by hard consequences. The only good thing lately was getting this little house for such a small amount of rent. Now she'd be able to build up her emergency fund. Buy a new bike for Abby. Save for school. Lizzy envisioned a time where she could study interior design and have a studio.

Roman snapped his fingers, bringing her back to the present. "Where'd you go? You stared off into space."

Lizzy's face grew warm. "Sorry. Sometimes I do that."

"So, you said last night."

Lizzy sprang to her feet. "More coffee?"

Roman held out his cup. "I haven't met anyone else who drinks coffee at night. They say it keeps them awake. Not me, though."

"Me neither. It never has." Lizzy filled their cups and sat down, staring at the paper. Why not enter the contest? What did she have to lose?

Roman's voice interrupted her thoughts. "You're doing it again."

"Sorry. I was thinking about the essay contest. I mean, someone has to win, right?"

Roman nodded. "Right. As my dad would say, 'nothing ventured, nothing broken.'"

Lizzy raised an eyebrow. "Isn't it 'nothing ventured, nothing gained?'"

"Yup. But my dad likes to change things around." He shook his head. "My parents are weird."

Huh. That's where the geek vibe came from. "What do you do for work?"

"Computer security software."

Of course. "Sounds…interesting."

Roman leaned forward. "It is. Really. My whole job is to find holes in companies' security procedures, then write code to strengthen it. You wouldn't believe how vulnerable most companies are to hackers."

He talked for a few more minutes, but Lizzy couldn't concentrate on his words. Instead, she watched his face become animated and his eyes shine with excitement. He wasn't your typical Liam Hemsworth. More Ryan Reynolds meets Matt Damon meets the geek from Scooby-Doo.

"What do you do for work, Lizzy?"

"Huh?" She'd done it again. "Oh, I work for the drug store. You know, The Pill Shoppe." She shrugged. Hard to get excited over a clerk's job paying barely over minimum wage.

Roman bit into another cookie. "These are good. Thanks for sharing. I never buy junk food."

"Oh, I'm sorry. Should I put them away, to keep you from being tempted?" Lizzy half-rose from her seat.

"No, don't do that. I don't buy them because I'd end up eating them all in one sitting. Sugar is my kryptonite," he said, his tone serious before his mouth widened into a grin.

Lizzy's stomach fluttered a little when he smiled. Then she remembered her vow. No men until Abby was an adult. And perhaps not even then. She would not, repeat, would not go down that road again. If sugar was Roman's kryptonite, Lizzy's was cute guys. It's how she got into trouble the first time. And it would be the last.

Roman drained his cup and stood. Carrying it to the sink, he said, "I should go. I'm sure you're beat after moving yesterday and having to work today."

Lizzy had forgotten about being exhausted. It was a relief to have a normal conversation with another adult. Especially one who had gorgeous blue eyes.

She was doing it again; getting pulled in by blue eyes. She gave herself a stern warning *Stop it!*

"Thanks for bringing over the info on the contest. I'll think about it more when I'm not working. Or unpacking."

Abby skipped into the room. "Hey, you had cookies, and you didn't tell me?" She put her hands on her hips with a defiant look.

"You can have one, Bug. That's it." Lizzy opened the back door to let Roman out.

"Bye, Abby. See you soon," Roman said as he stepped outside. "Thanks for the coffee. And cookies."

Lizzy watched his back as he crossed the yards and headed into his house. Nice guy. Not that it mattered. Not one bit.

While Abby readied herself for bed, Lizzy opened her sketch pad to a new page. As per her habit, she bowed her head and prayed for the Lord to guide her hand as she drew.

Pencil in hand, Lizzy let her mind guide the

strokes. Several minutes later, a picture emerged of a man, hair falling over his brow, with a faraway look in his blue eyes.

Chapter 2

Roman hunched over his laptop, searching for a chink in his client's firewall. It was there, and he'd find it. A yellow pad sat next to the mouse on his right side, covered with bits of code and equations. To the left was a warm half-drunk soda and his cell phone. The client's current software was good, but not great. He was so close he could feel it.

He raised his eyes to stare out the sliding glass door, concentrating on his next move. As he did, the curtains covering Lizzy's slider opened. She stood there for a moment before moving away.

Concentration disrupted, Roman picked up his pen and chewed on the end. What excuse could he use to go over to her house again? A present for Abby? Too obvious. And creepy. A housewarming gift? He made a face. Again, too obvious.

Forget it, his inner geek said. *You're way out of your league.*

Roman reached across the table to stroke Millie's fur.

"Help me out, Millie." Millie yawned, stretched, and settled back down behind his laptop.

What if he took Lizzy some of his premium roasted coffee, the kind he special-ordered because it tasted like honey and molasses. She might appreciate it. Then she could make some the next time he visited instead of the generic stuff she'd served last night. Ugh. He was becoming a coffee snob.

You are much more than a coffee snob, his inner geek said.

Roman stood and stretched, telling his inner geek to pound sand. Sitting at the kitchen table and being able to see outside was better than his ergonomically arranged office. But his neck and back felt the brunt of the hard wooden chair.

Moving into the kitchen, he pulled the bag of whole bean coffee from the cupboard over the Breville coffee maker. He'd paid way too much for the machine, but it did make an amazing brew.

Roman measured some beans into the grinder and ground enough coffee for a couple of pots. He pulled open the bottom drawer for a plastic container, then reached for the matching lid, neatly stacked next to it.

The clock on the microwave showed 5:35. He'd wait until six-fifteen before heading to his neighbor's house. With the coffee.

Reality check, his inner geek said. *Why would a beautiful woman like Lizzy be interested in someone like you?*

Lizzy was everything he wasn't. Outgoing, upbeat, and artistic. He'd seen some of her sketches the night before when they'd had coffee. It was open on the table, and he couldn't help but peek.

She had real talent. And the way she'd decorated the house. It was warm and inviting. A far cry from his sterile bachelor pad.

She was also an excellent mother. He could tell by the way she looked at her daughter, Lizzy loved Abby with every fiber of her being. Seeing them together evoked feelings he thought he'd buried along with the past broken dreams. Feelings of wanting to get married, have kids, live happily ever after. Hallmark movie stuff. A sliver of longing slid between his ribs.

Could he pursue a relationship with Lizzy, beginning with friendship?

His inner geek guffawed.

Roman sighed. At least he could be a good neighbor and take some coffee as a welcome gift. Then retreat to his man-cave and forget all about the brown-eyed beauty and her pixie little girl.

In the meantime, there were forty minutes to fill until he'd allow himself to go over to her house. First, a clean shirt. Tee or button-up? Roman chewed on his lips, deciding. Tee shirt.

Then a quick swipe of the toothbrush. Aftershave? No, better not. A little hair product to keep the too-long strands from falling over his eyes.

Roman headed to the living room and sank onto the sofa, tapping his foot while composing a text to his younger brother. Millie jumped on the sofa next to him, then clambered onto his lap.

Roman: **What are you up to?**

Rory: **Hanging with the old folks. You?**

Roman: **Housewarming gift for my new neighbor.**

Rory: **What kind of gift?**

Roman: **Genuine Guatemala Antigua Gold coffee**

Rory: **She must be special. You never share your coffee**

Roman: **What makes you think it's she?**

Rory: **(smiley face with heart eyes)**

Roman: **TTYL**

Sheesh. Rory was worse than his sisters. Why couldn't a guy be almost thirty and single without constant grief from his family?

What was it about Lizzy that made him think of giving up his singleness? Could he open his heart again after the last time? Shayna had broken his heart into a million shards of glass, then made him walk barefoot over them. Relationships meant risk.

Need some help here, God.

The clock on his phone changed to six-fifteen. He ran his hands through his hair, loosening the strands which always seemed to fall. Once on his feet, he grabbed the plastic container, looked around at his colorless living room, and headed out the door.

"Wish me luck, Millie," he said. Millie yawned in response.

-*-

Once again, Abby beat her to the door. "Abby, you've got to be careful not to open the door for just anybody. We don't know this neighborhood."

Abby spoke over her shoulder as she unlocked the slider. "It's Roman."

Lizzy's heart beat a little faster at the sight of their neighbor filling the doorway. He looked good.

Too good.

"Come on in," Lizzy said, setting the last of the dinner dishes in the drainer. "We just finished eating."

Roman stepped into the kitchen with a smile. "Hi, Lizzy. Hi Abby. How was school?"

Abby shrugged. "All right, I guess."

Roman turned to close the door behind him. "What was the most exciting part of your day?"

Lizzy kept a watchful eye as Roman interacted with her daughter.

Abby put one hand on her hip and rubbed her chin with the other. "Hm. I guess when Micah threw up after lunch."

"What?" Lizzy exclaimed. "You didn't tell me that." How had Roman managed to wiggle the information from Abby? She hadn't mentioned it on the way home. Was Abby so starved for male attention she'd immediately bonded with their neighbor? Once again, Lizzy was filled with self-doubt. Had her decision to avoid men completely robbed Abby of a felt need?

Abby giggled. "It was super gross. He was spinning in circles and him and Mason tried to outdo each other. But Mason didn't barf. Only Micah."

Lizzy sighed. Oh, the drama of fourth grade. She turned her attention to Roman. "What do you have there?" she asked, pointing toward the container he carried.

Roman's cheeks turned slightly pink. "I thought I'd, you know, bring a little housewarming gift." He shrugged and shifted his weight from foot to foot. "It's not much. Some coffee."

Lizzy grinned. Anyone bearing coffee was welcome any time. "Awesome. Let's have some now. If you want to." She tamped down on her eagerness. She wasn't eager to share a cup of coffee with him. Not really.

Sure, tell yourself that. When was the last time she'd sat and had a normal conversation with someone of the opposite sex? Before last night, not often. Her boss, Josiah, didn't count.

"Okay," Roman replied. His Adam's apple bobbed up and down as he swallowed. "You don't have to use much per cup. It's pretty strong."

"Thanks for the warning."

Roman thrust the container toward her. Lizzy set about filling the pot. "Have a seat in the living room. Let's drink it out there."

Abby led Roman into the next room, chattering like a magpie about her class, after-school daycare activities, and her favorite Minecraft game. Roman seemed interested and continued to ask questions to engage her. Lizzy's heart warmed to him. He had a way with kids most men didn't.

While the coffee brewed, Lizzy slipped behind the sofa where Roman and Abby chatted and tiptoed to the bathroom. She cringed at her reflection. Loose hairs sprang from the scrunchie, and a spot of spaghetti sauce dotted her cheek. A quick swipe of a hairbrush and a washcloth to her face and she was presentable. Grabbing a tube of pink lip gloss, she twirled it between her fingers, undecided. Shrugging, she swiped it across her lips.

"I think the coffee's ready," Lizzy said,

passing through the living room again.

"Need any help?" Roman asked, starting to rise.

"No, I've got it."

Lizzy filled two mugs and sniffed appreciatively. "I hope this tastes as good as it smells," she said, handing one to Roman.

"You won't be disappointed."

Lizzy watched Roman's face become animated as he extolled the virtues of the brew. How could a person be awkward in normal conversation, yet talk about the growing region of coffee beans with ease?

Abby interrupted her thoughts. "Mom, can I use your iPad?"

"Did you do your homework?"

"Um," Abby tilted her head down to hide behind her hair. "Almost finished."

Lizzy tried to look stern. "Homework first, then iPad." Abby's shoulders slumped as she shuffled to her bedroom. "And show me your work when you're done."

Lizzy turned back to Roman. "Sorry."

"Nothing to be sorry about. Parenting is difficult."

Lizzy rolled her eyes. "You have no idea."

"I do have a slight idea. I've watched my sisters with their girls. It's a tough job. But important."

They sipped for a moment in silence. "This coffee is amazing," Lizzy said. "A girl could get spoiled."

A few minutes later, the doorbell rang. Lizzy

jumped up to answer it.

"Simone! Come on in."

Simone and her boyfriend, Adam, swept into the room. "Oh, sorry. Didn't know you had company," Simone said, eyeing Roman with a sly grin.

Lizzy closed the door behind them. "Simone, this is my neighbor, Roman. Roman, this is my best friend, Simone, and her boyfriend, Adam."

Simone held both hands behind her back as her grin spread from ear to ear. "Adam is no longer my boyfriend."

Lizzy raised her eyes. "What?"

Simone swept her left hand out and waggled her fingers. The diamond on her ring finger sparkled in the lamplight.

Lizzy squealed. "You're engaged! Awesome."

Abby ran from the bedroom. "What's going on?"

"Simone and Adam are engaged," Lizzy told her.

"Congratulations," Roman said, reaching out to shake Adam's hand.

"Let me see the ring," Abby asked, pulling Simone's hand down to eye level. "Wow. It's beautiful."

Lizzy and Abby admired the ring, then grabbed Simone in a group hug. A tiny spark of jealousy tickled Lizzy's chest. Would she still be single when Abby left home for college?

Yes, she'd told herself to stay away from men. Yes, she'd vowed to stay single until Abby was older. Still there bloomed a tiny spark of envy for her best friend's happiness.

Lizzy pulled away and took another moment to admire Simone's ring. The diamond was cut in an unusual almost triangular shape, set in a wide frame of yellow gold. Clean, yet dramatic.

"Gorgeous," Lizzy breathed.

Simone sighed as she looked up at her fiancé. "Adam has great instincts. I couldn't have picked out anything as fine."

Adam brushed a strand of hair out of Simone's face. "Something almost as unique as my beautiful bride-to-be."

Lizzy pressed her lips together as tears filled her eyes. Rabid jealousy and ecstatic joy for her friend fought for dominance in Lizzy's heart.

Later, after everyone had gone and Abby was asleep, Lizzy sipped lukewarm leftover coffee. What a difference between this and the bulk coffee she bought on sale at the grocery store. It tasted expensive. Not something she'd ever be able to purchase on her limited income. Yup, a girl could get spoiled drinking this.

Perhaps it was possible to be friends with her geeky neighbor. Just friends. Nothing more. The road to romance was a dead end with a huge "Road Closed" sign. And a chain-link fence covered with razor wire.

Meanwhile, she'd enjoy making this snug little house a home for her and Abby. Unless she entered the house lottery offered by the city. And won. Wouldn't it be something?

Lizzy grabbed her sketch pad and started to draw.

-*-

"A girl could get spoiled," Lizzy had said.

I'd like to be able to spoil you.

Where did that thought come from? Not from his inner geek.

Roman looked around his sterile place remembering the warmth of Lizzy's small living room. Splashes of color brightened what would have been a dark room. Lizzy had made Mrs. Carmichael's house her own. What a huge difference from his place.

What would it be like to have a woman's touch in his house, his kitchen, his life? Why was he suddenly thinking about it? Sure, his family would love to see him find someone and settle down.

It had everything to do with the beautiful and kind woman living near him. He had to get to know her better. He'd seen an emotion flash across Lizzy's face when Simone presented her engagement ring. Looked a little like jealousy. Roman understood the feeling. His then-best friend had snatched Shayna out from under his nose. After two years, the ache resurfaced from time to time. He should have known, should have seen the signs he and Shayna were drifting apart.

Shayna thought he was too rigid, too logical. So what he hated clutter. So what his cabinets were neatly arranged and his spices alphabetized. Did it make him rigid?

Uh, yeah, his inner geek said.

Roman couldn't come up with a response.

The next day, Roman struggled to put his thoughts into words for the house lottery contest.

Not that it mattered. He had zero chance of winning. His strength was in the language of computer code.

Lizzy on the other hand, oozed creativity. She'd be a finalist for sure. Glad they'd exchanged phone numbers 'in case of an emergency.' He sent a quick text.

Roman: **Working on my essay. You?**
Lizzy: **Not even. Can't think of what to say**
Roman: **Try to draw it first, then write**
Lizzy: **Great idea!**
This was followed by several smileys.

Roman sat back with a satisfied sigh while mentally patting himself on the back. Time to move from neighbor/acquaintance to friend zone.

Or not, his inner geek said.

He told his inner geek to be quiet.

Two days later, his hopes were answered, though not in the way Roman expected. His phone rang early Saturday morning. He groped for the annoying instrument and glanced at the screen. Lizzy's number.

"Good morning," Roman answered with a sleepy groan.

"Roman, good I'm glad you're awake. You are awake, aren't you?" Lizzy sounded rushed, breathless.

He debated a sarcastic, 'I am now,' but decided on the simplest answer.

"I'm up."

"I have a huge favor to ask. You can say no."

Roman's brow furrowed. "Ask. If I can do it, I will." Without that first burst of caffeine, his thoughts scrambled for footing.

"My babysitter bailed on me, and I have to work." Her voice came out in a rush. "Can you watch Abby for a couple of hours until my backup is available?"

Roman walked to the window and glanced out. Rain slashed at the window, each droplet like a pebble on a tin roof. The storm howled, a high-pitched shriek, punctuated by a crack of thunder.

Nobody should have to go out in weather like this. "Sure. Do you need me to take her to your backup sitter?"

"I can run home on my break and get her. My boss is okay with that."

Roman considered what was on his mental list of things to do and what could be postponed while he watched Abby.

Lizzy's voice broke the lengthening silence. "You know what? Never mind. I'll figure something out."

His pulse quickened. "No, of course, I can watch her." This was a perfect opportunity to advance from neighbor to friend.

See? Roman said to his inner geek. *I'm not rigid.*

"You sure?" Lizzy asked.

"I'm sure."

Lizzy exhaled into the phone. "Thank you. I'll bundle her up and bring her a few minutes before nine."

Roman disconnected and set the phone on the table, breathing a sigh of relief. He'd almost blown it.

Roman thought back to the day she'd moved in, and he'd worked up the courage to walk over and introduce himself. Not his best moment. But at least he'd conquered his nervousness and went for it.

What would it be like to get married and start a family?

Slow down, bubba, his inner geek said. *Remember the last time.*

The last time he'd been down that road with a woman, he'd crashed and burned. Getting dumped six months after he was engaged wasn't something he looked forward to again.

With a sigh, Roman checked his watch. He had exactly thirty-two minutes to shower, shave, and get dressed before Lizzy showed up at his back door.

Later, as he and Abby colored with the fine-tipped felt pens she'd brought, Roman took a breath to overcome his natural reticence. Learning more about Lizzy's private life had almost become an obsession.

Sounds creepy, his inner geek said.

Yeah, it kinda did.

"Where did you live before?" he asked, as they filled in the tiny details of the coloring book.

Abby scrunched her face in concentration on the task at hand. "We lived in the mouse house."

Roman scratched his head. "Mouse house?" Like Disneyland? That couldn't be right.

"That's what my mom called it. The apartment was next to a vacant lot. Mice used to get in." Abby capped the pen she'd been using. "You should have seen my mom. This one time she was standing on the couch with a broom, trying to hit one." Abby covered her mouth and giggled.

Roman smiled. He could imagine the scene. Lizzy, terrified yet determined to rid her space of a rodent.

"Is Simone your mom's best friend?"

Abby nodded. "They've known each other since school."

Roman chewed his lips, trying to determine how to ask his next question. "Does your mom have any male friends?"

"You mean like a boyfriend?" Abby's brown eyes gazed up at his. Total innocence.

"Well, yes." Subtle, Roman. Even his inner geek was shocked into silence.

Abby giggled again. "No. My mom says boys are yucky. I'm not allowed to date until I'm twenty."

"Really?" Roman raised an eyebrow in mock protest.

"Guess what?" Abby asked, taking the conversation in a different direction. "My birthday is in two weeks. "I'm turning ten."

"No way! Not ten."

Abby nodded, her curls bouncing around her head. "Yup. And my mom is going to tell me about my dad."

That was something he hadn't considered. That Abby had a dad somewhere and Lizzy had a, what, a boyfriend, ex-husband, or something. "What about your dad?"

Abby set down her pen and folded her hands

on the table. "Well, my mom said on my tenth birthday she would tell me about my dad. Like his name and where she met him and stuff."

Roman let her words roll over him. Imagine growing up and not knowing who your father was. His dad had always been there for him, going to his Little League games, helping with Science Fair projects, letting him tear apart their computer. And try to rebuild it. Good times.

What kind of history did Lizzy have that she couldn't talk about Abby's father until now? Roman's mind traveled down a dark path before he brought it back to the present.

"What will you do with the information, once your mom tells you?" Roman picked up a red felt tip and concentrated on the design.

"I dunno."

The innocence of kids. Roman hoped there wasn't a bunch of drama involved with Abby's dad. He'd like to get to know Lizzy better without having to fight with some guy who may want to lay a claim from Lizzy's past.

Roman glanced up to see Lizzy striding through the rain across their two yards.

"Abby let's clean up. Your mom's here."

"Aw, can't I stay with you while she's at work?"

Roman smiled. "I wish you could. But I have tons to do."

Abby's shoulders slumped. "That stinks."

"Hey," Roman replied. "Maybe you can come over next week and we can finish these pages then?" He doubted they'd finish the intricate design in the adult coloring book he'd bought, but perhaps it would mollify her.

"Okay," Abby answered without enthusiasm. "I wanted to finish it today." She sniffled loudly and reached for a tissue.

Lizzy poked her head in the back door. "Time to go, Ladybug." To Roman, she said, "I hope she wasn't any trouble."

"Not at all."

The rain had lessened to a drizzle. "Looks like you and Abby won't get too wet."

Lizzy felt Abby's forehead. "She woke up with the sniffles. I hope you don't catch anything."

"I'll be fine," Roman said. "I never get sick."

Lizzy looked up at him. "She doesn't feel hot. Sometimes I feel like I'm the worst mom ever. I should be home, feeding her chicken noodle soup, not heading back to work."

Roman laid a tentative hand on Lizzy's arm. "You're a great mom. And Abby's fine. Aside from the sniffles, she's been chatting up a storm."

Lizzy's eyes filled with tears. "Thank you." She used the sleeve of her hoodie to wipe her face. "And thanks for watching her."

"Anytime. How are you coming with your essay?"

"Ugh. Slow."

Roman took a breath and blurted, "We could work on them together."

"That'd be great," Lizzy exclaimed. "Tonight?"

Roman experienced a moment of panic. What had he done? "Uh, yeah. Sure."

"I'll text you when I get home from work."

Roman spoke around his suddenly dry tongue. "I'll, uh, bring a pizza."

"Awesome. Abby and I love pizza."

"Pepperoni," Abby chimed in.

Lizzy zipped up her daughter's coat. "I have to run. C'mon Bug, let's go."

Lizzy checked to be sure she'd gathered up all Abby's things, then leaned in to give Roman a quick hug. "Thanks again for watching her."

Roman nodded, his mouth unable to form words. Feeling Lizzy close to him affected him in a way he hadn't expected. As soon as she'd gone, he sank onto the sofa with a whoosh and rubbed his face.

A little help here, Lord? Roman pulled open a leather-bound Bible that had seen better days. His parents had given it to him when he'd first committed himself to Christ. Although Roman usually used the Bible App for iPhone, sometimes it helped to hold the actual book. The pages fluttered as his fingers ruffled the edges. The Bible fell open to Proverbs. Roman began to read.

"Death and life are in the power or the tongue, and those who love it will eat its fruit."

Okay, Lord. I know my words have power. What are you trying to say? After a moment, Roman continued to read. Then stopped.

A man who finds a wife finds a good thing and obtains favor from the lord.

Wow. Did God speak to him? Goosebumps rose on Roman's arms. Was God telling him Lizzy would be his wife?

His inner geek guffawed.

Chapter 3

Lizzy breezed through the hours at work. There'd been no call from the back-up sitter about Abby's sniffles progressing to something more. What a relief. Pizza and an evening of adult conversation sounded heavenly, even if she and Roman were technically competing for the same prize.

Lizzy knew what she wanted to say in her essay, but the words wouldn't translate from the pictures in her mind, through her fingertips to the paper. English hadn't been her best subject in school. Neither was Math. The only thing she'd excelled in was Art class.

Someday she'd study interior design and finally put her gift to use. The drug store job supported her and Abby, but it required zero creativity. At least now she had an actual house, some of the pent-up desire could be expressed. Mrs. Carmichael had given her the go-ahead to draw a mural on a wall in Abby's bedroom. Lizzy had been working on designing a jungle scene, complete with a giraffe peeking over green vines and a lion crouching on a low tree limb. In two or three months, she'd have saved enough to buy the paint.

Or maybe, just maybe, she'd win the house lottery and have no rent, which each month seemed to come due way too quickly. Lizzy imagined what she could do with several hundred dollars extra every month. Design school, a more reliable car, braces for Abby. Giving her church ladies some money to supplement their limited income. They'd been super generous when Abby was a baby, letting her live with them rent-free. Helping her learn to be a mom at seventeen. Coaching her through the GED ·exam.

Lizzy had a dream, and it didn't involve working for minimum wage as a clerk for the rest of her life. Until the dream became a reality, she'd give Abby the stable home Lizzy herself had been denied.

"How are you feeling, Ladybug?" Lizzy asked in the car on the way home from the babysitter.

Abby sniffled loudly from the back seat. "Okay. Are we still going to have pizza tonight?"

"I sure hope so." But were they? Did Roman mean it when he'd said they could work together? Lizzy could handle the disappointment and letdown if he'd forgotten, but Abby might not.

"You're gonna text him, right Mom?"

"As soon as we get home." Lizzy pulled up to the front of the house and parked. It had started to drizzle again, and the rain quickly covered the windshield. The last thing she needed was for Abby to get a worse cold. "Put up your hood before you get out of the car."

They bundled up and dashed through the gathering storm to the door. Lizzy closed and locked the door, then turned on the heat. "Go get your jammies on, Bug."

"But it's not time for bed," Abby protested.

Lizzy hung their coats on the hooks behind the door. "I know. But your clothes are wet, and your pajamas will be nice and dry. And warm."

Abby headed into her bedroom, calling over her shoulder, "Don't forget to text Roman."

Lizzy had no intention of sending him a text until she'd had time to change her clothes and do something with the mess she called hair.

Twenty minutes later, she felt sufficiently prepped to see a person of the opposite sex.

Lizzy: **We're home. Did you still want to work on the essays?**

Should she have mentioned the pizza? She chewed on her lip while waiting for his response. The little dots indicated he was typing.

Roman: **Yes**.

Yes? That was it? Lizzy let out a groan.

Lizzy: **We haven't had dinner. Have you?**

Roman: **I said I'd bring pizza. Be there in two minutes.**

Lizzy breathed out a sigh. "Abby, wash up. Pizza will be here in two minutes."

She heard the water run in the bathroom. A moment later, Abby trudged into the kitchen in her jungle print pajamas and thick socks. Lizzy's heart swelled with so much love for her little girl she thought it might burst. How God had blessed her with such a beautiful child, she didn't know. The circumstances of her conception could have been better, but Lizzy was reminded of the verse in Romans, *"In all things, God works for the good of those who love him and are called according to His purpose."*

Even though she hadn't had a relationship with God at the time, He'd become real to her through the miracle of Abby's birth and the gentle nudging of her best friend, Simone. On the days when she was overwhelmed by being a single parent, and money seemed to leak out of her bank account, Lizzy knew God would always be there for her. Unlike her dad, who left when she was a baby, and her mom who'd turned to alcohol to cope.

Getting pregnant at sixteen hadn't been part of her plan. At that age, her only interests were getting high, smoking, and finding unique ways to miss class. Having a baby at seventeen was an epic jolt into adulthood.

A light knock on the sliding glass door interrupted her thoughts.

Lizzy grinned at Abby's dash for the door. "Pizza time!"

Abby let Roman in, and the house immediately filled with the aroma of herbs, spices, and marinara sauce. Lizzy inhaled with satisfaction.

Abby was already clawing at Roman's arm. "What kind did you get?"

Roman set the box on the table and opened the top with a flourish. "Half pepperoni for the child, and half combo for the adults."

Lizzy grabbed some plates and paper towels and plopped them on the table. "Only half?" she teased.

Roman's face remained serious. "Did I do okay? I thought—"

"Stop worrying. I was kidding. This is awesome."

They sat and Abby reached for a slice.

"Uh, uh," Lizzy warned. "Grace first."

Abby held out her hands. Lizzy grasped one and Roman held the other. He reached across and took Lizzy's hand in his larger one. A frisson of. . . something teased up her arm and settled in her chest. Was it nerves? Or something less frightening. The last time a man had touched her, other than hugs from older men at the church, had been Abby's dad, Dylan, over ten years ago.

Before she had time to unpack the feeling, Abby had rushed through prayer and said, "Amen." She was the first to dig into the pizza.

After Abby snagged a piece, Roman pushed the box toward Lizzy. "You first."

Lizzy pursed her lips, contemplating. Pepperoni or combo? No way Abby would eat more than two pieces of the pepperoni side. Roman was more than capable of consuming all the combo. But he'd said half for Abby and half for him and her.

Why was she over-thinking this? Because it was different sitting here sharing a casual dinner with him than with Simone. This felt a little like a date.

-*-

Lizzy was taking way too long to grab a piece of pizza. Should he have asked what kind she liked before ordering? Roman's head swam with scenarios; one where he'd blown it; another where she was one of those women who wouldn't eat in front of a guy; still another where Lizzy pretended to like his choices, while silently condemning him for being obtuse.

Good job, loser, his inner geek said.

"Is everything okay?" he asked, rubbing his sweaty hands down the legs of his jeans.

Lizzy turned her head toward him with a confused look in her brown eyes.

"Yeah. Fine."

Uh oh. When a woman said 'fine' she meant anything but. Epic fail on the pizza choice.

"I can order something else," he offered.

"No, this is fine. I can't decide which to take."

"Have one of each." Obvious solution. Roman shook his head. He'd never understand women.

Lizzy smiled and his heart sped up a beat. Roman held her gaze until Lizzy broke it by reaching into the pizza box.

"Great idea." She plopped a slice of each onto her plate and dug into the one covered in greasy pepperoni.

"Hey. Roman said 'Pepperoni for the kid.'" Abby glared at her mom.

"Nice try, Bug. You'll never be able to eat half a pizza. Besides, sharing is caring."

Abby rolled her eyes and Roman laughed. This reminded him of the bantering around the table at his family dinners. His loud, crazy, Italian family. It had been too long since they'd all been together.

Note to self: Call Rory and check on the fam.

"You know," Lizzy said around a mouth of

pizza, "I checked on you."

Roman froze. "What do you mean?" This could be bad. Why would she check on him? Like, stalk him?

Lizzy smiled at his discomfort. "Before I called to see if you could watch Abby today, I asked my church ladies if they knew you."

He hadn't seen that coming. "What did they say?" He hoped his reputation as one of the Sunday School teachers was good.

Lizzy had eaten all but the crust. She set it on the plate. "They said you were fairly new at the church, but you'd already volunteered in Children's Church." She giggled. "They said you did a mean impersonation of Moses. The kindergartners were scared out of their wits."

Roman raised himself up to full height. "Let my people go!" he commanded in a deep voice.

Abby laughed so hard she almost fell out of her chair. "Do it again!" she said with a giggle.

"Once is enough, Ladybug," Lizzy said.

"You decided I was safe to leave your daughter with?" Roman held his breath, waiting for Lizzy's answer.

Lizzy chewed a piece of crust with a thoughtful look. "I don't leave Abby with many people. She's the only thing I have, and I have to protect her." She looked across the table at him. "I hope you understand. It's not you, it's anyone."

Roman nodded, honored she'd allowed him to watch her daughter.

"Besides," Lizzy continued. "I prayed for a while before calling you."

Roman shifted on the chair. "I'm glad God said I was okay." He smiled.

Abby finished the last bite of her second piece of pizza and sat back in her chair with a sigh. "My mom prays a lot. I mean, *a. lot.*"

Lizzy's skin darkened with a blush. "It's important to me," she mumbled.

Warmth spread through Roman's chest, making his arms tingle. A woman who shared his faith. As if by its own accord, his hand reached out and touched Lizzy's. "It's important to me, too."

-*-

Lizzy stared at Roman's hand, resting lightly on hers. That feeling was back. This time she recognized it as something comforting.

Lizzy pulled her hand away. This was not the time to start . . . Whatever this was. Abby was her top and only priority. When Abby was older, Lizzy might date. But not now. Better to turn the conversation around.

"Have you written anything on your essay?"

Roman reached for another slice of combo pizza. "A bit. My writing skills are sorely lacking."

Lizzy smiled inwardly. Roman talked like someone much older than he was.

"Same. I haven't written anything except a thank you note since high school."

"When did you graduate?"

Lizzy's stomach tightened. Roman probably had a master's degree in computer programming or something. Once she mentioned her lack of graduation status, he'd probably drop his pizza and run back to his house.

So what? She'd told herself not to get involved. Who cared what he thought?

"I, um, didn't graduate." Lizzy let her hair fall over her face while she picked at a few pieces of onion abandoned on the plate. "I dropped out before Abby was born. I got my GED when she was five."

Roman was silent for a beat. "Good for you. Lots of people would have given up at that point. It must have been difficult for you."

Lizzy's eyes filled with tears. Not the response she expected. She sniffed. "You have no idea."

Abby's voice interrupted the silence following. "Mom, can I watch your iPad in bed?"

"Brush your teeth first."

Abby slipped off the chair and raced to the bathroom. Lizzy heard water running.

Lizzy stood and gathered hers and Abby's plates. "Are you finished?"

Roman eyed the last piece of pepperoni in the box. "I shouldn't, but I'm going to." He snagged the slice then handed Lizzy the empty box.

Lizzy straightened up the kitchen, then wiped down the table. "Let me get a pad of paper and we can get started."

"I'm going to run home and get my laptop," Roman said, standing to his feet.

While he was gone, Lizzy checked on Abby, who was fast asleep, iPad still clutched in her hands. Lizzy gently pulled it away and kissed her daughter on the forehead. "Good night, Bug."

Roman returned and opened his laptop on the kitchen table. Lizzy dropped a lined yellow notepad on the table, followed by a mechanical pencil.

"Here's what I have so far," Lizzy said, pushing the pad in Roman's direction.

"Why I like living in a small town," Roman read. "By Elizabeth Greene." He shot a grin in her direction. "Great start."

Lizzy shrugged, pulling the pad back in front of her. "Not my best work," she said with a grin.

For the next thirty minutes, they bounced ideas off each other until the subjects became more and more outlandish.

"I haven't laughed this hard in a long time," Lizzy said, breathless.

"Me neither. But now we know how *not* to win this contest."

Lizzy tapped her pencil against her cheek. "You know we're competing against each other, right?"

Before he could answer, Lizzy's phone beeped with an incoming text.

Simone: **Finished my essay for the contest.**

This was followed by several emojis. Hm. Simone was entering the contest too? What if she won and Lizzy didn't? Jealousy reared its ugly head once again.

Before she could dwell on the possibility, Lizzy answered the text.

Lizzy: **Good for you. I'm working on mine.**

She hesitated, then added: **With my neighbor, Roman**

Little dots appeared, indicating Simone was typing an answer.

Simone: **What?!**

More emojis, mostly hearts and flowers.

Lizzy turned the phone over and set it on the table out of Roman's view.

"Sorry. That was Simone. She's entering the contest too."

"And why not?" Roman said. "Someone has to win."

"I guess." Lizzy rested her chin in her hand.

Roman closed his laptop and peered over at her. Lizzy watched his blue eyes darken. "You have as much of a chance as anyone," he assured her. He stood and picked up his laptop. "Besides, God is in control."

With a rueful grin, Lizzy said, "Right."

She watched him head out the door. Why did he have to be so nice? Her heart softened, remembering how good he was with Abby. Why couldn't he have come along in a few years, when she might be ready to have a relationship? Right now, Abby had to be her top priority.

"Right, Lord," she said aloud, looking at the ceiling.

-*-

Roman glanced at the clock on the microwave as he entered the back door. He'd been at Lizzy's house for over three hours. How was it even possible? It had been the most comfortable he'd been around a woman since, well, Shayna.

He set his computer on the kitchen table, then plopped onto the sofa to send his younger brother a text.

Roman: **What's up?**

Rory: **Hey, old man. Isn't this past your**

bedtime?

Roman: **Not true. How's the fam?**

Instead of answering, his phone rang, and his brother's familiar face filled the screen.

"Hey," Roman answered.

"Why are you texting me at nine-thirty at night to ask about the family?"

Roman couldn't answer. He'd never been good at expressing his feelings. How to explain the high he was on simply by spending the evening with his neighbor?

"I'm . . ." Roman's words faltered.

"You're what?"

Roman could hear his brother's bed squeak as he shifted.

"Are you in trouble?" Rory asked.

"No! Nothing like that."

"Am I going to have to play twenty questions with you? Come on, Ro, spit it out."

Where to begin. Roman remembered the Bible verse he'd read the other day about finding a wife. Then the spark of electricity he'd felt when he'd taken Lizzy's hand when they'd said grace. The way he was able to let down and laugh with her. Lizzy's smile shining out of her brown eyes. Her . . .

"Ro? You still there? You're starting to scare me."

"Yeah. I, well, there's this neighbor-"

"Male or female?"

"Female."

"Young or old?"

Roman thought about Abby and smiled.

"Young."

"The one you took your carefully guarded, top-secret, uber-expensive coffee to?

Roman felt his face grow hot. "Yes."

"Ah-ha! I knew it. You're twitter pated."

"Twitter pated?" Roman pushed his hair back.

"Yeah, you remember the animated movie Rose's twins made us watch, like, seventy times. The one with the dogs"

"Uh, no."

Rory huffed in frustration. "Never mind. So, this young, female neighbor has you befuddled?"

"I guess you could say that." Befuddled was a good word. Confused, perplexed, puzzled. Disoriented. Now he was a walking Thesaurus.

Rory's laugh grated on Roman's nerves. "It's about time, bro."

"I don't know why I called you. I gotta go."

Rory laughed again. "Call me when you figure things out. Oh, wait, I'm talking to my brother, Roman. You'll never figure it out, Captain Logic."

Roman disconnected with an irritated sigh. Why even bother talking to his brother. Rory had an easy way with both men and women. With his swarthy looks and sanguine personality, he didn't know a stranger. Rory would never understand the courage it took for Roman to walk across the expanse between his house and Lizzy's to introduce himself. Never mind that he offered to take pizza to her and Abby.

You're in way over your head, his inner geek said.

You're probably correct, Roman answered.

Chapter 4

A few days later, Lizzy stood in line in the cramped post office between her best friend, Simone, and her archenemy, Mariah. Mariah's black mane gleamed in the weak sunlight poking its way through the angry clouds gathering for yet another downpour. Lizzy hoped it drenched Mariah and her perfect, straight hair.

A quick pat of her own locks revealed several errant strands had come loose from the ponytail she'd gathered in the morning with one of her daughter's scrunchies. With dismay, she noticed some dried peanut butter on her gray hoodie. It refused to be pried off by an unpolished fingernail. She sighed and pushed her glasses back up her nose.

"Looks like half the town is here," Simone commented as the line inched forward.

Lizzy half-turned to glance over the queue snaking through the lobby and around the corner out of sight. "It's the most excitement we've had this year." In a small town like Main, Oregon, this was bigger than big.

Mariah pivoted toward them with a smug smile. "You might as well go home." Her voice, sweet as maple syrup, made Lizzy want to gag. "I'm going to win." She waved the large, white mailing envelope like a flag. She'd used a color combination of purple, pink, and orange pens and fancy calligraphy. Interesting color combination. Lizzy would have to try it on her color palette when she got home. The P in P.O. Box had squiggles at the top and bottom. The "S" in Salem resembled a musical treble clef.

"Huh," Lizzy responded, looking at her plain, manila envelope in comparison. A third grader could have written the block letters. A drop of grape jelly clung above the address. She picked it off. Would it have made a difference if she'd used fancy pens? Lizzy's stomach sank. Too late. Mariah had one-upped her again. Mariah didn't need a free house like she did. Her family owned a successful ranch on the edge of town. They could—and—did buy their little girl everything.

Writing this essay used every ounce of Lizzy's creativity. So much was on the line. If she won, her life would drastically change. Could she handle the disappointment if Simone won instead? Or Mariah?

The rules were simple enough. Out of all the entries, five would be picked as finalists. Out of those five, there would be a random drawing for a lucky winner. All previous property taxes would have to be paid, with the agreement the winner would live in the house for at least a year and would make the necessary improvements to fit with the rest of the neighborhood. Since the property sat next to hers, she had more than a vested interest in winning.

As did most of the residents. Who wouldn't want a free house. It was beyond her ability to own a home, that was for sure. She barely made rent most months.

Simone's voice interrupted Lizzy's thoughts. "Who's watching Abby?"

Lizzy's daughter was the biggest reason she had for wanting to win the house. She wanted to provide a stable place for Abby to grow up. Never again to be subject to the whim of a landlord who increased the rent. Or decided to sell. Or who didn't allow pets. Abby begged for a dog. Then a cat. They couldn't even afford a hamster.

"Roman," Lizzy answered. "He dropped his essay off early so he could watch her for me."

Simone raised an eyebrow. "How convenient."

"Oh, come on, Simone. You know nothing is going on between us. We're friends. That's all."

The line snaked forward. Mariah turned again.

"If I wasn't in a relationship… I'd make sure we were more than friends."

"I'll bet you would," Lizzy muttered as Mariah sashayed up to the counter to purchase the postage needed to mail her essay. Her red leather boots clicked on the faded linoleum. Lizzie's two-year-old tennies looked shabby by comparison.

Lizzy hated Mariah since fifth grade. Mariah had been an early bloomer and made sure all the other girls knew she'd gotten her first bra. It didn't matter it was a sports bra. She lorded it over all her flat-chested classmates.

Mariah had it all. Both parents worked to

provide her with everything a girl could want. She was the Barbie in the dream house. They took vacations to Hawaii, Europe, and cruises to Alaska and the Mediterranean. By high school, the divide between Mariah and her clique, and Lizzy was firmly established.

Lizzy's mom worked two jobs to keep them afloat. Dad left when she was a toddler. Lizzie's mom struggled to keep a roof over their heads. She did the best she could but left to her own devices, Lizzy started hanging out with kids who were not of the best character.

At sixteen, she was pregnant and dropped out of high school. Abby's dad moved to Portland and hadn't paid a dime of child support in nine years. If it wasn't for the help from her church ladies, Lizzy would never have gotten her GED. They babysat Abby while Lizzy studied. They held her when she thought she'd lose her sanity when Abby cried from colic.

To say Lizzy turned her life around would be an understatement. The church became her solace.

After all this time, she still compared herself to Mariah. Lizzy watched the other woman lay a hand on the white, purple-penned envelope, eyes closed as if in prayer. Lizzy's undecorated parcel didn't stand a chance.

Simone leaned close to whisper, "You can write circles around her, Lizzy."

Lizzy smiled. "Thanks," she answered, leaning against Simone, drawing strength from her friendship.

Outside the post office, rain-spattered the

parking lot. Lizzy tore her eyes away from the blue BMW Mariah drove.

"Want to grab some coffee?" Simone asked.

Lizzy shook my head. "I'd better not. I gotta get to work. Plus, I should rescue Abby from Roman."

Simone laughed. "Your girl talks more than any kid I know."

Lizzy slung her purse over her shoulder, preparing to dash through the rain which had turned into a deluge. "Don't I know it!"

Before she headed into the downpour, Mariah's car backed up, coasting to a stop where Lizzy stood. The passenger window lowered. Mariah leaned over the center console.

"You should be careful who you leave your daughter with," Mariah said. "People are not always what they seem."

The window went back up. Mariah pulled out of the parking lot, tires spinning on the wet asphalt.

Lizzy froze on the sidewalk, a sick feeling in her stomach. Had she made a terrible mistake by leaving Abby with a man she barely knew?

Lizzy dashed to her car. She couldn't get to Roman's house quick enough.

-*-

Roman and Abby sat side by side playing a game on Roman's laptop. He'd welcomed the opportunity to watch Lizzy's daughter again, even if for a short time. Abby's infectious energy made him forget his lonely bachelorhood.

"Your mom should be here soon," Roman said.

"One more game, please." Abby ran her fingers over Millie's fur, releasing a puff of loose hair. He'd have to vacuum again.

Roman couldn't resist those liquid brown eyes. "Fine. Last one, though."

They finished the last game when someone banged on his front door. "Who could it be?" he asked. "It can't be your mom." Lizzy usually came to the back door.

Roman stood and walked to the front door and swung it open. Lizzy stood on the doorstep, rain-soaked and shivering.

"Come in." He grabbed the sleeve of her hoodie and pulled her inside.

Lizzy jerked her arm away. "Where's Abby," she demanded.

"I'm here, Mom. Roman and I have been playing."

Lizzy strode into the dining area. "What have you been playing?" She placed her hands on her hips.

Roman ran a hand through his hair. Lizzy seemed upset, and he didn't know why.

Abby jumped up and ran to her mom. "It's cool, Mom. Roman has this online game. We played a gazillion times and I won."

Lizzy's face still wore a frown.

Abby didn't seem to notice. "And Roman let me drink coffee."

Lizzy's dark gaze swung to Roman's. "You let my daughter drink coffee? She isn't even ten years old."

"I thought—" Roman stuttered.

Lizzy glanced around Roman's living room. "What else should I know about?" her foot tapped the wood floor.

"Well, I—"

"Come on, Abby. I have to get to work." Lizzy bundled Abby into her jacket and was gone before Roman could form a word.

Nice job, dude, his inner geek said.

Roman sank onto his sofa. What just happened?

-*-

An hour later, Lizzy rushed into the drug store, still seething. She strode toward the register while pinning on her name tag. Mariah's suggestion Roman might not be all he appeared had rattled her. Abby's explanation the coffee concoction had been mostly milk and sugar hadn't mollified her. Lizzy was too trusting. Time to stop relying on her cute but geeky neighbor. She'd done fine for ten years without any male help.

"Elizabeth."

"Good morning, Boss."

Josiah glanced at his watch. "Glad you're on time today."

Lizzy rolled her eyes. "I'm always on time." Her declaration was a stretch, but it was their morning ritual.

Two chattering ladies approached her register.

"Did you see how many people responded to the house lottery?" Lizzy recognized the women from church.

"I did! My grandson made me write an essay, but I doubt I'll get into the final drawing. I haven't written anything except a recipe in over forty years."

"What about you, Elizabeth? Did you enter?"

"Of course, she did," said the older of the two.

Lizzy nodded while ringing up their purchases. She'd learned over the past years to say as little as possible. In a town as small as theirs, conversations were like the old game of telephone. By the time the words came to rest, they could be as twisted as a kite in a typhoon. Since getting pregnant with Abby, Lizzy vowed never to be the subject of gossip again.

Which made her think of Roman. How long before people began speculating about their relationship. Neighbors had probably seen them coming or going to each other's houses.

Yup, time to squash any rumors right now.

The women moved toward the door. Lizzy watched their retreating backs, thinking again about the house lottery and if she should get her hopes up to win.

With a sigh and a droop of her shoulders, she reminded herself this was the real world. People like her didn't win houses. Mariah would win. Although why Mariah entered was beyond Lizzy's imagination. She had a house. Her life was perfect. Beautiful ranch home on five acres, handsome boyfriend, a new car every two years.

Lizzy had heard her pastor preach about God's love and how hatred was like murder, but it seemed all too real when she encountered Mariah. From third grade until she dropped out of high school, Mariah bullied her relentlessly. Even now, whenever they ran into each other in town, Mariah still gave her the same cutting up-and-down judgmental look that made Lizzy feel small and unworthy. Even when Abby was with her, the disdain was clear. Lizzy wished she could forgive Mariah, but it was difficult to let go of the anger.

Lizzy shook off the dismal thoughts of Mariah to concentrate on her job. No use daydreaming about owning a house when it was obvious nothing like that ever happened to people like her.

When traffic in the store was slow, Lizzy worked straightening shelves and putting items back where they belonged. It never failed to amaze her how shoppers could take something from one side of the store and leave it in another. Nail polish in the diaper aisle, tissue abandoned in the kitchen implements.

"Customer service up front!" Josiah announced over the PA system.

Lizzy scurried down the candy aisle to the registers.

"Hi, Lizzy." Roman stood at the counter, holding Abby's stuffed dog. "Abs left this at my place this morning. Thought I'd drop it off before she misses it."

Lizzy's mouth went dry. How dare he show up at her work. As usual, his brown hair looked like he'd raked his hands through it more than once.

"Thanks," Lizzy said, her voice low with controlled anger. "You could have waited until we got home and given it to me then." She grabbed Abby's beloved Spot from his hand.

A blush crept up Roman's neck. "I had some

errands to do. I didn't, you know, make a special trip or anything."

Lizzy glanced over to see Josiah glaring at her from the prescription counter.

"I have to get back to work." Lizzy shoved Spot under the counter and clasped her hands behind her back.

"Oh, yeah, of course." The pink which started on Roman's neck rose to his cheeks. "I'll let you go."

He backed away from the counter and strode to the door. Lizzy's shoulders slumped as she exhaled.

After Roman left, Josiah cornered her in the detergent aisle. "Tell your boyfriend this is your workplace."

"Good grief, Josiah. Chill out already. Roman was dropping off Abby's stuffed animal she left at his house." It wasn't as if his friends never came into the store. Sheesh. "Besides, he's not my boyfriend." Not now, not ever.

Josiah exhaled through his nose, then turned on his heel without a comment.

Toward the end of her shift, Josiah's voice came over the PA. "Customer service to the front, please."

Lizzy headed toward the registers, only to slow her steps when she saw who stood at the checkout counter. Lizzy's nemesis, Mariah. She dawdled, hoping Ada would appear to help.

Josiah repeated his request over the PA, a little terser. Feet dragging, Lizzy made her way to the front of the store with a fake smile.

"Thanks for your patience. How may I help you?"

Mariah gave her a 'duh' look and shoved her basket a few inches toward the register. Mariah ignored her and pulled out what Lizzy assumed was the latest and greatest iPhone.

They were not allowed to comment on people's purchases - too invasive - but Lizzy paused when she grabbed a pregnancy test in Mariah's basket. Hm. Wondered if there'd be a little Mariah clone making an appearance in a few months. Seeing Mariah pregnant and uncomfortable might make her seem more human. Then again, she'd probably be like one of those celebrity types who looked perfect the entire nine months.

Lizzy finished ringing up her sale while asking God for forgiveness for her jealous thoughts. The words from her morning's devotional pinged in Lizzy's spirit. *Look at the heart, not the outward appearance.* But what if Mariah's heart was cold and brittle?

"That's sixty-four eighty-nine," Lizzy told her.

Mariah pushed her American Express Platinum Card into the reader without a comment. Even her credit card was better. Lizzy rolled her eyes. It was time to stop tormenting herself with comparisons to Miss Perfect.

Mariah signed the signature pad with a flourish and took the plastic bag out of Lizzy's hands.

"Thank you, Lizzy," Mariah said with a fake smile. Her eyes focused on Lizzy's name tag. "Or should I say, Elizabeth?"

Lizzy gritted her teeth to keep from saying something un-Christ-like.

As she swept toward the exit, Mariah spoke over her shoulder. "You should think about getting contacts, Lizzy. It might make a difference."

A difference of what? She sighed, pushed her glasses back up her nose, and went in search of Josiah.

"It's about time for my shift to end. Is there anything else you need me to do?"

Josiah pulled the clipboard he'd been holding to his chest. "No. Sign out of your drawer and let Ada know she's number one on the register."

Lizzy nodded her assent and went in search of the elusive Ada. How she managed to disappear while working was an ongoing mystery.

Once she won the house lottery, she could work part-time and go to college. Lizzy didn't want to end up like poor, ancient Ada. She'd worked at the drug store forever. She was in her late seventies, with swollen, arthritic fingers. She was so slow, Josiah avoided putting her at the register. He didn't dare fire her, age discrimination, and all that. Not like Ada would sue, but still. Ada knew everyone in town. Someone was bound to encourage her to sue the company.

Lizzy had bigger plans. Interior design school, then start her own business. Everyone said she had a knack with color, feng shui, the whole enchilada.

Yup, if she won the house, she'd enroll in college. No, not *if*. *When* she won the house. The church ladies said to speak of those things which are not as though they are. Her church wasn't a name-it-and-claim-it church. They simply believed in the power of prayer. Why not ask God to let her win? Lizzy was his child, after all.

She mentally brushed off her dislike of Mariah and all negative thoughts concerning her and the job and headed home to figure out how to deal with Roman.

Chapter 5

What had he done wrong? Roman paced his living room, reliving the confrontation with Lizzy from the morning. Since then, he'd been unable to concentrate on his work. His inner geek had turned into a demon, taunting him over his lack of discernment and utter failure with the opposite sex.

Give it up, dude.

Forget even trying.

You could never be a father to that little girl.

The Scriptures which came easily to mind seemed to have disappeared. Roman jabbed a hand through his hair as he remembered how Lizzy had stormed into his house.

Something must have happened before her arrival which had angered her. But what? She'd gone to the post office to mail her contest entry. That much he knew for sure.

Think, Roman, think. What could have happened to set her off? No matter how hard his brain worked, Roman could come up with no logical circumstance.

Of course, the coffee thing with Abby exacerbated the situation.

Note to self: don't give a nine-year-old coffee, no matter how diluted it is with milk.

Roman picked up his phone, turning it over in his hand a few times. Finally, he entered Lizzy's number and sent a text.

Roman: **Sorry I gave Abby coffee. It won't happen again.**

He watched the screen for the telltale dots showing an answer was imminent.

He waited a long time.

-*-

Lizzy scrubbed the kitchen sink with more force than was necessary. Roman's text had come moments before.

How dare he think a text apology was acceptable. Was he trying to worm his way back into her good graces by a little "I'm sorry?"

She was an idiot by letting a stranger watch her daughter. Or was she more of an idiot by letting Mariah get into her head?

This situation needed an intervention. Lizzy abandoned the kitchen sink and sent a quick text to Simone, asking if she could talk.

Ten seconds later, Simone's face filled the screen.

"What's up, Buttercup?"

"Hold on, let me check on Abby." Abby sat in her bed, iPad firmly clutched with both hands.

"I'm going to be outside, on the back porch. You okay here?"

Abby briefly glanced up before nodding and resuming her game.

Lizzy dragged on a hoodie, stepped outside,

and sank onto one of the comfy patio chairs.

"Simone, I'm a mess."

"What did you do now?" Simone's forehead crinkled with concern.

"Ugh. Where to begin." Lizzy pulled the band out of her hair and let it fall loose. "You know my neighbor, Roman."

"The cute but nerdy one?"

Lizzy sighed. "I've had him watch Abby a couple of times."

"Go on."

Lizzy pursed her lips, deciding how to tell Simone how she'd gone off on Roman.

"He didn't do anything to her, did he?" Simone sounded like she was ready to launch a blast of fire. Bossy, straightforward Simone sometimes scared Lizzy with the strength of her personality.

"No, nothing like that. It's, well, today after we mailed our submissions at the Post Office, you'd already left. Mariah pulled up and told me I needed to watch out for Roman. Something about him not being who he appeared to be."

"The witch!" Simone exclaimed.

"I freaked out and I'm afraid I was kinda rude to him when I picked Abby up."

Lizzy pulled on a lock of hair, waiting for Simone's response.

She didn't have to wait long.

"Did you get any kind of creepy vibe from him?"

"No. And my church ladies vouched for him. Said he helped in Sunday School sometimes."

"You need to do some damage control."

Lizzy shrugged. "I guess."

"Why do you let Mariah get into your head? You know she's hated you forever. Her whole purpose in life is to stir up drama."

Lizzy sighed and slumped against the cushions. "I know. But I have to protect Abby. What if I let some random guy take advantage of her?"

Simone frowned. "Your neighbor is not some random guy. He's a card-carrying, church-going Christian. And a super nice guy, according to what you've told me." Simone wagged a finger at the screen. "Besides, you could use a little male attention yourself. This self-imposed quarantine from the opposite sex is getting old."

Simone could be right. What if it was time to see if she'd matured enough to be friends with a man without being tempted into sin. Ten years was a long time. But was it long enough?

"Thanks, Simone. I guess I'll apologize."

"You do that, girlfriend. And let me know how it goes."

Lizzy disconnected and sat for a few minutes, praying for the right words. Finally, she sent a simple text.

Sorry I snapped at you.
Roman: **Okay**

-*-

"Why are we stopping here, Mom?" Abby's voice piped up from the back seat.

Lizzy released her seat belt and turned, supporting her arm on the center console. "What do you say we take a peek at the house next door?"

Her heart quickened as she looked at the house, its white paint was peeling in spots, the windows dirty and a little green but it was the house she had always dreamed of. Someone had taken advantage of the break in the rain and mowed the lawn. The grass clippings and the wet soil smelled freshly cut and lingered in the air with a sweet tang.

"Is this going to be our new house?" Abby asked in a whisper.

"I hope so, Bug."

"Yippee!" Abby bounced up and down on her toes.

They peeked in the front windows, hands cupped around their eyes to block out the afternoon sun. The front door sat in the middle of what Lizzy assumed was the living room and dining room. The hardwood floors had dulled over time, but she pictured colorful area rugs in gray and navy partially covering the dulled wood.

"C'mon, Bug. Let's look in the back yard."

Abby followed on her heels as they walked around the side of the house. The windows were higher here as the side yard sloped downward.

"Lift me, Mom. I want to see!"

She hefted Abby up and they investigated the kitchen. The appliances were older. Lizzy hoped they were in working order. White cabinets sat above laminate countertops. Plain, but functional. She could live with that. A few colorful herb pots on the windowsill would draw the eyes away from the relentless white. Maybe a colorful vase. Excitement rose as Lizzy pictured a decorative spice rack sitting on the counter. Or…

"Oof, you're getting big," Lizzy exclaimed as Abby wriggled from her grasp. Abby took off toward the back yard.

"Look, Mom, you can see our house and Roman's from up here!"

Sure enough, they stood on a small rise overlooking her rental and Roman's. Had the previous owners known the owners known Mr. and Mrs. Carmichael? Probably. Main was a small town, friendly to a fault.

Lizzy continued around to the rear of the house. Wet leaves dotted the concrete patio, blown from the massive cedar trees in the adjoining property. Lizzy slipped, then righted herself with a laugh. The odor was faint but there. A musty odor carrying with it the scent of damp, rotting wood and old rags left in the sun too long.

The wooden pergola had once been painted white, but now chunks of paint peeled from it like sunburned skin. Curtains covered the windows along the back of the house, obscuring the interior.

She laid her hand on the trim of the sliding glass door, then bowed her head for a quick prayer. "Please, Lord, can I have this house?"

"What are you doing, Mom?"

"Praying we can get this house, Bug."

Abby placed her hand below Lizzy's and closed her eyes for two seconds, which was about the length of time her daughter could stay still.

Abby bounced up and down. "When can we go inside?"

"They're scheduling an open house soon. We

have to go online and make an appointment."

"Are we gonna?" asked her little pixie.

"Of course, Bug. As soon as we get home."

When they walked through the front door, Lizzy promptly forgot about making the appointment. Her stomach rumbled. She was starved and figured Abby was too. Seemed like all her daughter did was eat these days. What would she do when Abby was a teenager? Hopefully, by then, Lizzy would be a successful interior designer, creating beautiful rooms for model homes.

"Can I play on your iPad?" Abby asked, dumping her backpack on the floor.

"*May* I play. And yes, you may, as soon as you take your backpack to your room."

Abby sighed as only a nine-year-old could.

Lizzy headed into the kitchen and grabbed a package of hot dogs from the fridge. Her back pocket buzzed. Pulling out her phone, she saw a text from Roman.

You home from work yet?

Lizzy felt her heart sink and her body tense as she tried to figure out what she was supposed to do. She had already offered an apology, but it seemed inadequate. She felt ashamed of the way she had acted, and knew Roman deserved an explanation, but the implications of getting deeper into her feelings with him scared her.

Mariah had a way of pushing all the wrong buttons, and it was embarrassing to be vulnerable with Roman. But would he accept anything less than total transparency?

Lizzy strolled over to the large glass door and

pulled aside the curtains. Roman was in his dining room, clearly awaiting her response. Their houses were quite close to each other, about twenty-five yards apart, and it was hard to keep any secrets. If she opened the curtains, she had to be sure she was dressed appropriately, otherwise she'd be embarrassed. The lack of privacy bothered her at times, but it was nice to know there was someone of the opposite sex nearby. In case of an emergency. Nothing more than that. Like if she got locked out. Or something . . .

Her phone buzzed again, a reminder she hadn't answered his text.

Just got home. Hot dogs for dinner. Want some?

She held her breath. Had he accepted her brief apology? Perhaps by offering him dinner, he'd see she was sincere, without her having to go all transparent and vulnerable. She grimaced. This was why she avoided friendships with men. Too many minefields to dodge, waiting for a misstep to blow everything sky high.

Lizzy could count on one hand the number of dates she'd been on since Abby's birth. Most guys didn't want an instant family. Once they knew she had a daughter, they either ended the date early, or worse, ghosted her.

Roman's text jolted her out of her thoughts.

Sure! Be right over.

She sent a smile emoji, then contemplated his use of the exclamation mark after the word 'sure.' Roman didn't seem the excitable type, so why—

Another text popped up.

Simone: **How was your day?**

Lizzy sent a shrugging emoji. **Okay. Same old. R coming for hot dogs. You interested?**

Simone: **I'll let you two lovebirds have some alone time. Lol.**

Lizzy shook her head. Simone had been trying to connect Roman and her since she moved in. Even though Lizzy kept telling her she didn't think of him romantically, Simone was relentless.

Me: **You're killing me right now.**

Simone: **LOL.** Several smiling emojis followed, one with heart eyes.

Lizzy pulled out three brown and turquoise plaid placemats and placed them around the table. It wobbled when she set out ketchup and mustard. One of these days, she'd have to tighten the one loose table leg. Unless she dragged the whole thing to the dump.

Two minutes later, Roman tapped on the glass, then stepped into the kitchen.

Lizzy's glasses had fogged up from the pot of boiling water. She pulled them off and used the bottom of her tee shirt to wipe them.

"Hey," she said. "You look good. Do you have a date or something?"

His brown hair usually falling over his forehead, was slicked back. He wore a freshly pressed Oxford cloth shirt the same color as his eyes.

"Uh, no. Work and stuff." A blush rose to his cheeks. She turned, grinning to herself. Had he dressed up for hot dogs?

"I have some chili warming and I'm putting

together a salad. It's not haute cuisine, but at least Abby will eat it."

Roman seated himself at the table. "Where is Abs, anyway."

Lizzy stirred the chili, then reached into the fridge for a bag of prepared salad mix. "She's on my iPad in her room. Abby!" Lizzy called.

Abby bounded into the room a few moments later. "Hi Roman. Are you here to eat with us?"

"That's right, Abs. Hot dogs, chili, and salad are my favorites."

Abby jumped into his lap and gave him a fierce hug. "Yay! I like it when you eat with us." She lowered her voice to a whisper. "Sometimes it's boring with Mom and me."

Roman laughed, then whispered back, "Why don't you see if your mom needs help setting the table."

Lizzy and he exchanged an amused glance.

Between Abby's constant chatter about her day at school and excitement over her upcoming birthday, and Roman's amusing story about a Zoom meeting fail, Lizzy couldn't get a word in. Which was fine. It gave her a chance to observe Roman's interaction with Abby.

When the table was cleared and food put away, they moved to the living room.

"Hey, Bug," Lizzy said, handing Abby the keys. "Why don't you run out and check the mail?"

The neighborhood group mailboxes were a few houses down the street. If Abby stopped to pet the neighbor's dog, as she usually did, Lizzy would have a few minutes alone with Roman.

Abby pressed against Roman's knees. "Want to go with me?"

"No, he doesn't," Lizzy said quickly. "Let him digest his dinner."

"But, Mom, you said it's good to take a walk after a meal."

Her daughter, the girl who never forgot. "Go," Lizzy said pointing to the door.

"Fine." Abby huffed, then skipped out the front door, leaving it wide open.

Lizzy rose, crossed the room in three steps, and pushed the door closed.

"So, Roman," she said, picking at a loose thread on her sock. "I, um, feel really bad about the other day."

Roman's eyes were closed, and his head rested on the back of the sofa. "I understand your need to protect your daughter. I should have thought twice before giving her coffee."

Lizzy chewed on her bottom lip. "It wasn't only that. There's this woman. Mariah. She made me second-guess letting you watch Abby for me."

Roman's eyes opened. "What did she say?" He sat up and leaned forward, his blue eyes dark with some emotion Lizzy couldn't determine.

"She didn't say anything, not exactly."

Roman frowned. "I would never, ever do anything to hurt your daughter."

Lizzy's eyes filled with tears of shame and remorse. "I know."

Roman loomed above her, his eyes blazing with a storm of emotion. His silence spoke volumes of pain, a deep-seated hurt seeming to radiate from his body in waves. His voice was low and powerful as he asked, "Do you really know?"

Chapter 6

Roman slammed the sliding door hard enough to rattle the coffee mugs in the kitchen cupboard. How could Lizzy think he would do anything to hurt Abby?

This time no amount of Scripture quoting and pacing his living room would do. The only outlet was a trip to the gym to work off his hurt which was quickly turning into anger.

Roman changed into workout clothes and drove to the gym, ironically located between a bar and a restaurant. He climbed onto a treadmill and set the program for an intense running pace.

As the program ramped up, a woman stepped onto the machine next to his.

"Hi." Her smile revealed a mouth of perfect teeth, no doubt the product of expensive orthodontic work. Her red lipstick contrasted with the brilliant white of her smile, now directed toward him.

Roman nodded toward her.

"I'm Mariah." She tossed her black glossy hair over one shoulder.

Could she be the same Mariah who got into Lizzy's head? Roman punched a button to slow down the treadmill.

"I'm Roman."

Mariah practically purred her response. "Nice to meet you. Haven't seen you before." She thrust a dainty hand in his direction, and he noted the ruby nail color matched her lips. He took a moment to absorb her skintight workout pants and skimpy top that left her midriff bare, her thong line evident underneath the stretchy white fabric. He took in the warm smell of her perfume and felt the heat radiating off her body.

Roman ignored her outstretched hand. "Do you know Lizzy Greene?"

Mariah's smile froze. "You mean Elizabeth? Yes, I know her." She flicked a finger in his direction, as if to indicate Lizzy was of no consequence.

Anger bubbled in Roman's chest. "What did you tell her about me?"

"I don't know what you mean. I don't even know you." Her smile warmed. "Until now, that is."

"You said something about me to Lizzy that set her off. What was it?"

Mariah's laugh sounded forced. "Oh, Lizzy. You can't believe a thing she says. Anyone who knows her history knows about Lizzy Greene."

Roman watched as Mariah climbed down from the treadmill. It was clear Mariah had an agenda, one that involved Lizzy and Roman as well. He jumped off the treadmill, snatched his towel and water bottle, and sprinted out of the gym to his car.

He sighed and shook his head as he pulled out of the parking lot. Questions raced through his mind

- why did women get involved in these toxic relationships? Why would someone like Mariah take advantage of Lizzy's trusting nature? As he drove home, something else nagged at him – why did Mariah choose to involve him in her schemes?

The question remained unanswered in his mind: How could Lizzy have given a second's thought to what that horrible woman said? Roman realized with a sinking feeling it mattered to him what Lizzy thought about him. He was losing his heart to her, and he was powerless to do anything about it.

When he arrived home, Roman pulled his phone from his gym bag. A rush of adrenaline caused his fingers to tingle when he saw the text from his former best friend. The one who'd stolen Shayna from him.

Colin: **Can we talk?**

-*-

Abby burst through the door. "Here's the mail." She tossed the envelopes in Lizzy's direction and ran to her bedroom.

"Hey," Lizzy called. With a sigh, she gathered up the scattered pieces from the rug.

An official-looking return address caught Lizzy's attention.

'Lawson and Lawson, Attorneys at Law'

Lizzy tapped the edge against her bottom lip with a sick feeling. Why would an attorney contact her? This couldn't be good.

What if it was from Abby's dad, suing for joint custody after nine years of silence.

Lizzy felt completely paralyzed. It was like she had been struck by a wave of fear and was struggling to catch her breath. Her gaze was glued to the letter sitting ominously on the coffee table. Why now?

God, why couldn't this have happened later? But no matter how much she wished for it, Lizzy knew she had to face it. Like a Band-Aid, it was best to rip it off. She had no choice but to do it now.

Dear Ms. Greene:

We regret to inform you Margaret Carmichael has passed away. The ownership of her home at 1707 SE Marigold Avenue where you reside has been transferred to her heirs. They desire to sell the house.

Therefore, you are hereby given sixty days to vacate the property. Failure to do so will result in legal action, up to and including eviction.

We apologize for any inconvenience. Should you have any questions, please do not hesitate to contact us at the address below.

(Signed),
Mark W. Lawson
Attorney At Law

Mrs. Carmichael died. Lizzy knew she'd been in poor health after she broke her hip. But how sad to go downhill so quickly. At least she was in Heaven, away from all the struggling of this life. But where did it leave Lizzy? She pictured her and Abby, living in their car in the Wal-Mart parking lot. Tears filled her eyes and threatened to spill out.

Two months was all the time she had to find another place to live. When Mrs. Carmichael moved to Albany to live with her daughter, she'd offered to let Lizzy stay here at a rent so reasonable she could hardly believe it. What a blessing. Abby and she had been priced out of the apartment they'd rented. Right when she thought she'd have to beg her mom to let them stay with her in Salem, God had come through. Was it possible He'd do it again?

She had to win the house lottery.

Several cookies later, Lizzy paced from the kitchen to the living room, back to the kitchen. She'd tried to call Simone, but it went straight to voicemail. No doubt she was consumed with Adam and wedding plans. Her church ladies also didn't answer.

Lizzy put Abby to bed, trying her best not to show stress.

"Can we pray for Grandma tonight?" Abby asked as Lizzy tucked her in.

"Of course, Ladybug. What's on your mind?"

"I want her to go to church with us."

"I'm pretty sure she works Sundays. Besides, it's a long drive from Salem to here for church."

"I know," Abby said with a sigh. "But I want to show her my Sunday School project. It's Jesus feeding the five thousand."

Lizzy rubbed her daughter's curls. "We can take a picture of it and show her when she comes for your birthday."

"I guess."

Lizzy smiled, the letter momentarily forgotten.

"Mom, can we also pray for Roman? I really like him."

Lizzy's heart lurched. "Sure, Bug. You do that." The last thing Lizzy wanted to do right then was to think about how she'd hurt Roman's feelings. This whole man-woman-friendship thing was too confusing to deal with right now. It would be best to go back to her original plan of no male relationships until Abby was grown.

When they'd finished praying, Lizzy returned to the living room and sank onto the sofa. She pulled the letter onto her lap. It was time to emulate her daughter and pray about this new development in her world.

Her only priority was to keep Abby secure. Looking back, Lizzy thought she'd done an okay job. Although they'd bounced around over the past ten years, her love for her daughter had been constant. They'd never been hungry, and they'd always had a roof over their heads.

This house was supposed to be the answer to Lizzy's dream of having a forever home. Now the dream was being ripped apart. Added to the mix was this new friendship with Roman. Could they remain friends after she'd almost accused him of molesting her daughter? How would Abby react if Roman suddenly disappeared from their lives?

Lizzy sprang up and headed into the kitchen. The coffee pot held a cup of stale brew from the morning. Lizzy heated it in the microwave and sat at the table with her drawing pad.

After praying, she began to let her mind guide her hand. A peaceful scene took shape. A lake shimmered with light from a dawning sun on the horizon. Willow trees bent over the shore, dipping their leaves in the water. A lone white heron floated in the middle, her wake barely a ripple.

An hour later, Lizzy sat up and observed her drawing. She added the words 'John 14:27' to the bottom. The memory verse sprang to mind. "Peace I leave with you, my peace I give to you; not as the world gives. Let not your heart be troubled."

Lizzy's phone buzzed with a text. Finally, Simone was getting back to her. Pulling her phone toward her, she saw it was from Roman.

Saw your lights on. Everything okay?

Lizzy propped her chin up with her hand, wondering if this was his way of telling her he had forgiven her. This was all too complicated; should she tell him everything? Everything was great, but she would have to move again? Her daughter loved him, but she herself was uncertain about their status.

Lizzy typed 'yes' and then erased it. Be truthful with him, she thought to herself.

Lizzy: **Not really. Mrs. Carmichael died, and I have to move.**

It took several minutes for Roman to answer.

Roman: **I'm sorry. What can I do to help?**

She was tempted to answer "Give me a house" but opted for: **Nothing right now. Thanks**.

Roman answered with an emoji of praying hands.

Lizzy woke Sunday morning with a warm breath on her face. She cracked open one bleary eye. "Good morning, Bug."

"Mom it's time to get up. Let's go!"

Cool air hit her bare legs when Abby threw back Lizzy's cozy cocoon. "Hey, give me a moment, please," she begged. She smelled coffee brewing and thanked God she'd set the timer on the coffee pot before finally going to bed the night before.

Abby grabbed her hand, pulling her upright. "We have tons of stuff to do today," she announced.

"Like what," Lizzy teased, letting herself be pulled into the kitchen.

Abby stopped and put one hand on her hip. "Like plan my birthday party. I'm turning ten."

Like Lizzy needed to be reminded. She poured herself a cup of hot coffee, wondering how ten years could have passed since this little bundle of energy was born. Lizzy should have known she'd be a whirlwind since she started kicking inside her at six months and didn't stop until her birth.

Lizzy took a sip and spoke over the rim of the mug. "Are you sure? I think you're turning nine."

Abby's eyes widened with a look of outrage. "Mom! Stop it."

Lizzy pulled her in for a hug. Resting her chin on Abby's brown locks, she said "I love you very much, Ladybug."

Abby danced away, twirling. "What's for breakfast?"

Lizzy sighed. In a few years, she'd be dating, driving, and leaving her for good.

"Don't forget," Abby called from the living room. "This is the year you tell me about my dad."

Oh, right. She should never had made the

promise to tell Abby about her dad – the deadbeat who Lizzy hadn't heard from in ten-plus years. Right after she'd gotten pregnant, his family moved to Portland. Rather than finish his senior year at Main High, he'd chosen to run away. Lizzy knew for a fact one of his friends offered to let him stay at his house so he could graduate with the class. But, noooo, he didn't want to face her or his responsibilities. Lizzy figured he owed her ten years' worth of child support. The problem was Lizzy couldn't find him. Even if she did, there was the chance he'd want joint custody. She couldn't take the chance.

Lizzy took a small sip of her coffee and winced. Her mind raced, searching for the right words to tell Abby about her dad. But no matter how hard she thought, she couldn't think of a single redeeming quality Abby would cling onto. Lizzy knew the pain of betrayal all too well, but she didn't want Abby to experience it too. She had to talk to Simone today to see if she remembered something that could make things better. After all, who could forget Dylan James.

In the meantime, Lizzy needed to figure out what to do about the eviction letter.

She sat at the table, drawing pad in front of her while Abby munched on her cereal. Sundays were sugary cereal days, a treat replacing the trying-to-be-healthy breakfasts she encouraged the rest of the week.

"What are you drawing, Mom?" Abby asked, slurping the last of the milk from her bowl.

Lizzy slid the pad sideways into Abby's line

of vision. "I'm working on the mural for your bedroom." She'd sketched a jungle scene, complete with a mother and baby giraffe—Abby's favorite animal.

"For the house we're going to win?" Abby asked, bouncing on her chair.

"I hope so, Bug." If they didn't end up homeless first.

Abby grabbed Lizzy's cheeks in both of her hands. Her milky breath was warm on her face. "We're going to win. I know it."

"Really?" Lizzy said, trying to keep the sarcasm to a bare minimum. "And how do you know?" She waggled her eyebrows. "Do you know one of the judges? Did you bribe her with candy?"

"Mo-om." Her two-syllable use of "mom" sounded more like a sixteen-year-old than an almost ten-year-old. "I prayed and told God we really need the house."

As if it were that easy.

"All right, Miss Ladybug. Let's get ready for church, and we'll do some planning after."

The pastor droned on about the first chapter of Revelation, but Lizzy felt her concentration wavering as she thought about the letter from the attorney. Anxiety coursed through her as she contemplated what a move would mean for her and Abby. But even amid such fear, a spark of hope lit within her—this time, things would be different. Perhaps this time, she'd find a forever home.

Lizzy glanced across the aisle and caught Roman looking her way. She sent him a closed-mouth smile and looked away, to see Mariah and her boyfriend sitting two rows behind him. They were the perfect Barbie and Ken. Except why did they attend church regularly if they were sleeping together? Lizzy remembered the pregnancy test Mariah had purchased. Was it for herself? Or someone else?

Lizzy put Mariah out of her mind as she smoothed out the cotton button-up shirt she'd thrown on in the morning, regretting she hadn't taken the time to iron it.

After church, she hustled Abby out to the car, avoiding Roman and any chance of running into Mariah.

-*-

He should have saved Lizzy a seat at church, but she was usually late. It would be awkward if he saved her a place, and she didn't show up. People would think he was uncomfortable about sitting next to someone. He bandied the idea back and forth before deciding to let Lizzy find her own seat.

Were they back on speaking terms? Were they ever *not* speaking?

He'd left her house rather abruptly the night before, his feelings hurt by her comment about that woman, Mariah.

You're an idiot, his inner geek said.

Yeah, I know, he answered.

Her text said she had to move.

He wanted to find out how she was doing. If she had to move, and they wouldn't be neighbors, he wouldn't get to see her practically every day.

Roman felt the familiar tug of despair, and he fought against it fiercely. He had worked hard over the years to stay off anti-depressants, despite the fact Shayna had left him for his best friend. The counseling sessions he had attended in Salem had provided some reprieve from the darkness, but it was still there, waiting to overtake him.

With hands clenched together in his lap, Roman prayed, asking God to help him focus on the sermon. He looked over and saw Lizzy had found a seat on the other side. He glanced her way, hoping to send an unspoken bit of encouragement, to himself as well. Her closed-mouth smile told him nothing.

Why did he let himself get down? Jesus said to cast all your cares on him. Why was it difficult to do? He had no problem believing God would work everything out for her. But for himself, not so much.

Focus on the good things, his counselor had said.

Roman breathed in and out, repeating the familiar words.

I have a good job I enjoy.

I have a family who loves me.

I live in a good house I can afford.

I have a faith which can't be shaken.

Are you sure? his inner geek said.

Roman switched his attention back to the sermon, focusing on the words and missing the message.

Chapter 7

Lizzy heard a familiar voice at the front door. "Knock knock!"

"Simone!" Abby jumped off the chair and bolted for Lizzy's best friend, practically bowling her over.

"Hey, there, rug rat." Simone dropped a cloth bag and her purse and bent down to hug Abby. "How ya doin?"

"Mom's drawing a mural for my new bedroom. It's cool!"

Simone straightened. "Your new bedroom? Are you moving?" She looked across the room at Lizzy, her face unreadable.

Abby's head bobbed up and down. "Yup. When we win the house, she's going to paint it in my bedroom."

"What if I win?" Simone asked, speaking to Abby but looking at Lizzy.

Lizzy felt a chill go up her spine. Simone winning wasn't something she'd seriously considered. She'd been so caught up in the excitement of submitting her entry, she didn't give a thought except she didn't want Mariah to win. And now the letter from the attorney.

"What's in the bag, Simone?" Abby's voice pierced the silence hanging between them.

"Wouldn't you like to know, rug rat?" Simone smiled down at Abby. "Go ahead and take a peek."

Abby squealed with excitement as she pulled party supplies from the bag and set them on the rug.

"Look, Mom, giraffe plates and napkins!" Abby held up the treasures.

"Oh, Simone, you shouldn't have." Lizzy rose from the table and crossed the room to kneel beside her daughter.

Simone sank onto the sofa with a shrug. "I can't let my favorite little person not have the best tenth birthday ever."

The chill evaporated as they talked about Abby's party. Later, after Abby went outside to enjoy some rare Oregon sunshine, Lizzy grabbed the letter from the attorney.

"Look at this, Simone. Can you believe it? I'm getting evicted."

It took only a minute for Simone to scan the letter. When she was done, it fluttered to her lap. "Wow."

"Wow is right. I had no idea Mrs. Carmichael was ill. She told the church ladies she wanted to live nearer her grandkids."

"Do you think she might have had the virus?"

Our community had only recently reopened businesses after the Covid-19 pandemic. "I suppose it's possible." Lizzy shrugged. "The thing is, I can't afford to rent anything else right now. I don't have enough saved for a security deposit."

"I hear ya. Every time I save a few bucks, something happens."

"I know, right? Like a flat tire or a broken tooth." Last time she'd drained her meager savings to pay for Abby's overnight school field trip to Portland.

Simone let out a sigh. "We need to find rich husbands. Too bad Adam is so devoted, or I'd have to dump him and find someone with money."

"Ha. Like that'll happen. You two are perfect for each other." Lizzy thought about Roman. Would she let him pass the 'friend zone' boundary?

"I'll probably never find someone. No one wants a woman with a kid."

Simone gave her a look.

"What?" Lizzy demanded.

"Girl, you are dumb." She pointed a thumb toward the sliding glass door. "Your neighbor would marry you in a New York minute."

Lizzy swatted Simone's arm. "Roman? You're kidding, right?" But Lizzy's heart fluttered.

"I've seen the way he looked at you and Abby when we came over."

Lizzy scrunched her face. "Uh-uh. We're just friends."

Simon shrugged. "As I said, you are dumb."

Lizzy shook her head and let it go. She had bigger issues to think about than whether Roman thought of her as more than a friend.

There was Abby's party to plan, what to tell her about loser Dylan James, and where she was going to live if she didn't win the house lottery.

For Lizzy, the next days passed as usual.

Work, pick up Abby from daycare, church, laundry, and all the minutiae that came from being a single mom.

Her solace was walking through the front door of her little rented home. No one would ever know her sofa was a garage sale find. She'd made a cover from lightweight denim to hide its flaws. The rug was another find, a floral pattern with splashes of red, yellow, and green. A couple of silk trees added some texture to the room, along with a tabletop fish tank. After they won the house, Abby could get a real pet. The alternative was unthinkable. All their stuff would have to go into storage if she was homeless.

Thinking along those lines, Lizzy pulled out her iPad to see if there was any update on the lottery. Her phone pinged with an incoming text, duplicated on the iPad.

Roman: **Did you make your appointment yet?**

Lizzy: **??**

Roman: **They're taking appts to look at the house Thursday and Fri**

The website opened and there on the landing page was a place to submit your name for a tour of the house. She tapped in her information and waited.

Not more than a minute later, she received confirmation and immediately texted Roman.

Lizzy: **Thursday 3:30**

Which worked out perfectly because she had Thursday off.

Roman: **I'm Friday at 4**

She sent a smiley emoji, then added: **Beat ya!**

Her stomach sank. After what Simone said, she shouldn't joke with him. Simone had to be way off base. Lizzy thought back over their recent encounters, looking for any clue Simone could be right. They'd gone back to their easy friendship, neither mentioning the night he'd left in a huff.

Simone had to be wrong.

Thursday arrived and Lizzy was a bundle of nerves. She'd finally get to see the inside of the house. Once she'd had a chance to look around, what if she hated it? What if it needed more elbow grease than she could manage.

Lizzy sat at the table, trying to sketch. It usually calmed her, but not today. The finished product looked like some of Picasso's later work. With a groan, she slapped the drawing pad closed and shoved it away.

Her second form of therapy was baking. She searched through the kitchen cupboards for all the ingredients for peanut butter cookies.

The day was warm for April. Lizzy opened the windows and turned on some Christian music. Making cookies would keep her centered for the next couple of hours until the appointment.

Halfway through the second batch, a voice called through the open back door.

Lizzy jumped at the sound of Roman's voice. "I smell cookies!"

"Come on in."

Roman's grin widened like he had a secret, exposing his straight white teeth and creasing the corners of his blue eyes. His light brown hair was slicked back from his forehead, a few long strands hanging down his neck and brushing against the collar of his crisp cotton shirt. His jaw was strong and angular, giving him a nerdy but handsome look. Lizzy couldn't help but smile.

"Quit staring at me and give me a cookie," Roman said, reaching for the cookies cooling on a rack.

"Sorry. Was I staring?"

He spoke around the bite he'd taken. "Like I was a bug under a microscope. Or an Algebra equation. Or—"

"I get it." Lizzy grabbed a cookie and leaned back against the counter. "I'm nervous about seeing the house. What if I hate it?"

Roman reached for another cookie. "You're getting way ahead of yourself. You don't even know if you've won. None of us do." He looked thoughtful as he munched. "There are several possibilities. One, you love it, and you win. Two, you love it, and you don't win. Three, you hate it, and you win. Four, you hate it, and you don't win."

Good old Roman. Logical. That's why Lizzy liked him. As a friend. He was the yin to her yang. Wait, no. There was no yin. No yang either. Darn Simone. Still, Roman was a good person to lean on.

"Come with me today," Lizzy urged.

He shook his head. "My appointment isn't until tomorrow."

"So? Who's going to care? Tell them you can't go tomorrow."

"I don't think so."

"Don't be such a rule follower. Haven't you done anything, ever, against the rules?"

Roman's face clouded over. "I gotta go," he said, grabbing another cookie on his way out the door.

Lizzy's heart stirred with excitement as she walked the few hundred yards from her current house to the house she hoped to win. Someone, presumably the City Council, had decorated the front of the house with balloons and a banner stretching across the door saying "Welcome!"

An older gentleman Lizzy recognized from church greeted her from a card table set up on the porch.

"Hi, Lizzy. Let me get you checked in." He put an X next to her name on a list.

To Lizzy's dismay, Mariah's name appeared beneath hers.

"Speak of the devil," Lizzy murmured under her breath as Mariah climbed out of her BMW. Today Mariah wore red heels costing more than what Lizzy paid in a month for childcare. Tossing her hair back, Mariah sashayed up the walk toward her.

"Hello, Elizabeth." The barely veiled sarcasm of her use of Lizzy's given name oozed from her like hot oil.

"Mariah." *Please God, don't let me react.* Lizzy instinctively looked down to make sure there were no holes or food stains on her clothes.

The older gentleman seemed oblivious to their mutual dislike. "Good afternoon, Mariah. I have you both checked in. Go on in."

Lizzy nodded, turning her back on Mariah. The front door of the house was already open, letting in a cool breeze. The walls carried the scent of old books, the pages crisp and yellowed. The smell of musty insulation lingered in the air, of a basement or attic untouched for decades, once the home of a family with four children and a dog, now nothing but memories. She stepped into the living room as her inner decorator kicked in. The first thing Lizzy noticed was the real hardwood floor. This was no laminate, no fake wood trying to look real. It would take a lot of work, but she could see it restored to its original state. A couple of area rugs wouldn't detract from its beauty, but rather accentuate it.

The walls were plaster, painted white. Lizzy envisioned a light blue over a white chair rail, darker blue below. Nautical colors were all the rage right now.

"Oh my gosh." Mariah's voice cut through Lizzy's meanderings. "This place is ugly."

Lizzy swirled, mouth open. "Wh-what?"

Mariah scowled. "I can see my contractor will have his work cut out for him when I win."

"Contractor?" What was Mariah blabbering about?

Hands on hips, Mariah turned in a slow circle. "This floor has got to go. Look how uneven it is. And those walls. No one has used plaster since, oh, I don't know, the Fifties. All these walls will have to be torn down to the studs."

Speechless, Lizzy gazed at Mariah's back as

she entered the kitchen.

Lizzy followed on Mariah's heels, nearly plowing into her as she stopped dead.

"Horrid!" Mariah exclaimed.

Lizzy had seen the white cabinets from the window when she and Abby had peeked in. Close up, she could see all they needed was a new coat of paint and modern handles. She pictured the cabinets in the same navy blue as the living room, with the doors and drawers white. The dark blue would pull the attention away from the cabinet's age.

"Yuck," Mariah said. "This will have to be gutted as well." She shook her head and examined the appliances as if she expected a horde of roaches to come pouring out.

"It's not too bad," Lizzy said.

Mariah's look dripped with condescension. "Oh, Lizzy. You are too cute." She brushed past her to return to the living room. Over her shoulder, she said, "Don't bother dreaming. I'm going to win."

As if. As her church ladies often reminded her, *dreams are free.*

A short hallway off the living room led to two small bedrooms with a bathroom in between them. While Mariah inspected one of the bedrooms, Lizzy stepped into the bathroom. With a grim smile, she wondered what Mariah would say about the bathroom.

The porcelain tub was seafoam green. Lizzy hadn't seen a real porcelain tub in forever. Everything now was fiberglass. The sink was the same color, and both needed a good scrubbing. Laminate countertops in dark and light green pattern completed the look. Lizzy thought hard about how to incorporate the blues from the living room and kitchen into this green monstrosity. She'd have to do some research, but Lizzy was confident it could be done.

Lizzy barely escaped into one of the bedrooms before she heard Mariah's shriek. She must have seen the bathroom, Lizzy thought with a grim smile.

There was a door at the end of the hall. Could be a closet. Lizzy's pulse sped up when she opened it and found a set of narrow stairs. Ducking her head, she crept up. The stairs made a sharp turn to the left and she found herself in a large open room. The roof pitched high in the middle, sloping down on each side to a small window. She'd never noticed there was a second story in this house.

She pictured a workspace for her designs and a play area for Abby. She could put in a corner reading nook on one side and finally have space for her to leave her sewing machine up all the time.

Footsteps sounded on the wood stairs. Mariah's head appeared as she ascended the last few steps. Her mouth dropped open.

"Wow."

"I know, right?" Lizzy said with a grin. "Isn't this place fantastic?"

Mariah crouched down to peer out one of the windows, then turned and straightened. "I mean, the carpet would have to go, but you could do a lot with this space."

"The possibilities are endless," Lizzy said.

"Agreed. A home office."

"A design studio."

"Nursery."

A thick silence fell between them. Lizzy remembered the pregnancy test Mariah had purchased a few days ago. Was she…?

Mariah's face darkened as she turned away. "Don't get your hopes up, Elizabeth."

Lizzy thought they'd shared a moment, Mariah and she, but apparently not. Mariah was back to being her snippy self. With a sigh, Lizzy clumped down the narrow stairs. She found Mariah deep in conversation with a man she didn't recognize. When Mariah caught Lizzy staring, she turned her back. Lizzy headed out the front door.

"Thanks for letting me look around," she said to the man checking people in.

"You're welcome. Glad you could come. Good luck!"

Lizzy passed the next group of people on the sidewalk. They were a young couple with two kids who came into the drug store weekly. Lizzy didn't know what their thing was, but they bought something at the prescription counter every time. She hoped one of the kids wasn't desperately sick. She'd feel bad if they needed the house worse than her.

At home, she pulled her phone from the pocket of her jeans and plopped down on the sofa, then started a text to Simone.

Lizzy: **You should see the**

Her fingers hovered over the phone. Lizzy remembered the day when Simone stood in the living room. "What if I win?" she'd said. The thought chilled her. What *if* Simone won. How would it affect their friendship? Could Lizzy be happy for her?

What if Roman won? He submitted an essay as well. Somehow, the thought of Roman winning didn't affect her the same way. Hm. She'd have to think about it more in depth. In the meantime, she backspaced what she'd typed, laid the phone on her chest, and stretched out on the sofa to daydream about the house.

She could incorporate some of the green from the bathroom with throw pillows of the same color to add a splash in the blue living room. At least the green wasn't the avocado color from the seventies. That would be horrid, to quote Mariah.

As for the kitchen, Lizzy knew where she could get some cabinet knobs to add a bit of a farmhouse feel. Eventually, the counters could be replaced with stained concrete. She'd seen a cool sink on a website resembling an antique washbasin.

She must have dozed off because she was startled when her phone vibrated on her chest.

"Hi, Mom. What's up?"

Mom's voice sounded tired. "I'm checking in. What's new with my little granddaughter?"

Lizzy smiled. "Abby's doing great. You'll be here Saturday for her birthday?"

"Of course. Wouldn't miss it. I bought her a kid's Fit Bit."

Lizzy rolled her eyes. "Why?"

"She's turning ten, for heaven's sake, Elizabeth. Time for a big girl watch. And stop rolling your eyes."

Mom always knew.

"But a Fit Bit, Mom? It's a slippery slope. First a Fit Bit, then her own iPad, then a phone, then—"

"What, then she's cyber-bullying some poor girl who isn't as beautiful as my granddaughter?"

Lizzy rolled her eyes again. "Okay, Mom. I get it."

At least cyberbullying hadn't been a thing when Lizzy was in school. She'd have been a target for sure. Especially by you-know-who and her friends. There was enough chatter when she'd started to show a baby bump. she could imagine what it might be like now with Facebook, Instagram, Snap Chat, and whatever else was the flavor of the month. Lizzy wanted to protect Abby as long as possible.

"She'll be thrilled, Mom. Thanks."

"Oh, by the way. I ran into Simone's dad the other day. He told me they're moving to Idaho to be near Simone's oldest sister. Did you know Ava is expecting triplets?"

Simone hadn't mentioned it. Had Lizzy been too focused on Abby's birthday to notice something bothering her best friend? Simone was super close to her parents. If they weren't around, well, Simone would be lost.

"What about Olivia?" Simone's youngest sister was still in high school.

"Cassius told me she's staying here with Simone to finish high school."

Oh. My. Goodness. No wonder Simone wanted to win the house. She lived in a one-bedroom apartment on the outskirts of Main. If

Olivia was going to stay with her, Simone would have to move.

But the bigger thing was, why had Simone kept it from her.

"I'll see you Saturday, Elizabeth. You can tell me all about this house lottery thing then."

They disconnected, and Lizzy realized with a start it was time to pick Abby up from school. Abby's chatter on the way home in the car distracted her from the bombshell Mom had dropped about Simone. As soon as they pulled up to the house, Abby was out of the car and running for the swing set in Roman's back yard.

"Thirty minutes!" Lizzy called to her as she unlocked the front door.

From the kitchen, she could keep an eye on Abby as she prepared dinner. Cooking meals wasn't her thing, leaving her to stick to the basics. Spaghetti, tacos, beans, and rice. She could burn off some frustration baking cookies, but the main way she de-cluttered her brain was with a pencil and sketch pad.

Since it was still two days until payday, they'd have to settle for meatless spaghetti, which was noodles with a jar of sauce dumped over it.

As the water heated, Lizzy sank onto a chair and pulled the sketch pad toward her. After taking a moment to pray, she gave her hand free will. A storm began to take shape. Dark clouds dumped rain on a raging sea. A tiny boat looked ready to capsize as the lone passenger struggled to stay upright.

The sound of boiling water sizzling on the

stove pulled Lizzy back into the kitchen. She broke the long sticks of dry spaghetti noodles in half and dumped them into the water. As she stirred them, she eyed her drawing. Many times, the Lord spoke to her through what she drew. This one was obvious. She was the one in the boat. A storm was coming, and she'd have to struggle to keep from getting dumped into the water.

But the picture wasn't finished. she dashed back to the table, sat, and grabbed the pencil. On the far left of the page, she drew a lighthouse in the distance.

Chapter 8

Roman hopped on his bicycle to clear his head. Nothing like fresh, spring air to blow away the cobwebs after working for hours on his latest contract. Plus, the fact he hadn't answered Colin's text. He couldn't imagine what his former best friend could want to talk to him about. Roman had mentally severed the tie the moment Shayna told him she was in love with Colin.

He'd answer the text the minute he got home from his ride. Or after dinner. Or tomorrow.

Roman looked forward to the silence of the road as he pedaled his bike through Main, the small town where he'd lived for only a few months. The narrow lanes were lined with two-story Victorian houses, and it was nice to be able to ride without worrying about getting hit by a careless driver. He'd lived in Salem and in Portland, where riding a bike could best be described as a death wish. Traffic was minimal, and the air smelled like coffee and cardamom and grilled meat.

The signs of the change of season were evident by the fresh pots of flowers hanging in front of the downtown businesses.

Roman coasted to a stop in front of The Main Bean, parked his bike, and went inside.

The manbun-wearing barista greeted him as Roman stepped through the door. "Hey, Roman, haven't seen you for a while. Your usual?"

Roman experienced a flutter of panic at Daniel's easy familiarity. He ducked his head and flicked a bug off his tee shirt. "I've been busy."

"Keeping the world safe from hackers?" Daniel asked as he prepared Roman's Columbian pour-over.

"That's right."

"What's the latest on the house lottery?" Daniel asked.

"I'm not sure. I think the finalists will be announced next week. Did you enter?"

Daniel laughed. "No way. As soon as I graduate from Oregon State, I'm outta here."

Roman thanked Daniel for his drink, paid, and escaped. Small talk. Ugh.

He sat on a bench in the sun, sipping his coffee with a sigh of appreciation. His phone buzzed with his mom's number.

"Hi, Mom," Roman said as he answered his cell.

"Roman, you have been a very, very bad boy."

Mom was born in the United States, but she liked to pretend she was from the 'old country.' Roman's great-great-grandparents had emigrated from Italy in the late 1800s.

"What now, Mom." As the oldest son, he was used to his mother's scolding.

"We have not seen your little house. When

were you going to invite us? Are you ashamed of your *genitori Italiano?*"

"No, Mama. I'm not ashamed of my Italian parents. I've been busy."

"Psh. Busy, busy. Always busy. Your Papa and I are coming to visit."

Roman's shoulders tightened. "When Mama?" Now he was doing it, calling her Mama instead of Mom.

"Next month, of course."

Roman spoke through gritted teeth. "Great. I'll reserve a room for you and Dad at the hotel."

"Hotel?" Mom's voice ratcheted up an octave. "You would put your *genitori* in a hotel? We are not good enough to stay in your home?"

Roman cut her off before she could explode into an angry Italian monologue.

"Okay, Mom. I thought you might be more comfortable having your own space. Of course, you can stay here."

Mollified, she said, "*Bennissimo.* Your papa will let you know when we are coming."

Roman disconnected with a guilty hope one of his parents might get sick. Or one of his sisters might need an emergency babysitter. Or he'd get hit by a falling tree.

Too many pitfalls to avoid with his parents here. If Lizzy didn't live close, he'd be able to avoid her for two or three days. But with mom and dad here, they were bound to bump into each other, especially if Abby danced her usual way across their two back yards to play on the swing.

As soon as Mom caught a glimpse of his

neighbor, and discovered they were friends, she'd be ordering wedding invitations.

He had to warn Lizzy. But how? The wood bench creaked under his weight as he wrestled with several options before coming up with a plan.

Pastor Roy sank onto the bench next to Roman. "Roman, how are you?"

"I'm fine, Pastor," Roman said. They shook hands.

"Beautiful day," Pastor Roy commented. "God's handiwork evident."

Roman nodded. Sweat formed on his brow as he struggled to make small talk.

"Will you be joining us at the sing-along tomorrow evening?"

Roman swallowed. "I'm not sure." The thought of being in a room full of people was enough to give him hives. But it might be tolerable if Lizzy went with him.

Like a wingman? his inner geek asked.

Pastor Roy pulled his cell phone from the front pocket of his shirt. "Text me your number, and I'll send you the directions to the VanDuker farm."

Roman did as he asked and moments later received the response.

"It's a bit of a drive out of town, but the view from their place is magnificent." Pastor Roy smiled. "You'll need to bring a lawn chair. We meet in the barn on the property."

"Sounds, um, good." Roman tucked his phone into the back pocket of his jeans.

Pastor Roy slapped Roman on the back as he stood. "It's a hoot, son. You'll have a great time."

Doubtful. Roman watched his pastor stroll up the street, calling greetings to people outside enjoying the sun. What would it be like to have such an easy way with people? Like his brother, Rory. And Lizzy.

Again, his thoughts turned to the woman he couldn't keep out of his mind. She invaded his day as he watched her comings and goings. Sometimes she made a cameo appearance in Roman's dreams.

With a start, Roman realized he was falling for her.

That ship has sailed, his inner geek said. *You've fallen and you can't get up.*

Roman took a sip of his now lukewarm coffee and grimaced. As he stood to toss the cup in a nearby trash can, an older woman ambled along the crosswalk in front of the coffee place. She wore dark blue slacks and a flowered top stretching across her ample frame. She passed Roman with a smile, stopped, and backed up.

"Hello."

"Hello." Roman thought he'd seen the woman in the church, but he couldn't be sure.

The woman leaned toward him. "You're the nice young man from church, aren't you?"

Roman took a moment to decide how to answer.

"From Main Community Church."

The woman nodded vigorously. "I'm Sarah. With an 'h.'"

"Roman." He grabbed her outstretched hand, surprised by the strength of her grip.

Sarah's eyes bored into his. "You're Lizzy's

young man."

Did she expect him to answer? Was it a question or a declarative statement?

"I, uh," Roman stammered.

"Don't you worry. I told Lizzy you were trustworthy. After all, you had a background check before working with the kindergartners in Sunday School." Sarah smiled as if he were Moses coming down from the mountain.

"Thank you." What else could he say? Sarah must be one of Lizzy's 'church ladies.' At least he'd passed the sniff test. His dad had said if a dog sniffs you, then lets you pet it, you were an okay person. He'd never had a dog, but it sounded logical.

Sarah switched her massive purse from one shoulder to the other. "Let me give you some advice," she said, leaning even closer. Roman resisted the urge to take a step back. "Lizzy has had a rough time of it. Since that rascal Dylan James left her high and dry with a baby to raise on her own, she's closed herself off to all but a few people. You seem to be someone she's allowed into her life."

Roman nodded, pleased to hear he was one of the few chosen in Lizzy's life.

Sarah shook a finger in Roman's face. "Don't hurt her."

Now Roman did step back. Before he could answer, Sarah trundled down the street toward the row of shops. He slumped onto the hard bench.

What just happened? How had he gone from 'that nice young man' to 'don't hurt her?'

Roman had no intention of hurting Lizzy. He intended to get closer to her and, hopefully, have a relationship with her. One which would possibly be permanent.

In your dreams, his inner geek said.

-*-

Lizzy opened her eyes Saturday morning and shrieked. she shot up and bonked foreheads with Abby, who was staring into her face, willing her to wake up.

"Holy moly, child. You scared me to death."

"Wake up, Mom. We have a lot planned today."

Lizzy pursed her lips and rubbed her chin. "Are you sure? I can't think of anything we *have* to do today."

Abby grabbed her hand and attempted to pull her out of the warm covers. "Come on. You have to make my favorite breakfast. Then we're going to decorate, then you have to hide all the animals for the scavenger hunt."

"Scavenger hunt?" Lizzy asked, letting her feet hit the carpeted floor.

"Mo-om. You can't have forgot already. It's my birthday!"

"Oh, that." Lizzy grinned and chucked her under the chin. "Give me five minutes to grab a sweatshirt and find my glasses."

By the time she shuffled into the kitchen, Abby had already pulled out the pancake mix, a package of blueberries, and an egg.

"Maybe you should fix *me* breakfast," Lizzy said. "If it wasn't for me, you wouldn't even have a birthday.

Abby put her hands on her hips. "Nice try

Mom. Now get to work." She pointed to the stove with a stern look.

This child would be the death of her.

While Lizzy fixed blueberry pancakes, she told Abby the story of the day she was born. Abby loved this tradition, and Lizzy had to admit, she did too.

"So, about three in the afternoon, my back started to hurt. I thought I'd strained it, so Grandma made me lie down. I couldn't get comfortable."

Abby bounced up and down on her chair. "Then what happened?"

"Well, I had to go to the potty. I pulled myself out of bed and waddled to the bathroom."

Abby giggled. This was her favorite part.

"When I got there, all this water poured out of me and onto the bathroom floor. I thought I'd wet myself!"

This brought on a gale of laughter.

"I yelled for your grandma. She came running, saw what had happened, and rushed me to the hospital."

"Were you scared?"

"Oh, yes," Lizzy said, warming to her story. "I was terrified. I was about to give birth to the most amazing human being ever."

Abby grinned and pointed at her chest.

"You were so little and wrinkled I knew I had to name you after my great grandmother, Abigail. She was a dancer way back in the day."

Abby laughed. Then her face turned serious. "Was my dad there?"

Lizzy's heart sank. She'd never asked the

question before. "No, he wasn't, Ladybug."

"Why not?"

Lizzy exhaled through pursed lips. How much to tell her? He was a deadbeat loser. When she told him she was pregnant, he asked if it was his. Should she know when his mom decided to move to Portland six months before his graduation, he took the easy road and went with her?

"Good luck with the kid," he'd said. "Whoever the father is."

Lizzy had tried to forgive him many times over the past ten-plus years, and she still struggled with the concept.

"Hello? Mom?" Abby snapped her fingers in front of Lizzy's nose.

"Sorry, Bug. Trying to remember some of the details." She shoved a piece of soggy pancake around on the plate. "Your dad couldn't be there when you were born. He moved out of the area."

"What did he look like? What is his name?"

Abby's questions came at her like tiny darts. She took a deep breath. She did promise to talk about him when she turned ten. "His name is Dylan."

"Dylan," Abby whispered.

"When we were in high school, I thought he was the cutest guy in school. He was two years ahead of me, and I was flattered he'd noticed me." Which was true. What Abby didn't need to know was all the stoners hung out together, regardless of age. There weren't too many in Main's small high school. She also didn't need to know they got drunk a lot and cut school. A lot.

"What else?" Abby was relentless. What other crumbs could Lizzy toss her to satisfy her ten-year-old curiosity?

"Well, let's see. He was about five foot ten, and super skinny."

"Like Roman?"

"A little shorter than Roman, and a lot skinnier." Due to the fact he hardly ate, preferring instead to get high.

"What color are his eyes?" Abby batted her long lashes. Lizzy had to smile. Even though she never expected to be a mother at seventeen, she was grateful Abby had come into her life. Not only had Lizzy grown up in a hurry, but she'd also discovered unconditional love. Her love for her daughter had opened her up to the unconditional love of a Father in Heaven. Lizzy couldn't remember her own dad, and God's love filled the aching hole in her heart.

"His hair is reddish-brown, like yours, and his eyes are blue." Why was she talking about him in the present tense? For all she knew, he was dead from an overdose.

"When can I meet him?" Abby's question threw her for a hot minute.

"Well, Bug, I don't know where he is or how to get a hold of him."

"But you said he moved to Portland. Why can't you track him down with Facebook or something?"

Lizzy rubbed her hands across her face and shoved her glasses up. With a sigh, she said, "I'll see what I can do." She pushed her chair back and stood. "Time to get moving. We have a party to prepare for."

Later, after settling an exhausted and cranky Abby into bed, she and Simone relaxed on Lizzy's back patio with a mug of hot cocoa.

"I'd forgotten how close the houses are in this neighborhood," Simone said, glancing over at Roman's back door.

Lizzy shrugged. "I'm used to it. I have to remember, though, to make sure the drapes are closed across my slider first thing in the morning. I wouldn't want to have Roman see me in my Pj's."

"Well, not yet anyway."

Lizzy practically spewed out a stream of cocoa. "Simone!"

"Kidding! You've made it abundantly clear you're remaining celibate until you get married."

"Not when, *if*," Lizzy corrected her.

"Oh, come on. You could get married someday. If you crooked your little finger toward you-know-who," Simone gestured toward Roman's house with her mug. "Speaking of whom, why was your mom rude to him?"

Lizzy shook her head. "I don't know. Seems like since she stopped drinking, she's lost her ability to filter."

When Roman arrived at the party, front door this time, Mom looked him up and down then said, "Why would a young, single man be interested in a little girl's birthday party?" She'd made it sound creepy.

"I thought Roman was going to have a heart attack," Simone commented. "I thought he'd take it more in stride."

Lizzy chewed her lip as she thought about his reaction. He'd turned several shades of red, then lost all color as he stammered a response.

Lizzy didn't want to talk about Roman. What she wanted to talk about was the house. But she felt like it was off-limits. Lizzy wanted to win, Simone wanted to win, and one of them might lose. *Or both of us,* she supposed.

Changing the subject, Lizzy said, "Abby asked me about her dad today."

Simone frowned. "You mean Dylan the deadbeat dad?"

"The one. I made a stupid promise to tell her about him when she turned ten. The first thing out of her little mouth today was 'tell me about my dad.'"

"What did you say?" Simone set her now empty mug on a small table and tucked one of her legs under the other.

"As little as possible. I gave her a brief physical description and I might have mentioned his name."

"First, last, or both?" Simone fixed Lizzy with a laser-like gaze.

"First."

Simone relaxed. "Good."

"I said I'd try to find him." Lizzy held her breath, waiting for Simone's response. she didn't have to wait more than a micro-second.

"You did *what*?"

Lizzy bit her lip as she tried to contain her fear. She loved Simone and considered her her best friend, but sometimes her strong and demanding personality could be overwhelming. They had been friends since forever, but Lizzy felt like Simone was always trying to control her life. Even though she wanted to tell her everything, she couldn't bring herself to do it.

"What could I say, Simone? She's curious." Simone couldn't know what it was like to always question who your dad was. Simone and her family were super tight. She'd never stared at perfect strangers and examined them for any physical resemblance to herself.

Simone pulled her leg free and planted both feet on the cracked concrete. "Knowing what a druggie he was, he's probably dead." She stood and yawned. "I better go."

Lizzy stood and grabbed her in a hug. "Thanks for everything today. Abby loved the art set."

Simone pulled away and looked her in the eye. "Be careful if you're determined to look for Dylan."

She hugged Lizzy back, then headed into the house. "See you later."

Lizzy picked up her mug and sipped at the cold cocoa as she sat back onto the webbed chair. She wished she could go back two or three weeks in time, before all the house lottery drama. Her excitement grew over the possibility of winning the house next door, and she wanted to talk to her best friend about it.

With a sigh, she slurped down the rest of the cocoa and headed into the house. As she readied herself for bed, she realized Simone hadn't mentioned anything about her parents moving. Looked like she wasn't the only one to hold back from her friend.

Chapter 9

Roman drummed his fingers on the kitchen table. His heart beat a rapid tattoo as he considered the text he was about to send to Lizzy. But first, where was his phone? With a fond smile, he used two fingers to pull the device free from where Millie sprawled on the table.

Are you going to the church sing-along tonight?

Normally he'd stay home from group social events, then berate himself for not going. But if Lizzy was going, he wanted to be there too. Any chance to see her was a good reason to step out of isolation. Even if his stomach did flips and his hands shook.

Roman stared at this phone, willing Lizzy to answer. Ten agonizing minutes later, he saw the little dots indicating she was typing.

Yes. Going with Simone and Adam.

Roman's already queasy stomach dropped. He'd waited too long and now he'd be home alone. Again. Not that it had been a big deal before Lizzy had moved in. Working at home gave him the quiet he needed to concentrate on his job.

Everything changed when little Abby danced into his life, and then her mother.

Roman laid his cell phone on the table and slumped back in his chair.

Moments later, his phone buzzed with a new text.

Want to ride with us?

Roman's heart skipped a beat.

Yes. Thank you. What time should I meet you?

Lizzy: **Come to the house around six-thirty. I get off work at six. I'll barely be able to change before Adam picks us up.**

Roman: **Sounds good.**

His fingers hesitated over the phone. Should he say 'thank you' again?

Too eager, his inner geek said.

This time, Roman agreed.

The day went by with agonizing slowness. Roman got caught up on emails and did some work on one of his projects. Now, he stood in front of his closet, considering his options.

What did one wear to a sing-along in a barn? Jeans, of course. He swept the long-sleeved dress shirts to one side of the closet. What a relief not to have to wear those anymore, now he could work from home. He should move them to one of the other bedrooms. He'd do it right after his parents' visit.

He rejected a few of his favorites, shoving them aside. There on the last hanger was a shirt he'd never worn. Shayna had bought him the shirt.

She'd wanted to help him break out of his boring solid-colored choices. This one was a plaid button-down, loose-fitting, and made to be worn untucked. They'd broken up shortly after she'd gifted him with it. The tags still dangled from the collar.

Roman slipped it on, buttoned it, then turned right and left in front of the mirror. The blue in the pattern brought out the color of his eyes and the yellow and green kept the shirt from being boring. Perfect for a barn event. He hoped.

The clock on the nightstand read five-thirty-one. Fifty-nine minutes to wait. Roman ran both hands through his hair, then pulled the unworn dress shirts off the closet pole. He tossed them on the bed, then removed the hangers. The pile of shirts grew as he carefully folded each one, ensuring the collars weren't crushed. The now empty hangers went into his office closet, along with the pile of folded shirts.

He checked his cell phone for the time. That little chore took less than fifteen minutes. Forty-five minutes until it was time to leave. Roman sighed.

In the meantime, he'd grab a book and try to immerse himself in someone else's drama. For once his inner geek was silent. He settled onto the sofa, nudging Millie to the middle. She meowed in response before settling again.

At six twenty-nine, Roman strode from the back door to the front door, returning to the back. Should he cross the two yards to Lizzy's house or go to the front? Would it be weird for him to show up at her back door? Or weirder to wait out front?

Tick-tock.

It was now six-thirty on the dot. Roman

locked the back door and hurried out to the front, to the sidewalk, and around the block to Lizzy's house.

Simone rolled down the passenger window and motioned to him. "Come on and get in. Lizzy said she'd be out in a minute."

Roman slid in the roomy sedan behind Adam. Simone turned around with a smile.

"I'm glad you could join us. Have you been to one of these shindigs before?"

Roman shook his head. He'd never considered going to a church event alone. Or any community event.

"It's super fun," Simone said.

Roman hoped so. Abby barreled out of the front door and spun in circles until she reached the car.

"Hi, Aunt Simone." Abby grabbed the door handle and jumped into the car. "Hi, Roman. Hi Adam."

With all greetings dutifully made, she fiddled with the seat belt until it snapped into place.

Lizzy stepped over the threshold and turned to lock the front door. Roman's breath caught in his throat. Lizzy's jeans hugged her slim legs, and the slightly over-sized sweatshirt emphasized her petite build. She'd let her hair loose, and it fell in auburn waves over her shoulders.

Wowzer, his inner geek said. Roman agreed.

Lizzy poked her head in the car, smiled at Roman, and climbed in. "I wasn't sure if you were coming. I thought you'd come to the back door. Apparently, I was wrong."

"Oh, uh, sorry," Roman said.

Lizzy laughed. "No worries. Let's go have some fun and get our worship on."

"Amen," echoed Simone and Adam.

The three others began a spirited conversation about the last time the church had a worship sing-along night. Roman sat with his hands clenched in his lap, feeling as uncomfortable as a wool sweater on a ninety-degree day.

The talk turned to the upcoming house lottery.

"The finalists are going to be announced soon," Adam said.

"I'm excited," Simone said. "What if all of us are finalists."

Roman spoke for the first time. "I doubt it."

Lizzy fixed her gaze on his. "I read part of your essay. It was good."

Roman felt his face grow warm. "Thanks. But it wasn't as good as yours."

"Whoever wins," Simone said, "It is already known by God, right?"

"Right," Abby piped up.

Everyone laughed.

"What?" Abby asked. "Me and my mom are gonna win."

Tension mounted in the silence following. Roman rubbed sweaty palms on his jeans.

So, how about those Giants, his inner geek said.

Abby broke the silence. "My mom said the house is really cute."

Simone half-turned in her seat to face her. "I know, right? It has potential."

Lizzy made a face. "Can you believe Mariah

wants to tear the interior down to the studs?"

"Nothing that woman does would surprise me," Simone commented.

"You should have heard her when she saw the green bathroom." Lizzy and Simone shared a laugh.

"When am I going to get to see it?" Abby asked. "It's not fair you all got to go, and I didn't."

Lizzy tweaked Abby's nose. "You were in school, Bug."

"Well, it's still not fair." Abby crossed her arms and frowned.

When Simone turned back to the front, Lizzy asked, "What did you think of the house, Roman?"

"Uh, it was okay, I guess." Roman wiped sweaty hands down his jean-clad thighs.

Lizzy chuckled. "Okay, you guess?"

Roman searched his brain for the impressions he'd had when touring the house. "It's, uh, old."

He was saved from having to add anything more when Adam turned the car off the highway onto a gravel road.

"Only a few more minutes," Adam said.

They bumped along in silence as the road climbed upward. Roman saw a red barn in the distance. He hoped it was their destination. Tension knotted the muscles in his neck. He rolled them back to try to relax.

"Look," Abby exclaimed as she pointed out the side window. "There it is!"

A few moments later, Adam pulled to a stop along a line of cars parked in an unpaved area.

"Here we are." He turned toward Roman and Lizzy. "I brought extra chairs for you."

Simone patted him on the arm. "My hero." Her smile lit up her face.

"Thanks," Roman said, remembering too late Pastor Roy had told him to bring his own seating.

They piled out of the car and waited for Adam to pop open the trunk.

"Mom, can I go find my friends?" Abby asked.

"Sure, Bug. Don't go running off, okay? Stay close and when the music starts, I want you to check in."

"Okay," Abby said over her shoulder as she ran toward a small group of girls.

Roman watched the girls gather Abby into their group with hugs and excited exclamations. He sure loved that girl. And her mom.

Whoa. Where did that come from? He'd known Lizzy for such a short time, and yet he was absolutely sure he was in love with her. He wanted to deny it, his head told him it was crazy, but his heart knew it was true. The question was, did she feel the same?

The VanDuker farm sat on the top of a plateau. Lush green pasture undulated down toward the gravel road they'd ascended. The distant grey-blue peaks of the Cascades rose to the sky, visible through the trees. Horses grazed behind a fenced corral. Roman took a deep breath of fresh air and felt himself relax for the first time that day. No matter what the evening held, he needed this moment of serenity. Something about being outside made him feel closer to God.

Roman rubbed his hand across his chest as if

to reassure his heart it wouldn't be broken again.

Roman and Adam carried the chairs and set them next to a row of empty lawn chairs.

Simone stood on tiptoe and kissed Adam. "Thank you, honey." Adam grinned.

Roman and Lizzy exchanged an awkward glance. He felt his face grow warm.

"Nice shirt," Lizzy commented. "Is it new?"

Roman ran his hands down his front. "No. Yes."

Lizzy laughed. "Is it yes or no?"

Roman was saved from having to answer by an older woman who approached them with a plate of cookies.

"Would either of you like to try my homemade oatmeal raisin cookies?"

They each took one and offered their thanks.

"Would you like some coffee?" he asked Lizzy.

"Sure," she said. "But I bet it won't measure up to yours."

"No doubt," Roman responded. Normally he'd pass on coffee made in industrial-sized brewers, but at least he'd have something in his hand since he'd devoured the cookie.

They made their way to the table set up along one side of the barn.

"Welcome!" said a gray-haired woman in a plaid flannel shirt, jeans, and cowboy boots. "Help yourself to some coffee or water." She pointed to the next table. "There's cookies too."

"Thanks," Lizzy said. "And thanks for hosting this event."

"You're welcome, honey. We're glad to share the bounty of the Lord."

Roman smiled at her as he filled his Styrofoam cup with the hot brew. He took a sip and tried not to grimace.

"I saw that," Lizzy said, her voice teasing.

He tried to look innocent as they moved down the line toward a table groaning under the weight of cookies and small pastries.

"I have no idea what you're talking about."

They helped themselves to another cookie and munched in companionable silence. Roman gestured toward the stage where a band was setting up.

"What happens here? What's the agenda?"

Lizzy drew out her words with a sardonic smile. "The agenda is . . . the band will play a few songs to get warmed up. Usually some upbeat praise songs. People gradually join in. Then they'll slow down, and we'll have some time of worship. Then they'll play a few more upbeat songs. Then we'll break up and go home."

Roman nodded. It helped to have an idea of what to expect.

"Does that work for you?" Lizzy asked.

She was teasing him again. Roman didn't mind. "I guess," he answered with an exaggerated sigh.

"Come one, let's go sit."

The evening turned out to be exactly what Lizzy said. Roman couldn't remember the last time he'd enjoyed himself this much. Toward the end, Abby climbed into his lap and rested her head on his chest. Contentment filled him from the top of his head to the bottom of his feet.

This was what it was like to have a family, not simply be a part of a family. He missed his crazy loud parents and siblings. They'd pulled him out of himself and made him feel less like a misfit. Exactly like Lizzy and Abby were doing.

But did Lizzy feel the same?

You're kidding, right? his inner geek said.

-*-

Lizzy glanced over when her daughter crawled onto Roman's lap with a sleepy sigh. She was too big to sit on Lizzy's lap, but Roman's larger size created a comfortable nest. Lizzy realized with a start she hadn't experienced one bit of apprehension tonight about Abby attaching herself to Roman.

What if Simone was right? What if it was time to let someone into her life. Someone who would cherish Abby the way she did. If what Simone said was true, all Lizzy had to do was give Roman any indication she was interested in more than friendship.

But how to do that? She hardly dated since high school. It wasn't like she and Dylan ever really dated. They hung out. Partied. Then, surprise -- she was a teenage statistic.

Roman could give her and Abby the stability she craved. He had a good job. He owned his home. Went to church. Loved her daughter.

But could she feel about him the way a woman should feel about a man? Where was the elusive "I can't live without you" feeling?

Lizzy watched his profile as he sang along with the band. He was certainly attractive in his nerdy way. What if…?

Lizzy reached out a hand and laid it on Roman's arm wrapped around her daughter. He looked down and froze. Then he shifted Abby from one shoulder to the other and took her hand.

There was no bolt of lightning or spark of electricity. Just a warm feeling of safety as the worship song came to an end.

Chapter 10

The next few days passed in a blur. Everyone was on edge waiting for an announcement from the City Council about the house lottery. Lizzy continually monitored the city's website for any news. She let herself be optimistic she'd be one of the finalists. A girl could dream, couldn't she?

"I doubt I'll win," Roman said when he came over one evening when Lizzy got home from work.

"Why not? Everyone has an equal chance." Lizzy was helping Abby cut pictures out of old magazines for an art project due the next day. As her mom would say, 'The apple doesn't fall far from the tree.' Lizzy had spent many long nights working on a project she'd put off until the last minute. Lizzy would like to think she'd gotten better. But she remembered how she'd written the house lottery essay the night before the deadline. Yikes.

"Yeah, I guess." Roman raked his hands through his hair, making it stand up. "My major was computer science with a minor in eCommerce. My communication skills are sorely lacking."

Lizzy looked up at him with a smile. "I have

no problem understanding you."

"That's not what I'm talking about, and you know it." He reached for a magazine. "Hand me a pair of scissors and I can help."

With the three of them cutting, they soon had a pile of pictures for Abby to choose from.

"Okay, Bug, it's up to you now."

"Mom, I can't do it by myself." Abby laid her head on the table with a deep sigh.

"No whining. This is your project, and you need to complete it. Pick a few of the photos and arrange them on the poster board. I'll come in and help you glue them."

Lizzy motioned to Roman to join her on the back porch.

"Have you heard anything about when the winners will be announced?" Lizzy asked when they were seated on the plush cushioned chairs.

Roman leaned forward, resting his elbows on his knees. "What I heard is there will be a public meeting soon to announce the finalists."

"Soon? What does that even mean?" Nervous anticipation climbed up her arms.

Roman shrugged. "You know how things are in this town. Slow."

Lizzy sighed. "Half of me wishes I'd never entered. The other half wishes it was over."

"Me too. I heard some ladies in the Walmart arguing over who was going to win."

Lizzy thought of Simone, and the ginormous elephant in the room whenever they were together. If Simone won, Lizzy would struggle to be happy for her. Lizzy thought again of the letter from the attorney. The longer this lottery thing dragged on, the greater chance she had of being homeless. She hadn't made any effort to pack or to look for another place to live. Another thing she was putting off. Like looking for another job.

Roman sat back in his chair with a serious look on his face. "Not to change the subject, but I want to talk to you about something."

Lizzy's mind spun with the possibilities. Was he going to renege on his offer to help her financially if she won? Was he going to move? It was always a possibility, as the head office of his job was in Omaha. What would she do if he moved? His presence was a lifesaver when her daycare fell through. Lizzy felt safer knowing he was across the yard if something were to happen. Her breathing quickened as she waited for him to speak. Besides, Abby would be devastated.

Lizzy's stomach did a curlicue when Roman spoke.

"You know how we've known each other for a few months?"

"Yes. I moved in two months ago."

"Since then, we've become good friends, right?"

Oh, no. He was going to tell her about some girlfriend who was jealous of their friendship. Tears filled her eyes and threatened to overflow. All she could do was nod.

"Well—"

The slider opened, and Abby stuck her head out. "I'm done, Mom. Come see."

Roman's shoulders dropped.

"Sorry," Lizzy said as she stood and bolted for the door. "Can we finish this later?"

"Sure." Roman stood and shuffled across the two yards and headed into his house.

That night Lizzy's bed was an ocean, and she was a fish, tossed from side to side trying to sleep. What was Roman going to say? Her mind went to the worst possible scenario. He was moving. That had to be it. She'd say bye-bye to her friend. It was possible he was moving because of her, if Roman thought of her as more than a friend and suspected she didn't feel the same.

There was Abby to consider. She'd miss him like crazy. He was a big brother and uncle rolled into one. Then there was the issue of Abby's dad. The last thing in the world Lizzy wanted was to find Dylan James. It would be easier if he was dead. They could both move on and forget his existence. The only thing Dylan had given her of value was Abby. For that she was grateful.

The next morning, Lizzy's red and sandy eyes stared back at her from the bathroom mirror. She blinked, trying to bring some moisture to the tired orbs. Coffee would help.

Once the flurry of breakfast, fixing Abby's hair, helping her dress, and loading the art project into the car was complete, she swung through Dutch Bros on her way to work to caffeine-load. There was enough change in the car's cup holder to cover the extra expense of the mocha. As she pulled into the drug store parking lot, her cell beeped with an incoming text. Lizzy took a long sip of her drink to brace herself to read the text.

"Alert! House Lottery finalists will be announced on April 30, 2023, at Town Hall. 601 Main Street, Main, Oregon at 7:00 pm."

Her nerves jumped with a combination of fear and excitement. Finally! She bounced out of the car and practically danced into work.

"You're jangly this morning," Josiah commented as she clocked in. "Too much caffeine again?"

"Nope," she said, swirling around him as she headed for her locker. "The lottery finalists will be announced next week."

He nodded. "Ah. Think you have a chance?"

Lizzy shrugged. "No idea. But at least I'll know something one way or the other."

Josiah smiled. "Good luck."

When he left, Lizzy pocketed her phone in her smock, which was a no-no. She wanted to make sure she got any updates as soon as they happened. Sure enough, Simone texted with the link to the announcement. Soon after, Roman did too. Lizzy called her mom on her break to tell her the news.

"Well, at least you'll get your disappointment over quickly," Mom said.

"You don't think I can win?" *Thanks for the vote of confidence, Mother.*

"Elizabeth." Uh oh, when Mom used her given name, she meant business. "You didn't do well in school, remember? Certain, uh, circumstances kept you from learning. You were lucky to get your GED."

"Gosh, Mom. Thanks a bunch."

"I don't want you to be hurt, sweetheart."

Right. As if. Sure, mom wasn't the most supportive in the world. The two women Lizzy called the church ladies had mothered her more than Mom had. After she'd gotten pregnant, Mom pretty much threw up her hands. She'd been out of control for a long time and getting pregnant was her last straw. If Simone hadn't invited her to church, Lizzy didn't know where she'd have ended up.

"I want to talk to you about the guy, Roman. Why did you invite him to Abby's party?"

"Mom, I gotta go. My break's over." Lizzy disconnected, let down and frustrated. Was there anyone who would be happy if she won the house? And why would Mom be annoyed she'd invited Roman to Abby's party?

Lizzy's musings were interrupted by a constant flow of customers. The community buzzed with anticipation of the announcement.

Sarah approached the register with a basket of purchases to be rung up.

"Did you hear?" she asked. "The finalists will be announced next week!"

"I heard," Lizzy said without enthusiasm. Between Mom's obvious judgment of her writing skills, and her question about Roman coming to Abby's party, she'd lost all the caffeine-powered energy she'd had.

"I have to wonder," Sarah continued, "Why is there more than one finalist? I thought there'd be one winner and that was that."

"I dunno." Lizzy scanned her purchases and shoved them into the reusable bag Sara placed on the counter.

"I'll bet you win," Sara said with a smile. "I know how much you want the house. I've been praying it will be yours."

Hm. Lizzy relied on Sarah's wisdom in spiritual things, but she wasn't convinced God was interested in whether she won or lost the house. She'd prayed for a lot of things which never happened over the years. Something this big was surely beyond God.

"Thanks, Miss Sarah. I appreciate it." Lizzy handed her bag across the counter with what she hoped was a smile.

"Keep the faith, Elizabeth." Sarah patted Lizzy's hand and walked to the door, athletic shoes squeaking on the linoleum.

Lizzy finished the rest of her shift by rote. By the time she clocked out, her feet hurt, her back hurt, and her head hurt. Even Abby's after-school chatter failed to cheer her up.

They ate frozen waffles and scrambled eggs for dinner, then Lizzy sent Abby to her room for an hour of screen time with her iPad. She downed some aspirin and sat at the table with her sketch pad. The last page showed the ocean drawing, the lonely ship on an angry sea. The somber message life was about to become messy.

"Well, God, let's see what you have for me today." Lizzy had read a book, *The Story of With* a few months prior. The allegory was about creating with God. Since then, her drawings had taken on a deeper resonance. She believed God spoke to her through her pencil. Not always, but Lizzy knew when it happened.

She opened to a fresh page and started with a gray pencil. Her mind conjured up bars, like a jail. Then a woman, staring through the bars at a large animal. Something like a bear. It was difficult to tell if the woman was on the inside of the cell and the bear outside, or vice versa. Lizzy rested her chin on her hands.

She jumped at the sound of a knock on the sliding glass door. She swirled around to see Roman, holding a pink box.

"Come on in - it's not locked."

He stepped in, holding out the box. "I brought donuts. I know, it's typical breakfast fare, but I couldn't resist."

Lizzy smiled for the first time that day. "You know the key to my heart. Comfort food in donut form."

Roman looked like he bit back whatever he was going to say.

"Want some coffee?" Lizzy asked, knowing he'd answer in the affirmative. She bit into a cake donut with sprinkles as she filled the coffee pot.

"Where's Abby?" Roman asked, glancing into the living room.

"She's in her room, probably deep into Mine Craft. She'll be out the minute she smells the donuts. I swear she can smell sugar a mile away."

Roman chuckled, then reached for a glazed sugar-coated donut. They shared the same sweet tooth. Anything baked, fried, and filled with sugar was Lizzy's weakness. And his. A sigh escaped her. When Roman moved, who would be her sugar supplier? She couldn't afford to buy many extras like donuts. Some months she and Abby survived on mac and cheese and Top Ramen.

As soon as the coffee finished brewing, Abby bounced out of her bedroom and pirouetted through the living room and into the kitchen.

"I smell something great," she announced, spying the pink box on the table. "Yummy! Donuts. Can I have one?" she asked, reaching for the box.

"One and done," Lizzy told her.

"But you'll eat at least two," Abby complained.

"That's because I'm an adult. When you're an adult, you can eat as many donuts as you want."

Abby rolled her eyes, then smiled at Roman with chocolate-smeared lips "Thanks for the treat, Roman."

He winked at her. "No problem, Ladybug. I was driving home from Portland, and I saw this beautiful pink box lying by the side of the road. I couldn't help but pull over and check it out. Guess what?"

"What?" Abby asked, leaning across the table.

"There was an entire dozen donuts in the box. So, I picked it up and put it in my car."

Abby looked horrified. "These were on the side of the road? What if a bug got on them?"

"Oh, I brushed all the bugs off."

Abby dropped her donut on the table, then stood back, hands on hips. "You better be kidding."

Roman and Lizzy shared a chuckle. "What do you think?" he asked.

Abby narrowed her eyes and glared. Then she

picked her donut back up and examined it before taking another bite. "I think if you aren't kidding, then I might have to hurt you."

Oh, my goodness. Precocious and adorable. Lizzy's heart swelled.

"All right, Bug," Lizzy said, "Here's a glass of milk." She glanced at the clock. You have about twenty minutes before you start getting ready for bed."

"Okay." Abby drank down her glass of milk, then retreated to her room.

Roman and Lizzy sipped their coffee in comfortable silence as they each helped themselves into a second donut.

"Thanks for bringing these. I needed some comfort food."

"Why? I thought you'd be excited the finalists will finally be announced."

"Yeah, that." Lizzy closed the drawing pad in case Roman asked about the picture. She needed some time to figure out what her subconscious was saying. "I am. I was. The thing is, there's so much at stake. If I'm a finalist, how long will I have to wait until the winner is announced? I may not have a place to live by then."

"Hey, stop worrying. Have you ever been homeless?"

"No."

"Ever not had enough to eat?"

Lizzy thought of the boxed mac and cheese they'd sometimes had for days, but they'd never actually gone hungry. "No."

"Then why worry about something which

probably won't happen?"

"Probably won't happen isn't good enough," she said, getting up to refill their mugs.

"Okay, then, something which *won't* happen."

Lizzy let out a sigh. "I know. God's got this. But why did the attorney letter have to come now?"

Roman shrugged. "I don't know. But I do know one thing. Even if you lose the house lottery, someone will take you in and give you a place to stay. You won't be homeless."

"Right," she said. Her mom lived in a one-bedroom apartment in Salem. Simone would be taking in her sister. The church ladies, Sarah and Beth shared a mobile home in a fifty-plus community. The only one Lizzy knew with extra bedrooms was Roman.

Roman stood, drained his coffee, and moved toward the door. "I won't let you be homeless."

He was out the door before Lizzy could respond. What was that supposed to mean? And why hadn't she asked him about what he'd wanted to talk about? Her head ached from the stress.

The next morning, Lizzy rushed into work, buttoning her smock on the way through the door.

"You're late." Josiah's face was grim.

"Uh, yeah. Sorry. Abby couldn't find her shoes."

"I need to talk to you after you clock in," Josiah said.

Uh oh. Not good. Was he going to write her up for tardiness? Lizzy sighed as she logged onto the computer in the break room. Sometimes it was hard being a single mom. Most days she fell into bed, exhausted. She carried the weight of, well, everything. Food, clothing, shelter; all her responsibility. Too bad someone hadn't told her at seventeen how difficult it would be. Would she have listened? Probably not.

Lizzy thought of the song "Dear Younger Me" by Mercy Me. If she knew then what she knew now . . . Ah, well. Better go face the music with Josiah and get it over with.

Josiah's office was no more than a glorified broom closet off the back storeroom. Lizzy would never get any work done in such a mess. Gray metal shelves held manuals and binders, plus a lot of stuff she couldn't identify. The concrete walls may have once been painted, but the color had either worn off or faded. Her artistic sense was deeply troubled by the chaos.

"Have a seat, Elizabeth," Josiah said, motioning toward the one hard metal chair in front of his scarred desk.

Her stomach twisted. Any time her full name was used it usually wasn't good.

In middle school: *"Elizabeth, you are being suspended for fighting."*

In high school: *"Elizabeth, please go to the principal's office."*

At the crisis pregnancy center: *"Elizabeth, the test is positive. You are pregnant."*

Now, Josiah. Was she going to be fired?

Josiah stroked his clipped beard. His eyes were downcast as if he'd laid out a script on the desk. "Things here at the store have been exceptionally tight since the Covid-19 outbreak. Business has slowed down as more people go online to purchase goods and services."

This was it. She was being laid off. Lizzy was grateful her hours hadn't been cut during the height of the coronavirus closures. Theirs was deemed an essential business. What would she do now? She would have no job and potentially no place to live.

Josiah continued. "Management is forced to lay some people off —"

She knew it. She was being canned.

"— And others will have their hours cut. You will continue your employment here, and you'll be three-quarters time."

Lizzy managed to inhale around the band squeezing her chest. "I'm not fired?" she managed to squeak out.

Josiah shook his head. "At this time, no. Beginning next week, you'll be working thirty hours instead of forty. I'll post the new schedule after I've had the opportunity to speak to all the employees."

Lizzy nodded silently.

"And I'd appreciate it if you wouldn't mention this to anyone else yet. The information should come from me."

Lizzy had never heard Josiah this serious. Gone was the friendly banter. He was all business, and don't you forget it. Lizzy was tempted to say, "Yes, sir!" but it would probably come out snarky. No sense in giving him any ammunition to let her go instead of someone else.

"Okay," she finally said, stirring out of her

mental calculation of where she could cut back the already stretched-thin budget.

"Could you please send Alan in to see me?"

"Sure." Lizzy stood and made her way through the storeroom and out into the store. She found Alan restocking the paper products aisle.

"Hey, Alan. Josiah wants to see you in his office."

Alan's face turned white, then red. "What's up?"

Lizzy shrugged.

Alan's voice dropped to a whisper. "I heard a rumor they're closing the store. I can't lose this job." He took a furtive look around. "I'm helping support my mom. She has lung complications after contracting the coronavirus. Without this job, we'll lose the house."

Lizzy could relate. Maybe Alan, his mom, Abby, and she could all move into an apartment together. Lizzy liked Alan. He was a nice kid. But like her, he'd made mistakes in his past and had no real job skills.

"You'd better go, Alan. Josiah's waiting."

He looked ready to cry. Lizzy swirled around and strode to the front register. The last thing she needed today was some kid crying on her shoulder.

As she rang into the register, Lizzy thought about what Alan had said about the store closing. This reduction in staff might be the beginning. If things didn't improve, the store could eventually go out of business. People would have to go to Salem for their pharmacy services.

Where would it leave her? She should try to

find another job. Something full-time, with benefits. Surely with her three years of employment history here, she could find something.

If she won the house, it would at least take some of the pressure off. If she didn't win, well, it was a worry consuming most of her waking hours.

Mom's words rang in her head. She was right, Lizzy hadn't been a great student. The reality was, she barely passed her junior year before dropping out completely to have Abby. She'd been more interested in partying than in studying. She might as well get used to the fact a long line of poor decisions brought her to where she was today. Barely scraping by, practically homeless, and in a dead-end job.

At times like these, Lizzy was tempted to buy a bottle of whiskey and numb the pain, even if temporarily. If it was only her, she'd do it in a hot minute. But she couldn't do that to her daughter. Nor to God.

The more Lizzy thought about her situation, the more the vortex of depression sucked her around and around, deeper and deeper. God seemed like a distant, fog-shrouded dream.

As Lizzy went through the motions of ringing up purchases and straightening shelves, her thoughts turned again to what Roman had started to say the other night when Abby had interrupted. If he was moving, why hadn't he brought it up again last night? When he'd said, 'I won't let you be homeless,' what did it mean? Was he offering to let Abby and her stay with him? Not that she would. Appearances of evil and all that. Tongues would wag he and Lizzy were sleeping together, which would damage both of their reputations, not to mention the effect it would have on Abby.

On her lunch break, Lizzy grabbed her peanut butter sandwich and headed to her car. She punched in Sarah's number.

"Well, hello, Lizzy. What a pleasant surprise to hear from you." Sarah's voice oozed warmth, exactly what Lizzy needed.

"Oh, Sarah, everything is going wrong." Tears filled Lizzy's eyes and spilled down her cheeks.

"What is it, my dear? What's happened?"

Lizzy took a shuddering breath. "You know Mrs. Carmichael died, right?"

"Yes. I'm going to her funeral next week."

"Her kids are selling the house and I have to m-m-ove." Lizzy wailed into the phone.

"Oh, sweet girl. You know you and Abby always have a place with Ruth and me."

"Th-that's not all." Lizzy wiped her face with the hem of her work smock. "My hours got cut. I don't know how I'm going to make it." She bent over, resting her forehead on the steering wheel while tears coursed down her face.

Sarah's voice was no nonsense. "Stop that, Elizabeth. You know God is in control, don't you?"

"Uh-huh."

"Then let's take a moment to pray about this. The Lord loves you, Lizzy, and He won't let you down. Not now, not ever."

Lizzy took a deep breath and exhaled while Sarah prayed for her and the impossible situation she faced.

"There now, Lizzy. You need to remember all the times God has come through for you in the past, okay?"

"Okay." Lizzy wished Sarah could wave a magic wand and make all her troubles disappear. Since that wasn't going to happen, she'd take Sarah's advice and try to walk by faith.

"Thanks, Miss Sarah. I love you."

"I love you, too, Lizzy. And God does too."

Lizzy was anxious to get off work and sit down with her budget app to see if there was any place in her budget she could cut to make her new thirty-hour schedule work. Lizzy sighed. She could stop eating or cut off the internet for a few months. Ride Abby's ancient bike to work.

Adulting was hard.

Chapter 11

As Lizzy drove home after picking Abby up from after-school daycare, she mentally reviewed what she had in the fridge to fix for dinner.

"How about breakfast for dinner?" Lizzy said, hoping Abby was in a good mood. Like Lizzy, she became hangry if she went without sustenance for too long.

Abby stared out the side window. "Whatever."

Lizzy raised her eyebrows. "Excuse me?" Where did she learn *that*? It was textbook teen-speak-attitude, and Lizzy wasn't having any of it.

Abby turned, looked her in the eye, and repeated it. "Whatever."

Lizzy was almost too tired to deal with her daughter's little act of rebellion. Almost, but not quite. "Abby," she began, drawing on her last ounce of patience, "'Whatever' is not an answer. I would appreciate either a yes or no. Do you understand?"

Abby's eyes filled with tears.

Lizzy's mama's heart melted. "What's going on, Bug?"

Abby sniffled. "Some girls at school made fun of me. They said I was a loser because I only got a

Fitbit for my birthday, not an Apple watch like them."

Her mama's heart turned into a mama bear. Lizzy wanted to find those little brats and rip their hair out. Then set it on fire.

Lizzy took a deep breath to calm herself before answering. "First of all, you aren't a loser. There will always be other girls who have more than you, and some who have less than you. What you have or don't have doesn't make you a loser. It's who you are in the sight of God, your Creator."

Lizzy glanced in the rearview mirror to be sure Abby was tracking. "Second, you are incredibly gifted. You're artistic, fun, pretty, and a great dancer." This brought a slight smile to her daughter's face. "And you know what? You always beat me at cards."

Abby sighed and wiped her eyes with the sleeve of her tee shirt.

"I know it's hard, Ladybug. It's hard for me too sometimes."

Abby pulled the neck of her tee shirt over her mouth, holding it with both hands. "When you find my dad, he can come live with us and help us."

Lizzy couldn't speak past the ache in her chest. Her past mistakes always reared up and smacked her when she was most vulnerable. She should have tried to keep in touch with Dylan. Maybe he would have manned up and sent child support.

Lizzy braked to a stop in front of the house. Abby unbuckled her seat belt and hopped out of the car. Lizzy stared at the house without moving. Only a few more weeks before they had to move. She kept thinking if she ignored the letter, it would go away. Like she did when she got pregnant with Abby. As it turned out, ignoring a problem only makes it bigger. Welcome to adulthood.

Lizzy climbed out of the car as Simone pulled up in her Subaru. Lizzy wasn't sure she could face Simone right now. But Simone got out of her car carrying a pizza box. Yup, she could face her. Simone had her at pizza.

"Hey, friend! I brought food. Hope you're hungry."

Abby jumped up and down at the front door. "Yay! I'm starved. You're the best!"

Guess Lizzy couldn't expect much of an enthusiastic response with pancakes. Not when the spicy scent of marinara sauce wafted from the box in Simone's hands.

"Hey, Simone. Let me get the door unlocked and I'll get us something to drink. I have water, water, or water."

Simone grinned and followed, the pizza smell making Lizzy's stomach growl. She'd been too upset to eat the peanut butter sandwich she'd taken for lunch.

Simone deposited the pizza on the table and pulled out a chair while Lizzy grabbed napkins and glasses of water.

"Go wash your hands, Bug, and we'll say grace."

Abby rushed to the bathroom and came back ten seconds later. "Uh-uh, let me look at those mitts," Lizzy said, examining her hands for cleanliness. Abby fidgeted until Lizzy finally released her with a sigh. "Fine, go sit and we'll pray."

"I'll pray," Abby offered. "Thankyouforthefoodamen." Before either adult could stop her, Abby grabbed a slice and took a huge bite.

"Hungry much?" Simone asked.

Lizzy eyed Simone as she searched for the skinniest piece in the box. Simone's job as a personal trainer meant she had to stay fit as an example for her clients. Lizzy knew from experience Simone would have one or two pieces of pizza, then leave her and Abby with the leftovers. Although after the day Lizzy had, there might not be any leftovers. Lizzy needed comfort food and she wouldn't care about how tight her jeans fit tomorrow.

"How was your day?" Simone asked.

"Fine." Lizzy shook her head slightly and nodded toward Abby, whose attention was on choosing another piece of pizza. She and Simone had been friends long enough to know each other's signals. Lizzy's body language told her they'd talk after Abby left the room.

They'd met in middle school when Simone's family moved to Main to get out of the 'big city' of Salem. Simone's older brother had been hanging with some bad people, so her dad, Cassius, moved them to the little town of Main. As one of a handful of outcast kids in the school, Lizzy's group had quickly assimilated her into their band of miscreants. Until their sophomore year, Simone had been content to hang with them and do all the bad stuff they could think of. Besides drinking and smoking pot, they'd tag the random abandoned farmhouse, or let the air out of a rancher's tractor tires. Dumb stuff.

When Simone went to a summer camp after their sophomore year, she came back different. She'd spent the summer with her grandma in Atlanta and attended a church camp put on by her grandma's church. Simone came back to school talking about 'getting saved' and 'finding Jesus.' It was all foreign to Lizzy, but she loved Simone like a sister. Lizzy resisted Simone's efforts to get her to church. Until Lizzy found out she was pregnant. Simone stuck by her when no one else did.

That's why it hurt to have this house thing between them. Lizzy didn't want Simone to win because Lizzy wanted to win. Simone had her family to fall back on if she didn't win. Lizzy had no one. She'd be living in her car. That wouldn't be the kind of life Lizzy wanted for her daughter.

"Let's sit outside," Lizzy said, pulling open the heavy glass door. "We'll be outside," she called over her shoulder to Abby. No response. She probably had her face deep in Mine Craft by now. Or one of those Barbie-type dress-up games to keep her occupied, so Lizzy could vent to Simone about the unfairness of life.

"What's up," Simone asked as they stretched their legs out to catch the last rays of the early evening sun.

"Today was the worst," Lizzy moaned. "Management cut everyone's hours at the store.

Well, not everyone. Some people got laid off." Her chin sank to her chest. "I don't know how I'm going to pay rent, buy food, keep gas in my car," she ticked off the items on her fingers. "And utilities, cell phone, blah, blah, blah."

"That stinks."

"Thank you, Captain Obvious." She hadn't meant to sound sarcastic, but Simone usually had a quick fix-it answer. Lizzy loved her to death, but Simone always came across as the expert in everything. Where was all her advice now?

"Sorry. That was harsh." If she apologized, Simone would have some magic answer.

Simone gave her a closed-mouth smile. "I don't know what to tell you, girlfriend. Can you get a part-time job somewhere to make up the money?"

It was Lizzy's turn to shrug. "I guess. But childcare is difficult. My hours fit perfectly with Abby's after-school care. I'd probably end up getting an evening shift, which would mean I'd have to pay for someone to watch her." Lizzy chewed her lip, thinking of possibilities.

Simone leaned forward. "Look, I know it's none of my business, but what about him?" She gestured toward Roman's house with a thumb.

"What about him?"

Simone chewed on her bottom lip for a moment before answering. "Roman adores you."

Lizzy opened her mouth to protest.

"Hear me out," Simone said, cutting her off with a gesture. "You are blind, deaf, and dumb if you can't see the man is clearly in love with you. And with Abby. If you gave him even half a chance, no, a quarter of a chance, he'd ask you to marry him. All this," Simone waved a hand, and the house Lizzy was being evicted from. "Would be taken care of. You'd have a place to live, a man who worships the ground you walk on, and from what I can see, he'd be a great father for Abby." Simone raised her hands in surrender.

Lizzy slumped against the back of her chair. "I don't need a white knight to swoop me up and save me."

"Do you like him like that, even a little bit?" Simone probed.

"I don't know. I guess I've got to wrap my head around it." Lizzy raised her hands. "We're just friends."

Simone shook her head. "Girl, you are so lame." She stood and looked down at Lizzy. "Good thing I love you. I gotta go. I have a new client coming in at six a.m."

Anxious to change the subject, Lizzy asked, "Oh, yeah? Who?"

"A bride-to-be who wants to drop a size or two to fit into her wedding dress."

Lizzy laughed. "Don't they all?"

"Uh-huh. Wish me luck." Simone fluttered her fingers goodbye. "Keep the rest of the pizza. I happen to know you like it cold for breakfast."

Lizzy grinned. "You know me too well."

She watched Simone walk around the house toward the front where her car was parked. Someone a few blocks over was mowing their lawn and the roar of the mower invaded the silence. Lizzy pulled her legs up and wrapped her arms around them, resting her head on her knees.

While Simone's suggestion made sense, Lizzy had no interest in marrying someone because he owned a lifeboat. What Lizzy needed was a plan. She'd made it this long alone, she'd do it again. Sarah had a point; if God was truly in control, then He knew Lizzy needed a miracle, not a husband.

She poked her head in the house and called, "Abby!"

"Yeah?" came her daughter's answer from the bowels of her bedroom.

"Start getting ready for bed. I'll be outside."

"K."

Back outside, Lizzy flipped open the pad to a blank page. Bowing her head, she whispered a quick prayer. "God, things are such a mess right now. Please show me what your will is."

Keeping her eyes closed, Lizzy blocked out all the negative images of the past few weeks. The letter from the attorney, Abby asking about her dad, the job and resulting money issues, the house lottery, and finally, what Simone had said about Roman.

When she was ready, Lizzy let her fingers fly over the gleaming white page.

-*-

Roman paced from the kitchen to the living room and back. At each pass through the dining room, he glanced across the expanse of lawn separating his house from Lizzy's. Through the sliding glass door, he could see Lizzy, Simone, and Abby eating pizza.

"Wish they'd hurry up and finish," he

muttered. Probably getting caught up on girl talk, whatever that was. He wanted, no, *needed*, to talk to Lizzy. He'd been ready to ask her out a few nights ago until Abby interrupted. He adored the kid, but she had the worst timing.

Shoving his hands in the pockets of his khakis, he stopped in front of the glass slider and stared out. Finally, Abby disappeared, and the ladies stood up from the table.

Oh, no, they were headed to Lizzy's back porch. Roman quickly hid from view. The last thing he wanted her to think was he was a creepy stalker.

Well, aren't you? His inner geek could be super annoying.

Roman turned and sat at his laptop, forcing himself to concentrate on breaking past the firewall of his company's recent client. They'd hired his firm to beef up their online security. After Simone left, he'd tell Lizzy about the possible solution to her problem of having a place to live.

Roman took a deep breath, slid open his back door, and headed across their yards. Lizzy looked up as he approached. Before he could get close, she slapped the drawing pad closed. Was she blushing? Interesting.

"Hey," he said, dropping into the chair Simone had vacated. "Hope I didn't interrupt you."

Lizzy placed her palm on the sketch pad. "Not at all." She kept her eyes glued to the back of her hand.

"Did you and Simone have a good time?" he asked. What a lame question. Of course, they 'had a good time.' He mocked himself. Something in the atmosphere between them had changed and he was helpless to figure out what it was. If only there was a program, an algorithm to decipher relationships. Or the atmosphere hadn't changed, his feelings had changed.

"Uh-huh," Lizzy answered. "We had pizza."

Roman nodded. "Good." Roman struggled to break the uncomfortable silence. "How was work today?"

"Don't ask."

Uh oh. "What happened?"

Lizzy finally looked up and he saw tears sparkling in the corners of her eyes.

"My hours got cut. I'll be working thirty hours."

Roman floundered for an answer. "That's good, right? You'll have time now to study for your interior design classes."

Lizzy's face turned bright red. "You don't get it, do you?"

She was angry. What had he said? "Uh, I guess not."

Lizzy leaped to her feet. "I can barely afford to pay rent as it is. How am I supposed to support Abby and myself on thirty hours?"

"But—"

"I can't talk to you right now," Lizzy said, brushing past him and heading into the house. She slammed the slider closed, rattling the glass, and he heard the decisive click of the lock.

Roman rubbed his face. Where had he gone wrong? The better question was, how could he fix this?

He slapped a bug that landed on his arm and looked up at the sky. "God, are you listening? Need a little help here."

With a sigh, he stood and headed back to his house in the gathering darkness.

Roman's phone pinged with an incoming text. His heart jumped. What if it was from Lizzy. An apology or an explanation.

Neither. Another text from his former best friend.

Colin: **Did you get my text?**

Roman slumped onto the bench and stared at the screen. Might as well get it over with. Finally, he tapped out a response.

Yes. What's up?

Colin: **I need to talk to you. Can we meet for coffee?**

Ugh. That sounded worse than having a root canal. Without Novocain. There was nothing Colin had to say Roman wanted to hear. He'd closed the door behind Colin and Shayna and double bolt locked it.

A teeny-tiny voice whispered in Roman's ear.

"First go and be reconciled with your brother or sister, and then come and offer your gift." The exact reference escaped him, but Roman recognized the nudging of the Holy Spirit. Totally different from his nagging inner geek.

He pinched his lips together and tapped out an answer.

Sure. When.

They decided to meet the following afternoon in McMinnville, about half-way between the Main and Beaverton.

Roman tossed the phone onto the other end of the sofa and scrubbed his face with his hands. This couldn't be good. If Colin asked him to be the best man for his and Shayna's wedding, well, that wasn't going to happen.

Hard no, his inner geek said.

Yup, Roman agreed.

Chapter 12

Lizzy locked the back door to keep Roman from thinking he could come inside. She grabbed a rag, wet it, and scrubbed the pizza crumbs off the table, muttering to herself.

"What an idiot. Sure, he's got the six-figure income and can't imagine what it's like to be broke."

Once the table had been scrubbed within an inch of its life, Lizzy sank onto a chair and flipped open her pad. She prayed, then let her hand go.

"You're joking, right God?" Lizzy asked when the drawing was complete.

On the page was a Norman Rockwell-style drawing of a house. A dog played in the yard, and a family of four held hands beneath a tall oak tree. Two adults and two kids. A boy and a girl.

"What did I miss, Lord?" If He was speaking to her about Roman, it should be a family of three. The two kids looked remarkably close in age. This drawing was weird. It wouldn't be the first time she'd missed Him.

With a sigh, Lizzy headed to Abby's bedroom to kiss her goodnight. After, she planned to take a couple of Aspirin and fall into bed. Tomorrow things would look better.

With a twinge, Lizzy realized she should apologize to Roman for her outburst. Tomorrow.

Lizzy made sure she was a few minutes early for work the next day. She didn't want to give Josiah and any senior management the idea she wasn't a valuable employee. She'd dragged Abby to school with her hair unbrushed and mismatched socks. Despite Abby's sullen attitude, Lizzy had pulled into the parking lot at the drug store a full five minutes before she needed to clock in.

"Good morning, Josiah," she called out as she breezed by him to clock in on the workstation computer.

Josiah's eyebrows rose as he made a show of looking at his watch. "Who are you and what did you do with Elizabeth?"

Lizzy shrugged, determined to have a positive attitude, no matter what. She'd sent off a quick text to Roman with two words. "I'm sorry." He hadn't answered. He needed some time to forgive her. Or he was still mad. Or he was driving to Portland for his weekly staff meeting and couldn't text back.

She was over-thinking the situation. Last night it had been easier to blow up at Roman than to watch for any signs of attraction on his part.

Lizzy shrugged into her work smock and headed out to the floor. It was her turn to check the bathrooms. It was everyone's least favorite job. Alan was already on the floor, checking inventory.

"Hey," she called to him.

Alan smiled. "I still have a job."

"That's good." Lizzy smiled back.

"I'm relieved," Alan gushed. "My hours were cut, but it's cool with me. I was offered a part-time job doing yard work for some neighbors. It will keep me from losing any money."

Lizzy struggled to keep her smile. "That's great, Alan. Good for you."

Stay positive, she told herself. "Well, I'm off to check on the bathrooms," she said with forced cheerfulness.

"Have fun."

Lizzy did a quick touch-up on the restrooms, then headed back to the front register. She pulled a dust rag and a can of cleaner out from under the counter and started dusting the displays behind the register.

God's got this, she reminded herself. He'd help her find a place to live if she didn't win the house. He'd help her figure out this thing with Roman. The thing was, Roman was a cute guy. He had the nerd vibe going for him, which was endearing. His blue eyes always smiled, even if his mouth didn't. He'd been a huge help when Lizzy needed an emergency babysitter. Abby loved spending time with him, and he was good with her.

An impatient tapping on the counter pulled her out of her thoughts. She whirled to face Mariah.

"Oh, sorry. I didn't hear you."

"Obviously," Mariah sniffed.

Today Mariah wore skinny jeans, ripped in all the right places to be stylish. The silk tee shirt screamed expensive. Lizzy ran her hand over the front of her smock, grateful the other woman couldn't see the faded tee she wore underneath.

"How's your day going so far," Lizzy asked, trying her best to show good customer service as she'd been taught.

Mariah's lips thinned into a straight line before she spoke. "You're not going to win, you know."

Lizzy bit back the remark which sprang to her lips. Instead, she kept silent and scanned Mariah's purchases. In the bottom of the basket was a pregnancy test.

Again? She'd already bought one a couple of weeks ago. Lizzy kept her face neutral as she totaled the items.

Mariah slipped her American Express Platinum card into the reader, signed with a flourish, and took the bag Lizzy slid across the counter.

Lizzy tried to keep the sarcasm out of her voice as she said, "Have a nice day."

Mariah didn't respond. Lizzy watched Mariah's back until she exited. As soon as the doors swished closed, Lizzy slumped against the counter.

What was it about Mariah that brought out the worst in her? They were both adults, for heaven's sake. Why did she keep comparing herself to the other woman and find herself coming up short?

It was obvious the difference in their social status and income brackets. Mariah came from money. As a spoiled only child, she wanted for nothing. Lizzy, raised by a single mom, had struggled for everything. Getting pregnant in high school had set her back as well, both educationally and financially.

Lizzy sighed, then picked up the dust cloth, wondering why Roman hadn't returned her early morning text. She should have said more than 'I'm sorry.' This relationship, or friendship, or whatever, was becoming too complicated. Time to take a step back. Or ten.

As she moved things off the shelves and scrubbed away the dust and bugs which accumulated behind the display, her cell buzzed. Glancing around to be sure Josiah wasn't within eyesight, Lizzy pulled it out. Not a text from Roman, but a call from Abby's school.

Heart in her throat, she answered. "Hello?"

"Ms. Greene?" The admin's voice sounded stressed.

"Yes." Lizzy tried to calm her breathing. The school only called if Abby was ill or hurt.

"I'm calling to see if Abby is ill today?"

"Uh, no. Is she running a fever?"

"She isn't here. Usually, you call if she is home sick."

A jolt of adrenaline raised Lizzy's voice an octave. "What do you mean, she isn't at school. I dropped her off an hour ago." There had to be a mistake. She'd watched Abby hop out of the car. Had she seen her walk past the gate? She'd been in a hurry to get to work. What if someone snatched her? Lizzy's breath hitched as she imagined the worst.

"I'm sorry, Ms. Greene. Abby didn't show up for class. We've already checked all the other classrooms, the restrooms, and the playground. She isn't here on the school grounds."

Lizzy bent over as the blood drained from her head. The edges of her vision darkened. "Oh my gosh. What should I do?"

The admin's voice shook. "Go to the police department."

Lizzy disconnected and almost dropped her phone as she headed to the break room on wobbly legs.

Josiah intercepted her. "Your break isn't for another hour."

Lizzy glanced at him, unfocused.

Josiah grabbed her arm. "What's wrong? Your face is white."

"I have to go. Abby's missing."

"Missing?"

"She didn't show up for school today." Lizzy's voice caught. "I think she's been kidnapped."

"Oh, my gosh. Go." Josiah gave her a push toward the lockers. "Please keep me posted, Elizabeth."

Lizzy wasn't sure if she responded as she grabbed her purse.

She sped through the tiny downtown, breaking the twenty-mile-an-hour speed limit, and jerked to a stop in front of the police station. The air was heavy with the scent of wet pavement. Gray clouds scuttled across the sky as Lizzy grabbed her purse and dashed inside the brick building.

A uniformed woman sat behind the counter, pecking at a computer.

"My daughter's been kidnapped," Lizzy said,

her breath coming in puffs.

The officer's head swung up. "Excuse me?"

Lizzy's words came out in a rush. "She didn't show up for school. I swear I dropped her off, but the school called me and said she wasn't there. I think she's been kidnapped."

"Let me get someone," the officer said, standing and heading through a door with a distinct lack of urgency.

Lizzy drummed her fingers on the counter fighting nausea. How could this happen? Who would take her sweet little girl? Tears formed in the corners of her eyes as she imagined the worst.

A few minutes later, the female officer returned, followed by a man in dark slacks and a golf shirt. The gun holster at his waist was the only indication he was a police officer.

"Ma'am, my name is Detective O'Brien. I understand your daughter didn't show up for school today?"

"Yes, that's right. You have to find her."

"Come with me and tell me what happened." Detective O'Brien opened the gate and indicated Lizzy should pass through. "Let's go back to my office."

He led the way down a short hall and into an office barely larger than Josiah's at the drug store. Lizzy collapsed on the only chair as the detective sat in a metal desk chair that squeaked under his weight. He pulled a yellow pad toward him.

"Let's start at the beginning."

Lizzy took a deep breath to try to calm herself. "I dropped Abby off at school—"

"What time?"

"It was around eight." Lizzy thought back. She'd been in such a hurry to get to work. The tears spilled over, dripping down her cheeks.

"Is eight your normal time?"

Lizzy nodded, then shook her head. "It was before eight. I usually drop her off at eight, but I was. . ." This was all her fault. She should have waited until Abby disappeared into the schoolyard. Lizzy sniffed and scrubbed her cheeks with her hands.

"How much before eight?" The detective's words felt like pointed darts, accusing Lizzy of being a bad parent.

"A few minutes, I think. I dropped her off, then went to work."

The detective scribbled notes on the pad. "Can you think of anyone who would want to harm your daughter?"

"No!"

"How old is your daughter?"

"Abby is ten." Lizzy thought back to Abby's recent birthday party. They'd had a lot of fun celebrating the milestone of being in 'double digits.'

"Okay, let's backtrack a little. Your name?"

They went through the basics, name, address, Abby's grade in school, her teacher.

"Any behavioral problems at school?"

"No, she's a good kid. Not an A student, but solid B's."

"Is there anyone else living with you?"

"No, why?" Where was he headed with this line of questioning?

"Do you have a boyfriend or ex-boyfriend who might want to hurt you or your daughter?"

"No." Lizzy shook her head.

Detective O'Brien reached for the desk phone. "Let me call your daughter's school and see if she's shown up. Sometimes these things have a way of resolving themselves."

Lizzy's heart pounded a staccato beat as she listened to the one-sided conversation.

Please let her be there. Please let her be there. Lizzy's prayer was a mantra, willing it to happen.

"Okay, thank you," the detective said. "Let me know if she shows up." He laid the phone in the cradle with a grim look.

"Let's go over this again." He picked up his pen and pulled the tablet toward him.

"This is all my fault," Lizzy wailed, choking on her tears.

The detective reached into his desk and brought out a box of tissues. "This isn't your fault, ma'am," he said, shoving the box toward her.

Lizzy pulled out several tissues and pressed them to her eyes. "I was in a hurry to get to work. I usually drop her off at eight, but I wanted to get to work early. Because my hours got cut, and I wanted to show I was a good employee. I should have been more concerned about being a better mom. Now some creep has my daughter and is doing who-knows-what to her!" Lizzy burst into fresh tears.

Detective O'Brien's voice was calm. "We don't know that. Is there a family member who might have decided to take her out of school without letting you know?"

Lizzy looked up with a sliver of hope. "Let me call my mom."

She pulled her cell from her purse and hit the 'Favorites' button. After four rings, it went into her mom's voice mail. "Mom, call me. Please. It's important."

Lizzy set the phone in her lap. "She's probably at work. She doesn't answer when she's working. But if she's working, then she couldn't have picked Abby up." Fresh tears spilled out. "Where is my daughter?"

Detective O'Brien tapped his pen on the yellow pad. "What about Abby's father? Where is he?"

"I don't know," Lizzy wailed.

"What is his name?"

"Dylan James."

Lizzy recounted the sad story of her pregnancy in high school and Dylan's sudden departure. She should have at least tried to find him. She was the worst mother ever. Now Abby was missing. Sobs shook her shoulders.

"Ma'am, is there someone you can call? Another family member perhaps?"

Lizzy nodded and blew her nose. She pressed Roman's number into her phone, leaving sweaty fingerprints on the screen.

"Roman, call me as soon as you get this. It's about Abby." She stifled a sob before disconnecting. She tried Simone's number and got her voice mail also. Where was everyone?

Straightening her spine, she took a deep breath. She'd have to handle this alone, like always.

"What do I need to do?"

Detective O'Brien looked over his notes. "I'm going to head over to the school. See if anyone saw anything. In the meantime, we'll organize a search party, and go to all the parks. It's possible she ran away. Was she upset over anything?"

"No. Not at all." Lizzy remembered their conversation about being teased for not having a phone, but it wouldn't have made her run away.

"How would you describe your relationship with your daughter?" the detective asked.

"We're super close. She's a good girl, Detective. Never in trouble. She wouldn't have run away. You must believe me." Lizzy leaned forward in her chair. "You have to find her. She's all I have."

"I would suggest you go home and wait. She may turn up later today. If you're home when she gets there, call me." He dug a business card out of a drawer and pushed it across the desk. "Any time, no matter what when. Okay?"

Lizzy nodded.

She was shown the door and shuffled to her car. She climbed in, letting her head fall forward onto the steering wheel, fresh tears coursing down her cheeks.

Where could Abby be? Before turning the key in the ignition, she called Sarah. After giving her the brief rundown of the morning, Lizzy asked Sarah to start the church's prayer tree.

Driving home, Lizzy hoped to see Abby sitting on the porch, waiting. With a good explanation of why she'd walked away from school.

Abby wasn't sitting on the front porch, and she wasn't on the back porch either. Lizzy paced from the living room to the kitchen and back. Where could her little girl be? The pictures going through her mind were unimaginable. What if some sick person had abducted her? Tears coursed down Lizzy's cheeks.

She should have waited until Abby had entered the school gate. She was a terrible mother. If she'd been more diligent, in less of a hurry, Abby would now be in her classroom.

The doorbell startled her out of her misery. With a jolt of hope, she ran to answer it, hoping it was the detective with Abby.

Lizzy yanked open the door. Instead of Abby, Mariah stood there, clutching her two-hundred-dollar Michael Kors bag.

"What do you want?" She was in no mood for Mariah's constant put-downs.

Mariah frowned. "Can I . . .May I come in?"

Lizzy motioned to the room with an impatient gesture.

"This isn't a good time for me," Lizzy said as Mariah stepped in. Lizzy closed the door with a bang.

"I'm sorry to intrude." Mariah bit her lips as her eyes darted around the room.

Wait, was she apologizing for something? Bad timing, Mariah. That ship sailed a long time ago.

Lizzy waited with arms crossed while Mariah shifted her purse from one hand to the other.

"I might know what happened to your daughter."

"What? How?" Lizzy tamped down the urge to shake the woman.

"I drove by the school this morning on my way to the gym. I recognized your car a few cars ahead of me."

Talk faster.

"After you drove away, I had to stop for some kids to cross the street. There was a guy who looked like he called something to your daughter. Abby, isn't it?"

Lizzy nodded, silently imploring Mariah to hurry up.

"He approached Abby, and they had a conversation. Of course, I couldn't hear what they said. But then he put his hand on her shoulder, and they walked off the campus toward a car."

Lizzy's hand flew to her mouth. "Oh my gosh. No." She'd warned Abby numerous times not to talk to strangers. "Did she look like she went willingly?"

Mariah nodded. "Yes."

"Did you get a good look at him? What kind of car did he drive?" Lizzy peppered the other woman with questions until Mariah looked ready to burst into tears.

"I need to call Detective O'Brien. Don't move."

Lizzy grabbed her phone and the business card the detective had given her. He said he'd be at her house in less than ten minutes.

She and Mariah stared at each other while they waited. Mariah reached into her bag for a tissue and removed two, handing one to Lizzy.

"I can't imagine what you're going through," Mariah said.

No, you can't, Lizzy wanted to say. Because you have no heart.

"I've always wanted kids. But Scott doesn't. It's one reason we haven't gotten married yet."

Why did Mariah pick this time to spill her guts? Lizzy thought back to the pregnancy tests Mariah had purchased. Was she trying to trap her boyfriend into marrying her by getting pregnant? Lizzy wouldn't put it past her. But if she and Scott were intimate, why did she show up at church every Sunday looking all spiritual? At least during Lizzy's rebellious years, she didn't try to be something she wasn't.

Mariah fingered the MK logo on her purse. "All I've ever wanted was what you have."

She had to be kidding. How could Princess Mariah want what Lizzy had? A tiny house she didn't own she was being evicted from. A decrepit car that barely ran. A diet of Ramen and boxed Mac and Cheese. No money and a dead-end job.

Lizzy held up a hand. "Stop. Just stop."

"I'm serious," Mariah protested. "Look at you. You're beautiful. You have incredible style." She motioned to the room's decor. "You have a cute little girl and friends who love you for who you are, not what you can do for them." She paused. "And you have a man who would die for you."

Ah, Roman. He hadn't returned her phone call from the detective's office.

"Was it Roman who took Abby from the school?" Half of her wanted the answer to be yes, and half wanted it to be no. If Roman had taken Abby, there had better be a good reason for him to give her the scare of her life. But at least it would be Roman.

Mariah shook her head. "No, I didn't recognize the guy."

The doorbell rang. Lizzy dashed to the door to let Detective O'Brien in.

He nodded to Mariah as he pulled a notebook from his jacket pocket. "I believe you have some information for me?"

"Yes, I saw something this morning," Mariah answered.

Lizzy focused on everything Mariah said as she went through the story again with the Detective interrupting by asking questions. He asked Mariah to repeat it several times, asking the same questions in a couple of different ways. She was able to give him a brief description of the man, and a little bit of what kind of car he drove.

Forty minutes later, Detective O'Brien got up to leave. "I'll pass this on to my team. In the meantime, call me if you think of anything else." He handed his card to Mariah.

Lizzy let the detective out, then stood by the door, arms wrapped around her stomach. She half wished Mariah would leave, but she also didn't want to be alone. The irony didn't escape her of having her nemesis be a comfort.

Mariah stood and picked up her purse. "I should go." She slung the strap over her shoulder, then fiddled with the zipper. "Look, Elizabeth, I know we haven't always gotten along."

Thank you Captain Obvious.

Mariah glanced her way, then down. "I, um, can sometimes say things." She took a deep breath. "Anyway, I wanted to say I'm sorry."

Lizzy couldn't find words. Her daughter was missing, and Mariah chose now to apologize for years of belittling. She shook her head. Whatever.

Mariah walked to the door. "I hope Abby comes home," she said, opening the door and stepping across the threshold.

Rain pelted the sidewalk, immediately dousing Mariah. Any other time Lizzy would have been gleeful. Today, she was grateful to have a tiny bit of information about who had snatched Abby from the school.

"Thanks," she called out as Mariah climbed into her BMW.

Her phone pinged with a text as she closed the front door behind her.

Roman: **Got your VM. What's up?**

-*-

Lizzy left him a voice mail instead of her usual text. Her message sounded breathless, as if she'd run a mile before calling. She'd said it was about Abby. Was she ill and needed a sitter? Did Abby need to be picked up from school?

Was that all he was to her, a friend with the only benefit for her was a glorified babysitter for Abby?

As soon as the thought came, he brushed it aside. No, their friendship was mutual. And if his plan worked, they'd be more than friends.

Roman sent Lizzy a quick text. His phone immediately lit up with a call from her.

"Hey, what's up? Your voice mail sounded stressed."

Lizzy sniffled into the phone. "Abby's missing."

"Missing? What do you mean?"

Lizzy's sobs filled his ear.

"Unlock your back door. I'll be right over."

Adrenaline shot through Roman's veins. If anything happened to that little girl, Lizzy would be devastated. He would be too.

Roman sprinted across his yard and hers and reached the back door as Lizzy unlocked it. He stepped in and gathered Lizzy into a hug. She sobbed against his shirt, wetting it through to the skin.

With one hand, he slid the door closed and with the other, led Lizzy to the sofa. "Come on and sit. Tell me what happened."

Fear emanated from her in waves. "I dropped Abby off at school this morning. I was in a hurry to get to work, so I took her a little earlier than usual."

Roman pulled Lizzy's hand and held it between his two. "Okay. Go on."

"I should have waited. It's all my fault." Fresh tears erupted from her eyes.

"It isn't your fault. Tell me what happened next."

"Someone, some sick person took her. Mariah saw it."

Roman's brain kicked into overdrive. Mariah? The woman who seemed to cut Lizzy down at every opportunity.

"How do you know she was telling the truth?" Could Mariah be that evil? To upset Lizzy by either lying about Abby or having someone take her.

"She told the detective."

"Back up. What detective?" Roman ran a hand through his hair.

Lizzy got up and walked to the bathroom, returning with a wad of tissues. "The school called me at work and said Abby wasn't in class. When I got there, they said she hadn't shown up and she wasn't anywhere on campus. So, I went to the police department."

Roman inhaled then exhaled through pursed lips. "Did someone take a report? Are they looking for her? Should we organize a search party?"

Lizzy cringed at his questions.

Roman patted her hand. "Sorry. I'm worried too."

"Detective O'Brien told me to go home and wait for Abby in case she showed up. Then Mariah came over and said she saw some guy t-t-talk to Abby, and they left together in his car."

Roman softened his voice. "What did he look like? What kind of car?"

Lizzy pressed the tissues to her eyes with a shrug. "Medium height. Brown hair. Blue hoodie. She thought it was a Honda or Toyota."

"Could have been anybody." Who would pick Abby out of the dozens of kids going into the school? When they found him, Roman pictured himself punching the guy in the face. He tamped down the rage threatening to erupt to concentrate on comforting Lizzy.

"How about some coffee?" Roman asked. He needed something to keep his mind busy. Anything other than imagining what some pedophile was doing with little Abby.

Lizzy nodded, then blew her nose. "Sure."

Roman searched through the cupboards and found what he needed. The fragrant brew soon filled the kitchen. He filled two mugs and carried them into the living room. Lizzy hadn't moved.

She reached for the mug and took a small sip before putting it on the coffee table.

"Okay, let's think. Who do you know who fits the description and drives either a Honda or Toyota?" Roman asked.

Lizzy reached for the mug again, holding it in both hands. "I don't know very many men. I tend to avoid them, for obvious reasons."

Roman wondered what those reasons could be, as it wasn't obvious to him.

"Can you think of anyone in the church who might have taken her?"

Tears leaked out of the corners of Lizzy's eyes. "I don't know, Roman," she wailed. "I can't stand this."

Roman set his mug down and pulled Lizzy close. He took the mug out of her hands and set it next to his. Lizzy sniffled against his chest while he rubbed his hand in a circle on her back.

Then he prayed, "Lord, you know how worried we are about Abby. Please bring her safely home. Amen."

They both jumped as the doorbell rang.

Chapter 13

Lizzy wanted to stay in Roman's warm embrace. She gained strength from his strong arms encircling her, comforting her.

Then the doorbell rang. Roman's arms dropped as she leaped up and dashed to the door. She threw it open, then stepped back in shock. Abby stood there looking extremely pleased with herself.

"Hi, Mom," Abby said, grabbing a man's hand and pulling him into the house behind her.

But it wasn't simply any man. It was a ten-year-older version of the guy who'd gotten her pregnant.

"Dylan?" Lizzy blurted.

"Hi, Roman," Abby said. "This is my dad." Abby wore a grin stretching from ear to ear.

Lizzy battled between grabbing her daughter and never releasing her or screaming at Dylan he'd once again made her life a living hell.

Keeping her voice low, she said, "Do you have any idea what I've gone through today?"

At least Dylan had the grace to look embarrassed.

Roman stood and approached Dylan. "You gave Lizzy the scare of her life by your stunt. I'm tempted to call the police and report you for kidnapping. After I smash in your nose."

Lizzy laid a calming hand on Roman's arm. Abby didn't seem upset, and Lizzy didn't want her to witness any violence. Not yet anyway. "What were you thinking, taking my daughter without letting me know?"

Dylan spoke for the first time. "I wanted to see my daughter, and I knew you wouldn't let me."

"You got that right," Lizzy said. Anger burned white-hot. "Ten years, Dylan. I haven't heard from you, haven't spoken to you, and I haven't received one cent in child support in ten years." Lizzy ticked off the list on her fingers.

Abby pulled at Lizzy's shirt. "Don't be mad, Mom. Daddy and I had fun. We went to the park and McDonald's and the arcade. Look, I won a friend for Spot." Abby held up a stuffed animal.

Lizzy took a deep breath and looked over to where Roman stood with a scowl on his face. "What do you want, Dylan?"

"I want to see my kid."

Roman took a step closer. Dylan stepped back. "There are proper channels to go through to make it happen."

"Who are you, anyway?" Dylan appeared to have gathered some bravado.

Lizzy stepped closer to the two men. "None of your business. Nothing I do is any of your business. I need to call the police right now and let them know Abby is back."

Dylan's face filled with fear. "I'm leaving. But first, Abigail, come hug your dad goodbye."

Abby raced to him and gave him a fierce hug. "When will I see you again?" she asked, love shining from her eyes.

Lizzy focused her gaze on him like twin lasers. "I swear, Dylan, if you let this little girl down, I will find you and . . ." Lizzy bit back her threat, seeing Abby's look of confusion.

"This isn't over," Dylan said. "I have an attorney and I'm going to sue for joint custody."

"Why now?"

Dylan didn't answer. He ruffled Abby's hair and opened the door. "See you soon, Abigail."

Lizzy pushed the door closed behind him, then collapsed against it. As if she didn't have enough on her plate. Now this. After all this time, Abby's dad decided he wanted to be a father. After missing all the sleepless nights, mountains of diapers, spit-up covered clothes, nonstop crying.

"Mom?" Abby's voice broke through her whirling thoughts.

"Yes, Bug?" Lizzy pushed herself off the door with both palms.

"Thank you for finding my dad."

"Abby, you need to go get ready for bed, okay?"

Abby skipped to her bedroom, stuffed dog dangling from her fingers.

Lizzy wobbled to the sofa and slumped down.

"Wow," Roman said.

"Wow is right." Lizzy pulled out her cell phone and Detective O'Brien's business card. She left a message for him Abby had been returned safe and sound and she'd give him the complete story the next day. "I don't think I can talk to anyone right now," Lizzy said when she disconnected.

"Want me to leave?" Roman asked.

-*-

Roman hoped she'd say no. His arms ached to hold her and take the stress onto himself.

"Please don't go yet," Lizzy said, leaning back against the sofa and closing her eyes.

"Want to talk about it?"

"Yes. No. I don't know."

"How about I talk, and you listen?" Roman said.

"Sure. Tell me about your family. Or anything. Distract me, okay?"

"I'll tell you about my family. I have three sisters and one brother."

Lizzy cracked open an eye. "Seriously?"

Roman warmed to his story. He loved his family to pieces, though they drove him crazy at times. "My two older sisters, Rose and Rina, are both married with kids. All girls. Rose has twins, Rina has one kid. Then there's me and my brother, Rory. He and I are thirteen months apart. People always think we're twins."

Roman stopped when Lizzy opened her eyes. "Go on," she urged.

"Our youngest sister is Ruby. She's spoiled rotten by the way. She still lives at home while she's attending a community college."

"I've always wondered what it would be like to have a big family," Lizzy said wistfully.

"It has its pros and cons. My dad is your typical sports fan. He'll watch anything sports-related on TV, including bowling."

"No way." Lizzy sniffled, then gave him a watery smile.

Roman nodded. "My mom is another story. Her grandparents emigrated from Italy. She speaks fluent Italian. She takes on this Italian persona at the drop of a hat."

Roman sat up straight and squeezed his thumb and forefinger together, speaking in an Italian accent. "My little bambino. Why you doing thees?"

Lizzy chuckled. "She sounds fun."

Roman rolled his eyes. "She's also incredibly nosy and constantly tries to get me and Rory married off."

"Hm."

Roman wasn't sure what 'hm' meant. He slapped his forehead and continued in an Italian accent. "Mama Mia! That's crazy talk."

Lizzy laughed. "I can't wait to meet them."

Roman shook a finger at her. "Consider yourself warned. They're coming to visit soon."

Lizzy straightened. "Thanks for getting me to laugh. I needed it. What am I going to do about Dylan?"

Roman took her hand. "You're going to hire a lawyer and fight him. He can't waltz in here after ten years and say, 'I want joint custody.'"

"How am I going to afford a lawyer? I can barely afford to support both of us as it is. Plus, in a couple of weeks, I won't have a place to live."

"I can help."

Lizzy pulled her hand away. "No—"

"I know what you're going to say. But I have enough money saved. Consider it a loan." One he'd never make her pay back.

Lizzy sprang to her feet. "I need to check on Abby."

She returned to the living room a few minutes later. "She's asleep. All the excitement must have worn her out."

Roman stood and gathered Lizzy in his arms. "I'm glad she's home safe. Please don't worry, you know God's got this."

Lizzy rested her head against this chest. "Sometimes I have a hard time believing it."

"Could be he will turn out to be a nice guy, and a good dad for Abby."

Lizzy tightened her grip around Roman. "I hope so."

They stood for a moment, swaying gently. Roman's heart expanded. Somehow, this woman had broken through his barriers and had given him hope. After Shayna, well, her betrayal had shoved him back in his protective shell. Now his heart was out there again, and he was okay with it. He loved this woman and would do anything for her. Even if she only thought of him as a friend, he'd be okay with that. For now.

-*-

Lizzy felt her body relax in Roman's embrace, but her mind was spinning with uncertainty. On one hand, she felt a strong desire to be loved, something she had never truly experienced before. But on the other, the thought of trusting a man terrified her.

Could she open herself up again, and trust the outcome would be different this time? She was desperate for an answer, but at the same time, she was scared to death of what it might be.

Lizzy remained pressed against Roman's chest, drawing in the warmth and comfort offered by his muscular body. Would this man, who'd become one of her best friends, stick around when things got difficult? Or would he be like Dylan and run when she needed him most? Thunder rumbled in the distance. The dark sky flashed with lightning before the storm rolled in, shaking the house.

What are you doing, God?

It was time to crack open her heart. She'd bound it up tight when Abby was born, vowing to never be distracted by anyone who would take her attention away from her daughter. Everything changed the moment she'd seen Abby's perfect little face. All her wildness and rebellion evaporated in an instant. She'd be the best mother ever. And until recently, it had been enough.

With Abby's father in the picture, things would be complicated. Suddenly it was too much. With a sigh, she pushed away from Roman.

"I'm super tired," she said, eyes downcast.

"Of course. I'll let you go. Let's talk tomorrow."

Lizzy nodded, scared to meet his eyes. Scared of what she'd see reflected there.

She watched as he let himself out the back door. Roman looked over his shoulder once, then was gone.

Lizzy prepared for bed, then sat propped with

a Bible in her lap. Inside was a verse Sarah had written there when she'd gifted Lizzy with it after Lizzy began attending Sarah's church.

"For I know the plans I have for you, declares the Lord, plans to prosper you and not harm you, plans to give you hope and a future."

What plans could God have involving Dylan James? Abby seemed happy to have spent the day with him, blissfully unaware her mom had gone through seven levels of hell. How much would life change if Abby's father truly took responsibility? Ten years of back child support would certainly make Lizzy's life easier.

Then there was Roman. Could she love him the way he deserved to be loved? She was definitely 'in like' with him. Even a teeny bit of love.

Lizzy yawned and slipped under the covers. It would be something to think about tomorrow.

She woke the next day, grasping onto the edges of a dream involving Mariah. They'd been in the house next door but that's all she remembered. Rolling over, Lizzy grabbed her phone to check the time.

Springing up, she rushed into Abby's room to wake her for school. Abby was already awake, sitting up in bed. She was holding a phone.

"Where did you get that?"

"My dad bought it for me."

"No, no, no." Lizzy held out her hand. "Give it to me. You are much too young for a phone."

Abby held the phone against her chest. "No. My dad gave it to *me*." Her eyes glittered with unshed tears.

Lizzy took a deep breath. This was exactly why she didn't want Dylan James in her daughter's life. He had no idea what was and was not appropriate for her daughter.

"You need to get ready for school," Lizzy said. She'd deal with the phone issue later.

Abby jumped off the bed and headed to the bathroom still clutching the phone.

"Did your dad give you his phone number?" Lizzy asked, trailing behind her.

"Yes. And I don't want to be called Abby anymore. Dad calls me Abigail."

Lizzy couldn't help rolling her eyes even as her stomach clenched. "Can I still call you Ladybug?"

"I guess," Abby said with a dramatic shrug.

Lord help me, Lizzy prayed.

She'd finally gotten Abby to school after a fight over leaving the cell phone at home. This time, Lizzy parked and walked her daughter to the school before heading to work.

On her way to work, she returned the dozens of calls that had come in overnight asking about Abby. Detective O'Brien agreed to meet her during lunch break to talk about whether she wanted to press charges against Dylan.

As Lizzy walked through the door to the drug store, her phone vibrated with a text from Roman.

How are you doing today?

How was she doing? Confused, frustrated, anxious. 'Yes', to all three. "Fine" was all she could come up with.

Confused over her growing dependence - and

attraction - to Roman.

Frustrated over the way her life had turned into a soap opera.

Anxious over the future.

Why not add angry to the list. Angry at Dylan. And Mariah. And Simone. Why hadn't her best friend called, texted, or come over yesterday when she needed a shoulder to cry on? Yesterday had been the worst day of her life, and Lizzy had relied on . . . Oh, yeah, her nemesis, Mariah, who apologized for years of bullying.

The world had tilted on its axis and Lizzy felt every bit of her childhood nickname: Dizzy Lizzy.

Chapter 14

Roman lay on his living room floor, dangling a toy for Millie to grab. As soon as she snagged it with one claw, he yanked it away so she could pounce again. While Millie stalked the toy, Roman reflected on his conversation with Colin at the coffee place the day before. He'd intended to run it by Lizzy to get her input. Abby's disappearance had thrown a wrench into that plan.

He shook his head. How could Abby's dad think it was okay to grab her from the school property and keep her for the day without letting Lizzy know? He was pretty sure it was considered kidnapping. Lizzy had been out of her mind with worry. What kind of a guy does something like that? Roman pictured himself landing a punch on Dylan James' nose.

You could take him, his inner geek said.

Roman agreed. But first, what to do about Colin.

They'd met outside Flag & Wire Coffee, shaken hands, and ordered their drinks. Colin offered to pay, but Roman declined. They sat outside to enjoy the thin sunshine trying to break through the clouds.

Roman sipped his coffee, letting the uncomfortable silence lengthen. Colin had to make the first move.

Colin twirled his coffee cup in lazy circles. "I guess you're wondering why I texted you."

Roman shrugged. He refused to make this easy on the guy who'd yanked his fiancée away.

Colin met Roman's eyes, then looked down. "Well, I wanted to let you know Shayna and I broke up." A brief smile flitted across Colin's face. "Actually, she dumped me."

Roman let a brief frisson on glee course through him before he repented. "That's too bad."

"Yeah, she met some guy at work who had serious money. They're getting married in Greece next month."

"Hm." What was he supposed to say to that? *How does it feel, Bubba? What goes around comes around.*

Colin took a sip of his coffee. "So, anyway, what I wanted to talk to you about, is, well, something my counselor suggested. Do you think you can forgive me?"

Roman choked on his coffee. He grabbed a handful of napkins while coughing and sputtering. Colin stood and pounded Roman's back until the fit subsided.

Forgive Colin? Isn't an apology what he'd wanted these past months? Now that the words lay between them, Roman had a choice. Take Colin at his word he was truly sorry, try to forgive him, and, what? Move on? Go back to being friends?

As if it was that easy.

Or sweep away Colin's apology and tell him to pound sand.

What would Jesus do? Roman knew he had to forgive his former friend. But it would be a process. Like Lizzy having to forgive Dylan for showing up out of the blue and snatching Abby up.

Again and again, Roman's thoughts returned to Lizzy. Now he needed to come up with a plan to warn Lizzy about his parents. Many people didn't understand their idiosyncrasies. Once Mom met Lizzy, she'd put two and two together and come up with wedding invitations. There was no way he'd let Mom derail his plan. Like a string of computer code, once he initiated Plan Lizzy, it should be foolproof. He'd gone over it a hundred times, looking for any holes. Exactly like the security software he wrote, his idea was flawless.

Roman changed from the grubby tee shirt he'd worn all day, into a button-up shirt and his best khakis. The last time he'd worn the shirt, Lizzy's eyes had wandered from his face to the shirt and back up. He craved her look of appreciation.

Using a small amount of hair goo, he swept his hair back, patting it into place, mentally kicking himself. He should have gotten a haircut. Too late now. Lizzy's little red car pulled in front of her house and stopped with a shudder. Roman sighed. He'd love to pay for car repairs, but Lizzy refused to let him help. She'd only grudgingly agreed to let him loan her the money for back taxes if she won the house.

"A loan," she'd insisted, even though he would

have gladly given her the money. What else could a single guy with a six-figure income spend his money on? He didn't drink, gamble, or do online gaming. He had no real hobbies unless you counted going to the gym.

Could you be any more boring? his inner geek asked.

No wonder Lizzy wasn't interested in him beyond being friends. Her urging to break the rules of seeing the house when he wasn't scheduled gave him the willies.

Speaking of the willies, Roman paced from the bedrooms to the kitchen, down the hall again to the bedrooms. If he showed up at Lizzy's back door before dinner, she'd invite him in. Her generosity was one of the things he liked about her. She and Abby had almost nothing, yet she never begrudged him dinner, cookies, or anything else.

Generous to a fault. Yup, that's what he liked, no, scratch that, what he loved about her.

Twenty minutes later, Roman grabbed a windbreaker and ran through the rain from his back door to Lizzy's. The covering over the sliding glass door kept him from getting too soaked. He knocked on the door and waited.

"Mom – It's Roman." Abby clicked up the lock and pulled open the door.

Roman stepped in. "Hello, Ladybug."

Lizzy turned away from the sink where she was elbow deep in sudsy water. "Hey, Roman. What's up?" She eyed him as he shrugged out of the damp windbreaker and hung it over one of the kitchen chairs.

"Not much. Did you two eat dinner already?" he asked, though he knew the answer.

"Yup. I have some leftovers if you're hungry," Lizzy offered.

See, there it was, her generosity.

"No, I'm good, but thanks."

Abby sat across from him at the table, furiously working on what looked like math problems. Slightly awkward to initiate Plan Lizzy with her daughter in the room. But perhaps a good distraction.

"Don't mind me," Lizzy said. "I'll finish up these dishes."

Roman practically rubbed his hands together in glee. With Lizzy's attention directed away from him, it would be a lot easier.

"So, Lizzy, I was thinking . . ."

Lizzy grinned, glancing sideways. "Always a problem."

Roman smiled in return, his stomach pitching. She was beautiful when she smiled. Like she pulled sunshine out of her soul and set it free.

"What I was wondering was if, we could, like," This was more difficult than he planned. "What I mean is, my parents are coming this weekend and I'd like to talk to you about their visit."

"Excellent. I can tell you lots of fun things to do in Main. And even surrounding areas. The drive to the beach is especially beautiful this time of year."

Roman nodded, considering her answer. "So, here's my thought. Why don't we go out to eat somewhere to talk, without either one of us getting interrupted." Roman looked pointedly at Abby.

Lizzy's hands stilled in the dishwater. She looked down. "You mean, like a date?"

Roman leaned back in the chair. "Noooo, two neighbors, friends, having dinner to talk."

Lizzy's brow wrinkled as she gazed at him. "Isn't that the definition of a date?"

Roman didn't see that coming. Redirect, change course, breach firewall.

"Um, well, I guess it could be seen that way." He licked his dry lips.

Lizzy's smile was hesitant. "If it looks like a duck, walks like a duck, it must be a duck."

Time to circumvent the obstacle. Roman pushed back the chair and stood. "So, tomorrow night. Six o'clock. You can get someone to watch Abby for a couple of hours?"

Lizzy wiped her forehead with the back of one arm, leaving a streak of bubbles on her cheek. He'd love to wipe them off, then pull her close into a hug. But not yet.

"Yeah, sure. I guess I can do that."

"Great." Roman clapped his hands together, then inwardly groaned. Stupid gesture. "I'll drive around and pick you up at the front door."

Without waiting for her change of mind, he pulled open the back door, said goodbye to Abby, and sprinted to his house, the windbreaker forgotten.

As soon as he entered his back door, he leaned over, resting hands on his thighs, panting like he'd run a fifty-yard dash. His plan hadn't been as perfectly executed as he would have liked, but the outcome was what he'd wanted. Dinner alone with Lizzy.

-*-

Lizzy let the water out of the sink, rinsing the remaining soap down the drain before drying her hands.

Abby looked up from her homework. "You and Roman are going on a date?"

Lizzy scooped up Abby's hair into a ponytail and gave it a gentle yank. "It isn't a date. Two friends having dinner."

Abby rolled her eyes. "Whatever, Mom."

"Off to bed with you," Lizzy said with mock severity.

Abby giggled and danced through the living room. "Mom's got a date, Mom's got a date," she sang.

Lizzy couldn't help laughing. As soon as Abby was tucked into bed, she texted Simone.

Can I call you?

Within thirty seconds her phone rang. "Hi, Simone. You'll never believe what happened."

"Okay. Spill, girlfriend."

Lizzy walked to the farthest edge of the kitchen and lowered her voice in case Abby wasn't asleep.

"Roman came over a while ago."

"And?"

Lizzy's stomach did a little flutter. "He said he wanted to talk to me about his parent's visit this weekend. Over dinner."

"What?!"

Lizzy pulled the phone away from her ear at Simon's shriek.

"Like a date?" Simone asked.

"I guess." Lizzy took a calming breath. "He said it was two friends having dinner."

"Girl, it sounds like a date to me. That's awesome! What are you going to wear?"

Lizzy pursed her lips. She hadn't thought that far ahead. Her wardrobe consisted of black work slacks, tee shirts, jeans, and a few church dresses.

"I don't know."

"Did he say where he was taking you?"

"No, but I need a favor. Can you watch Abby while we're gone?"

"Of course. What time should I be there?"

Lizzy paused. "Could I bring her to you? I don't want you to be here alone in case you-know-who shows up." Lizzy had nightmares about Abby's father showing up and forcibly taking her.

"Can I apologize again for not being there when you needed me? I'm the worst best friend ever."

"Simone, of course, I forgive you. You can't help it if you left your phone at Adam's."

"Thanks. You're the best. See you tomorrow."

"Have fun."

Fun. When was the last time she'd been on a fun date? Never. After Dylan, after getting pregnant, she hadn't had time nor inclination to date more than a couple of times. Only on Sarah's insistence she needed a social life. As if.

Every moment she wasn't working was spent with Ladybug. No offense to her mom, but Lizzy wanted to be a better mother. Mom's drinking had allowed Lizzy to get away with more than she should have. Hence, teen pregnancy. Thank God for church ladies and Simone for pointing her in the right direction.

Now, what to wear to her not-a-date with Roman.

-*-

Roman woke the next day with dry eyes and a pounding headache. He'd barely slept the night before, reviewing his conversation with Lizzy. Should he have said this, that, or the other instead? He tried to remember every inflection of her voice, every minute bit of body language to indicate if she did want to go to dinner.

He spent the day immersed in computer security code, forcing himself to concentrate. Unfortunately, his mind didn't want to cooperate. The schematic he'd designed resembled something a high schooler could have done. His head swirled with random thoughts of Lizzy, Colin, Shayna, and Abigail. Millie kept trying to lie on the laptop keys, further distracting him.

Roman finally gave up, pushed his chair back and made a cup of espresso.

How to move out of the friend zone? And how to warn Lizzy if his parents met her, they'd add one and one, resulting in some uncomfortable moments for both him and Lizzy.

His brother, Rory, had let it slip to Mom and Dad he had an attractive neighbor, and he might be interested in her. Roman was pretty sure it was the reason Mom was anxious to visit. She'd want to make sure the 'girl' was worthy of her oldest son.

Mom had only recently forgiven him for the drastic mistake he'd made with Shayna. Shayna was the exact opposite from him. Bright, funny, always up for a good time. Roman had been drawn to her like a gamer to a seventy-inch TV screen.

Mom warned him she wasn't a keeper. Instead, Shayna had pulled him away from his Christian beliefs, then dumped him for Colin. Now Colin was on the receiving end of Shayna's disregard for others' feelings.

After Colin's belated apology for ruining Roman's life, Roman wasn't sure what to think about the situation. He'd mumbled something to Colin, then pushed his chair back and headed to his car.

What if he and Shayna had gotten married? Roman never would have met Lizzy and Abby. *Abigail*, he reminded himself. Perhaps God's hand was in the Shayna-Colin situation after all. If meeting Lizzy was the end result of all the heartache he'd experienced, it was time to let go of the bitterness he'd held toward his former best friend.

Then Lizzy moved in, and lightning struck. The fact her daughter entranced him only sweetened the feeling of rightness.

At three o'clock he finally gave up the pretense of working, took some pain reliever, and headed to town to get a haircut.

-*-

Lizzy knocked on Simone's door at five-thirty, with enough time to drop off Abby and get back to her house.

Simone opened the door and gave a low whistle. "You look great, Liz."

"You think so?" Lizzy ran a hand down the denim skirt she'd pulled from the back of her closet. Black leggings led down to a pair of ballet shoes. The black, long-sleeved silk tee was one she'd picked up at Goodwill a few years ago and had never worn. A chunky turquoise necklace completed the outfit.

Simone raised her eyebrows. "Nice outfit for your not-a-date with Roman."

Lizzy couldn't help but laugh through her nerves. "Thanks."

Simone pulled Abby into the apartment. "Come on, squirt. We have cookies to make and binge-watching to do."

"Yay!" Abby said.

Lizzy's stomach summersaulted. "You have my number. And my mom's. I'll text you the doctor's information. She has Spot in her bag, along with some games. I'll be back in a couple of hours. Call me if you have any questions."

Simone grabbed Lizzy into a hug. "Stop worrying. I've got this. Have fun."

Lizzy nodded against Simone's shoulder. "Okay." She took a deep breath, released her friend, then said, "Bye, Bug. See you soon."

Abby barely acknowledged her goodbye. She was already inspecting the ingredients Simone had laid out on the kitchen counter.

Lizzy arrived back at her house at ten to six and began to pace. Why had she allowed herself to get talked into this not-a-date. Why couldn't she and Roman talk about his parents' plans over the phone? Or over dessert. Or on the back patio. She was more excited about this dinner than she should be. Lizzy thought back to the night Dylan had shown up at the house with Abby. Roman had been her rock. He'd comforted her and distracted her with stories about his crazy big family.

How different her life would have been if she hadn't been an only child. Before her rebellious teen years, she'd read and reread Little Women, Little Men, and all the Little House series. Lizzy looked forward to meeting Roman's parents, his brother, and sister.

A tiny sliver of her heart hoped Roman would be the one to wrap her into a real and loving family.

As she plopped onto the sofa to wait for Roman, Lizzy's gaze fell on the letter from the attorney lying on the coffee table. She pulled it to her and read it for the ninety-seventh time. There was barely five weeks to pack and find another place to live. A place more expensive than this cute little bungalow. And on ten fewer hours per week. Any day a For Sale sign would appear on the front lawn, making her potential homelessness a reality.

The doorbell rang. Lizzy jumped up with a flutter of nerves.

"Hi," Roman greeted her, eyeing her from head to toe.

She should have worn something else.

Chapter 15

Roman slid his car to a stop, parking in front of Lizzy's house. His heart beat to the rhythm of a NASCAR race car, fast and furious. What if she'd changed her mind. Or Abby was sick, and she had to cancel. Why did he do this to himself? Second-third-and fourth-guessing the decision to take Lizzy to dinner. They could have talked at her kitchen table, over coffee.

Roman clenched his teeth, opened the car door, and headed up the path to Lizzy's front door.

Lizzy opened it seconds after he rang the bell. His breath caught in his throat as he looked her up and down. Breathtaking. Her hair, usually pulled up into a ponytail or bun, lay around her shoulders in soft brown waves. Without her glasses, he noticed the coffee color of her eyes and long, dark lashes. His heart was completely taken.

"You look great," he managed to say around the pressure on his lungs.

"Thanks." Lizzy stood for a moment before turning to close and lock the door.

Leading the way to his car, Roman opened the passenger door and waited for Lizzy to get in. After seating himself and fastening his seatbelt, he put the car in Drive and headed down the street.

"Your car is clean," Lizzy commented, looking around at the back seat of his Subaru. "Mine looks like I live in it."

From the corner of his eye, Roman saw Lizzy's lips clamp together. She was worried about the house being sold from under her.

"I don't have kids," he said, hoping to bring her back. "My sisters' cars are always a disaster."

"I forgot, how many kids do they have?"

"Let's see, Rose has twins and Rina has one. All girls." He grinned. "My dad is outnumbered. He keeps hoping one of us will produce a boy."

Lizzy chuckled. "Girls are easier. At least, it's what I've heard."

"You may be right," Roman commented. "Rory and I did a lot of things girls wouldn't think of."

Lizzy raised an eyebrow. "Oh really? Like what?"

"Like climbing on the roof of the school and pelting kids with rocks."

"Seriously?"

"They were small rocks. In my defense, it was always Rory. I went along with him to make sure he didn't kill himself."

"Right."

They'd been on the road about twenty minutes when Lizzy asked, "Where are we going, by the way."

"I'm taking you to Ocean Zoo. Have you heard of it?"

Lizzy's excitement was palpable in the confines of his car. The fruity smell of her shampoo wafted toward him, making it hard to breathe.

"I've always wanted to try it, but I've heard it's spendy."

Roman shrugged. "I guess." He'd spend a thousand dollars a plate to see the look on her face again. The look of carefree anticipation.

"I've heard they have lots of exotic meats."

"And seafood," he added. "I want to try octopus."

"Yuck. Hard pass." Lizzy made a face and Roman laughed.

"We should get there in time to watch the sun go down over the ocean. I reserved us a table at the window, overlooking the coast."

Lizzy smiled her brilliant smile, causing his heart to skip. "This is the best not-a-date I've ever been on."

Roman smiled back. If he could keep the smile on her face forever, he'd be a happy man.

Roman pulled into the restaurant, parked, and hurried around the car to open Lizzy's door. She looked up at him with surprise.

"Thanks. I'm not used to being treated so nice."

"My pleasure," Roman said. To his disappointment, Lizzy dropped her hand from his as soon as she was out of the car.

Roman gave his name at the hostess stand. They were ushered to a table overlooking a wide expanse of ocean.

"Welcome to Ocean Zoo," the hostess said.

"May I get you something to drink?"

Lizzy shook her head. "Water for me. Thanks."

"Same." Roman stared at Lizzy's profile as she looked out the window.

"Beautiful, isn't it," Lizzy commented.

"Yes, it is," Roman answered, keeping his eyes on her face. "Where are your glasses?" he asked.

Lizzy swiveled her head to meet his gaze. "Glasses? Oh, yeah."

Roman mentally whacked his forehead with a palm. Way to break the mood, dummy.

"I rarely wear my contacts. But I figured I'd pop them in tonight."

Roman cleared his throat. "Well, you look good either way."

Lizzy looked down with a shy smile.

A server appeared at their table. "Good evening, I'm Terry and I'll be your server tonight. May I interest you in our specials?"

The short, dark man rattled off a list of tempting dishes. Roman watched Lizzy's expression, trying to read if she was interested in anything he'd mentioned.

"Sounds intriguing," Roman told him. "Give us a few minutes to decide."

The server handed them each a heavy leather-bound menu and scurried off with a bow.

"Anything sound good?" Roman asked, trying to see Lizzy's face, hidden behind the huge menu. "I thought we could start with an appetizer. How about some scallops."

Lizzy lowered the book disguised as a menu. "I've never had scallops."

"What? You're kidding. You are in for a treat."

Lizzy raised an eyebrow. "If you say so." Her forehead wrinkled as she perused the food offerings. "Are you sure you can afford this?"

The server returned to their tables with a basket of bread and a small bowl of whipped butter. "I'll be back to take your orders in a few minutes."

Roman nodded, closed his menu, and set it on the table. "I've got this. Don't worry. Order whatever you want."

Lizzy shrugged. "I'll have the hamburger. Or the chicken."

They were the least expensive things on the menu.

He picked up his menu again. "Oh, no you don't." He took her menu out of her hands and set it down. "Let me read a few things off to you without you seeing the prices. Okay?"

"Okay."

He finally convinced her to try the surf and turf combo, bird's nest salad, and a side of au gratin potatoes.

"It's too much food! I'll never eat it all."

"Eat what you can and take the rest home."

They settled in to watch the sun make its slow descent toward the ocean.

Lizzy spoke wistfully, her chin resting on one hand. "I love how light it stays in the summer up here in the Pacific Northwest."

"Me too," Roman agreed.

Their scallops arrived and Roman scooped two of the four onto her plate. The garlic butter formed a beautiful pool around them.

"Oooh, cool," Lizzy said. She speared one after cutting one into fourths. "Mmmm. It's amazing." Her eyes closed as she savored the flavor.

"The texture takes some getting used to, but fresh scallops are God's gift."

They quickly finished their appetizer and sopped up the remaining butter with a piece of crusty bread.

Lizzy leaned back with a satisfied sigh. "I could eat those every day of the year."

Perhaps he could make her wish come true.

-*-

A girl could get used to this. Dinner at a white tablecloth sort of place, overlooking the ocean with a nice guy sitting across from her. Lizzy was aware of the looks Roman got from some of the women who had passed by their table. She scrutinized him more closely. His brown hair had come loose from the product he used to keep it off his face, and a few locks fell over his forehead. Robin's egg blue eyes, even features, and an easy smile. Tall enough to make her feel petite. Not buffed out like a gym junkie, but in good shape. No bad habits she knew of. Funny, in a geeky kind of way. Everything a woman would want in a boyfriend.

Lizzy had to admit, when he took her hand to help her out of the car, she felt something pass between them. His hand on the small of her back as they walked to the restaurant was comforting yet disturbing to her pulse. If Simone was right, did she have the courage to let him into her heart? There was also Abby to consider. It wouldn't be right to get into a relationship with someone who may not want the additional responsibility of a child who wasn't his. Especially now with Abby's father in the picture.

She sighed.

"Earth to Lizzy." Roman nudged her out of her thoughts.

"Sorry. I was enjoying the scenery."

Roman's face took on a serious look. "I wanted to talk to you for a minute about my parents."

Lizzy nodded.

"They're—" The server returned to set their plates in front of them.

"Here you go. I will be back to fill your water glasses and refill the bread."

Roman laid an arm on the table, palm up. "Grace?"

Lizzy set her palm on his, and he curled his fingers around hers. His warm hand sent shivers up her arm. She let her hair fall across her face to hide the blush she could feel rise from her neck.

"Amen." Lizzy echoed Roman. She looked at his plate, then her own. "I'm glad you didn't get for me what you're having." Her mouth puckered as he speared a section of octopus in some kind of red sauce.

"Sure you don't want a bite?" Roman asked with a grin.

"Hard no."

They both tucked into their meals. After a few moments, Roman set down his fork. "Now, about my parents. They'll be here this soon, I'm not sure when, and they'll want to meet you."

"Me? Why?"

"My brother, Rory, told them we were friends."

Lizzy lifted one shoulder. "Okay. Why is it a problem?"

Roman inhaled, then exhaled with a whoosh. "My parents are a little . . . Eccentric. My mom acts like she's a recent immigrant from Italy. She breaks into Italian at the drop of a hat."

"I remember you told me. She sounds delightful." Lizzy contrasted her own mom, who still carried baggage from decades of alcohol abuse and a string of not-so-great men. Roman's mom sounded fun.

"The thing is, once she meets you, knowing what I do about her matchmaking attempts, she's going to start planning a wedding."

Lizzy swallowed then set her fork down as well. "I'm not sure I understand." Her thoughts tumbled like rocks in a dryer. Was Roman saying his mom wanted to match them together? Anger rose and threatened to make her say something she'd regret.

"Explain," she said, her voice flat.

Roman looked toward the window, then out over the restaurant dining room. Seemed he couldn't meet her eyes.

"My mom has been desperate to see me

settled down ever since, well, for a while."

Lizzy narrowed her eyes. There was a story here.

"Whenever there's any mention of a female within a sixty-mile radius, mom starts looking at wedding invitations." He huffed out a laugh. "I don't want you to feel awkward when my mom starts eyeing you like the next Mrs. Rossi."

Lizzy cut a bite of her steak, put it in her mouth, and chewed. "Hm." The next Mrs. Rossi. She tried to picture what it would be like to be married. To have someone to rely on, encourage and support her. To cheer her up when she was down.

Roman set his fork down. "A year ago or so, I was engaged."

Lizzy swallowed hard. Roman had been engaged. A slow burn of jealousy started in her stomach and worked its way up. She took a sip of water, appetite gone. Who was this she-devil who had stolen Roman's heart?

"What happened?" Lizzy wasn't sure she wanted to know, but the question had to be asked.

Roman gazed out the window to the darkening sky. "Basically, she ran off with my best friend."

Lizzy's hands curled into fists. Roman's face turned to hers. "Classic, right?" he asked with a rueful smile.

Lizzy opened her mouth to comment, but Roman continued. "My former best friend reached out to me last week. We met for coffee; it was the day Abby's father took her from the school." He blew out a breath through pursed lips. "Anyway, he apologized and said Shayna, that's her name, did the same thing to him she did with me." He shrugged.

Lizzy shook her head. "How painful. I mean, first the breakup, then hearing she did the same thing. And having to work through forgiving your friend. I thought my life was messed up."

"Yeah. I don't think Colin and I will ever be friends like we were. I'm working on the forgiveness thing. It's a process."

"Totally. I thought I'd forgiven Abby's dad, until he showed up the other night without even a hint of remorse about dragging me through terror.

Lizzy didn't mention the situation with Mariah. She was still working through Mariah's apology.

-*-

Roman watched Lizzy's face as she pondered what he'd said about his mom. At least she didn't look angry. After her first response, he was afraid she would come unglued.

He breathed a sigh of relief and changed the subject. "Are you looking forward to the announcement of the finalists for the house?"

Lizzy's face brightened. "Yes, but I'm also nervous. If I'm a finalist, it ratchets up the suspense to a whole new level."

"I hear ya. I think you have a good chance, though. I read your essay. You have a way with words. Ever think about becoming a writer?"

"Nope, I'll stick to drawing."

"Your drawings are beautiful." Lizzy's creativity constantly amazed him. From the way she'd turned her garage-sale finds into a warm and inviting place, to the easy way she expressed her emotions through a charcoal pencil. He felt dull and blah in comparison.

Lizzy shrugged. "It's no big deal. I let God direct my hand."

"No big deal? It is a big deal."

She shrugged again. "I guess. The big deal now is to get my stuff packed and figure out what I'm going to do for a place to live."

Roman took a deep breath. "That's another thing I wanted to discuss with you.

Seriously, 'discuss?' his inner geek said.

No wonder Lizzy wanted to keep him firmly in the friend zone. He sounded like a college professor.

"I know you're worried about becoming homeless, especially with Abby's father trying to get joint custody."

Lizzy's face tightened. "Exactly. I'd have a hard time proving I'm a fit mother if I'm living in my car or couch surfing."

Roman ran a hand through his hair. "Here's what I was wondering. Why don't you move into my place?"

-*-

Lizzy set down her fork, appetite gone. Had she heard correctly, Roman asked her to move in with him? A heavy weight settled on her chest. She thought she knew him and knew his integrity. Yet, here he was, asking her to compromise her Christian beliefs.

This was why she didn't date. This was why

she refused to put her heart out there. Lizzy felt her heart shatter into pieces.

The server approached their table. "Is everything okay?"

Roman gestured to their uneaten food. "Could you bring the check and a couple of boxes, please?"

Lizzy felt tears form in the corners of her eyes. She slid out of her chair and stood. "I need a moment." She strode to the restroom and locked herself into a stall before allowing the tears to fall.

She should have known Roman was too good to be true. Lizzy let herself wallow for a few moments before mentally pulling up her big girl panties. She splashed cold water on her face, applied some lip gloss, and marched back to the table. It was time to go back to her original plan of keeping all men at arm's distance until Abby was an adult.

Roman was signing the bill when Lizzy returned to the table. Their to-go boxes sat like a wall between the two of them.

Roman set the pen down and frowned. "Is everything okay?"

Lizzy sniffed once. "Yes, everything is fine. I'm ready to go home now."

-*-

Roman wiped his sweaty hands down his thighs. Something in the atmosphere had changed and he didn't know what it was. While Lizzy was in the restroom, he replayed their conversation over and over. What had he said to upset her?

He thought his suggestion to move into his house was a great solution to her housing situation.

He'd stay with his folks in Salem, and Lizzy would have time to find a place she could afford. And if she won the house lottery, the problem would be solved.

Lizzy slid into her chair across from him. Her movements were stiff and her face blotchy. She'd been crying.

Nice going, his inner geek said. If only his inner geek could give him an instruction manual.

"Let's walk down to the beach," Roman suggested after the waiter picked up the leather holder.

"Fine." Lizzy stood and wrapped her arms across her middle.

The sun had hit the horizon, leaving a red glow on the ocean surface. The breeze died and he heard the waves crashing on the rocks. They picked their way down the sandy path to the beach.

"My happy place," Lizzy murmured. "I don't get down here often enough."

Roman watched her as Lizzy closed her eyes and breathed in. Even though he'd somehow blown it, he was determined to find a way into Lizzy's heart.

Lizzy kicked off her shoes and padded down to where the water rose to lap the beach.

"Cold!" she exclaimed as the ocean surged around her feet.

After a moment's hesitation, he sat on one of the rocks and removed his shoes, tucking the socks neatly into each shoe. His footprints looked large next to her smaller ones.

"Yikes! You're right. The water is freezing."

Roman backed up a few steps, away from the advancing tide.

"Look, the sun is going down."

They stood in silence, shoulders touching, as the sun sank into the ocean.

"Amazing," whispered Lizzy.

"Indeed." Roman glanced at Lizzy, whose hair foamed around her shoulders like the sea foam gathering around their feet. "We better go. The tide is rising."

Lizzy turned, reluctance on her face. "I need to plan a day trip out here to the coast. Maybe the Lord will give me some direction while I'm here."

They sat on a low stone ledge and brushed the sand off their feet. Roman cringed at the feeling of sand clinging to his feet as he pulled on his socks and shoes. He'd have to shower first thing when he got home.

The silence in the car on the way home could have been sliced with a dull steak knife. Lizzy concentrated her gaze out the passenger window.

When they neared Main, Roman asked, "Should I stop by Simone's to pick up Abby before I drop you off? It will save you a trip."

"No, that's okay. Please take me home."

"But it makes more sense for me to swing by Simone's on our way into town."

"Fine."

-*-

At Simone's front door, an enthusiastic Abby greeted her. "I had so much fun. "We made cookies and painted rocks and all kinds of stuff. When can you go out with Roman again so I can come back?"

Simone smiled down at her. "You can come back any time, even if your mom doesn't go out."

As Lizzy gathered Abby's things, Simone said, "Call me later? I want all the deets."

"You can count on it."

Simone's brow wrinkled. "Didn't you have a good time?"

"Yeah, up until he asked me to move in with him." Lizzy wished she could take the words back as Simone's mouth and Abby's dropped at the same time.

Abby jumped up and hugged her. "You're going to move in with Roman? This is so cool. Wait until I tell my friends."

Lizzy laid a hand on Abby's shoulder. "Not so fast, Ladybug. I didn't say yes."

Simone's eyes had gone round as saucers. "You had better call me the minute you walk through the door."

Lizzy nodded and ushered Abby to Roman's car. "Not a word, Bug. Hear me? This is between me and Roman."

"But Mom—"

"No."

Abby dozed in the back seat of Roman's car on the drive from Simone's place to Lizzy's. Roman's attempt to draw her out was met with sleepy mumbles. Roman pulled the car up to Lizzy's front door. She jumped out the moment he put the car in Park.

"Thanks for dinner." Lizzy gathered Abby's backpack and urged her daughter toward the front door. After one backward glance, she unlocked the door and headed inside.

It was well past Abby's bedtime by the time her face was washed and teeth brushed. Lizzy knelt by Abby's bed and stroked her daughter's hair. Abby's eyes drooped as she clutched her beloved Spot.

"Prayer time," Lizzy said.

Abby closed her eyes. "Dear God, thank you for the good time I had at Simone's. And please let Mom move in with Roman. And please bless my dad."

Lizzy groaned inwardly. Having her daughter involved in her personal life was awkward.

"Mom, are you going to move in with Roman?"

"Hard no. Christians don't live with people they aren't married to."

"Why not?" Abby's innocence pierced Lizzy's heart. A ten-year-old shouldn't have to learn about adult stuff like sex and sin. Her little girl was growing up way too fast. A phone, a dad in the picture, and now this.

Lizzy took Abby's hand in hers and gently stroked her arm. "The Bible has rules about men and women living together without getting married."

"Then why don't you and Roman get married?"

Lizzy huffed out a laugh. "Not happening."

"You should." Abby's eyes closed and her breathing slowed.

Lizzy stood on shaky legs and headed to the living room, sinking onto the sofa. She tossed her phone from hand to hand as she thought about what to say to Simone. A sudden thought had her jumping up and dashing to the kitchen table to her sketch book. With shaking fingers, Lizzy flipped to the most recent drawing.

A man, woman, and two kids, holding hands in front of a house.

"No way, God. That isn't how it's supposed to happen." Lizzy would never, ever compromise her life for a man. That's what got her into trouble when she was sixteen. She wanted it all. A true proposal from a man she couldn't live without. A real wedding with a white dress, three-tiered cake, and everything that came with it.

For a few moments she'd thought Roman might be the one. Lizzy rubbed her chest where her bruised heart beat despite its pain. Why did he have to go and ruin everything?

Lizzy ripped the drawing from the sketch pad and tore it into tiny pieces.

Chapter 16

Lizzy dragged herself home from work after stopping to pick Abby up from after-school daycare. She'd managed to avoid Roman since he'd blurted out what she'd started referring to as his 'indecent proposal.' She mentally prepped herself for the evening ahead.

Tonight, the mayor would announce the five finalists at City Hall. The entire town would be there, including Roman. The evening had turned into a huge event with food trucks, chalk artists, and face painting for the kids. Lizzy desired to crawl into bed and put a pillow over her head, but Abby had talked for days about how much fun they'd have.

"When can we leave, Mom?" Abby asked for the nineteenth time.

"Give me a chance to change my clothes, Bug. Then we'll leave."

Abby made a show of checking the time on her new cell phone with a dramatic sigh. "All my friends will already be there."

"Then you can meet up with them when we get there," Lizzy responded, trying to keep her last nerve intact. The whole house lottery thing had worn her emotions thin, plus the thought of being homeless, Dylan's sudden interest in being a father, and finally, Roman asking her to move in with him. It was all too much. Not to mention the loss of income from her reduced hours.

By the time she and Abby arrived at City Hall, the party was in full swing.

"Bye, Mom," Abby said, jumping out of the car.

"Meet me at the ice cream truck in one hour," Lizzy said, handing Abby a few dollars she'd managed to scrape together. "Food first, though, okay?"

"K."

Lizzy sighed. Life would be easier if she had someone to share parenting duties with. Not just anyone, though. Someone who she deeply and madly adored her, and she him.

"Hey." Roman's deep voice interrupted Lizzy's thoughts.

Her heart jumped as she turned to look into his baby blue eyes. "Hey."

"You've been avoiding me." Roman swept a lock of hair back, only to have it fall over his forehead again.

"Guilty as charged." Lizzy hugged her arms across her stomach.

Roman indicated a nearby food truck. "Taco for your thoughts?"

Lizzy frowned. Roman was the last person she wanted to see, but her stomach didn't agree with her heart. "Sure."

She stood to the side as Roman ordered a tray of fish tacos and two sodas. He wore a black tee shirt and jeans. For someone who worked behind a computer screen all day, he was in amazingly good shape. They'd talked about his gym membership, and apparently, he was a regular there. Lizzy pulled her blouse down over the slight muffin top she'd discovered when pulling on her favorite skinny jeans, then chastised herself. What did it matter? She would not – repeat – would not let herself be attracted to him.

Roman chatted with the server in a mixture of Spanish and English, occasionally laughing.

When he'd been handed the food, Lizzy said, "I didn't know you could speak Spanish."

Roman shrugged. "Spanish is very close to Italian. I've picked up a few words."

"That was more than a few words."

He shrugged again, looking uncomfortable. "It's no big deal. Let's sit over there," he said, pointing to an area set up with portable picnic tables.

Lizzy sat across from him, waiting while he dished two tacos on a paper plate for her. "Thanks."

She dug in, then glanced up to meet Roman's eyes. "Aren't you going to eat?"

Roman glanced away, then back. "Look, I want to apologize for the other night. I don't know what I said to make you uncomfortable. Whatever it was, I'm sorry."

Lizzy set her taco down. Her temperature rose several degrees as she thought about her response. How clueless could he be?

"Say something," Roman implored.

Lizzy took a drink of her soda then set it down. "Roman, I value our friendship." She glanced up to see him run his hands through his hair.

She picked at a loose splinter on the table edge. "I like you and Abby adores you. However, I am a committed Christian and I do not believe in living in sin." Ack! She sounded like the heroine in a Victorian romance novel. This was not going well.

"Lizzy—"

"Let me finish." Lizzy raised her hands, palm up. "What I'm trying to say is while I appreciate you have some notion I need to be rescued, moving in with you would go against all the values I have. When I meet someone I want to spend the rest of my life with, I want it all, flowers, romance, giddiness, everything. Not some living arrangement not honoring to God."

Roman tossed the remains of his taco on his plate and leaned back. "Are you serious right now? Is that what you thought?"

A frisson of panic swept through her at his look of disgust. "W-well, yes. Didn't you ask me to move in with you at dinner?"

Roman rubbed both hands over his head, dislodging the strands of hair falling over his forehead. "Oh my gosh."

"What?" Lizzy's head spun. What was happening?

Roman shot to his feet, then sat again as quickly. "Lizzy, I would never ask you to compromise your beliefs. When I said you could stay at my house, I meant *without me.*"

Lizzy leaned forward. "I don't understand."

Roman grabbed one of her hands. "I can stay with my parents in Salem while you figure out a place you can afford." He slapped his forehead with the other hand. "I can't believe you thought—"

Lizzy couldn't speak over the lump in her throat. How could she have gotten it so wrong? Was she so jaded from her past she couldn't see Roman's offer had been in her best interest?

Her shoulders hunched as shame hit her like a boulder. "I'm sorry. I thought—"

"I know. It's okay."

Lizzy stared down at her uneaten taco, feeling like an idiot. Of course, Roman had meant something different than what she assumed. The Roman she had come to know was a good man, decent, kind, and thoughtful. She was wrong. She'd have to make it up to him.

"Earth to Lizzy."

She raised her head to find his blue eyes fixed on her.

"I need to go find Abby."

-*-

Roman watched Lizzy walk toward City Hall. He shook his head to clear it. Several thoughts hit him at once. At least now he knew why Lizzy had been upset. But how could she have thought he'd meant he wanted to live together? Sheesh. He'd never understand the workings of the female mind. But he wanted to at least understand one woman.

Lizzy's. His carefully concocted plan to help her out of the house situation had blown back into his face. Time to formulate a different plan.

Roman finished his meal and wadded his napkin, then stood and carried the trash to a nearby receptacle. As he made his way through the crowd heading into the City Hall building, Roman stopped and pulled his phone from the back jeans pocket. A large woman crashed into him.

"Don't stop in the middle of the walkway," she admonished with a shake of her finger in his face.

"Sorry." Roman dodged couples, kids, and moms with strollers as he headed to the edges of the thinning mob. Surely there was a playbook or instruction manual on how to get a woman to fall in love with you. His search for 'Romance for Dummies' came up empty.

He returned his phone to his back pocket and determined to research the subject more fully when he was in front of his laptop. For now, it was time to find out if he was one of the five finalists.

Not that it mattered much. He owned his home; owning another wouldn't change his life. His motivation in entering the contest was if he won, he'd gift the house to Lizzy. She deserved to have a stable place to raise her daughter. He'd love to wipe away the worry lines that had taken up permanent residence on her face. She'd been correct in her statement he wanted to be her rescuer.

What he needed now was a white horse, flowers, candy, and a house to boot.

Roman stepped over the feet of other community members to sit in the middle of the second to the last row. He caught sight of the back of Lizzy's head on the other side, halfway back.

He'd recognize her messy ponytail anywhere. He couldn't see Abby, but he knew she was there when Lizzy leaned over to talk to someone.

"Ladies and gentlemen, we're about to get started." The mic squawked as Mayor Dorgan spoke. "Sorry about that." He grinned as some older people covered their ears.

The murmurs and rustles of the crowd became silent. Nervous anticipation was palpable in the air. Lizzy must be beside herself. Roman sent a silent prayer in her direction.

The mayor spoke again, thanking everyone for attending and supporting the community.

"The community of Main has never been stronger. When we work together toward a common goal, we embody the American spirit. Can you believe we had over three hundred entries into our little contest? The entry fee of twenty-five dollars brought in a total of over seven thousand dollars. For the winner, it means almost half of the past due property taxes will be taken care of." This brought a smattering of applause. Roman wished Mayor Dorgan would get on with it. How long would he drag this out?

As it turned out, Mayor Dorgan spoke for another ten minutes before turning the microphone over to the vice mayor. Everyone breathed a collective sigh of relief, as she was known for getting right to the point.

"Ladies and gentlemen of Main, it's time to announce the five finalists. I have to say, the judging team from Salem told me the quality of essays was at a level they had never seen before.

Their decision was difficult but unanimous. Now, without further ado, I will read the names of the five finalists, in no particular order."

Roman scooted to the edge of the hard chair, as did most everyone else. Vice Mayor McGlashan opened a sealed envelope and pulled out a folded sheet of paper. She took a moment to glance at the names, then nodded.

"Okay, here we go. The first of five finalists is William Spade."

Applause erupted from a row near the front. Obviously, family and friends.

"Can we please hold the applause until all finalists have been announced?" implored the vice mayor.

Like that's gonna happen, his inner geek said.

For once, Roman agreed.

"The second of the five finalists is Mariah Washington." This time an even louder celebration from somewhere ahead of where Roman sat. If Mariah was a finalist and Lizzy wasn't, she might go into a complete meltdown.

"Next is Simone Travis." There were some whoops and cheers for Simone.

Roman's stomach started to hurt. What if Lizzy didn't final? Would she be devastated? Relieved to be done with the suspense? Would she worry about the future? He ran both hands through his hair, hoping to hear her name called next.

The Vice Mayor rattled the paper. "Isn't this exciting?" She practically vibrated from head to toe.

"The fourth finalist is," there was an infinitesimal pause. Roman prayed to hear Lizzy's name. "Charles Wilcox."

Roman was sure he was going to throw up. The suspense couldn't possibly get any worse. He pictured himself jumping over the chairs and running to the front to grab the paper out of Vice Mayor McGlashan's hands.

"And now, the fifth and final name of the person who will have the opportunity to win the house, is. . ."

-*-

As the names of the finalists were called, Lizzy chewed on the fingernail of one hand and squeezed Abby's hand with the other.

William Spade

Mariah Washington

Simone Travis

Charles Wilcox

Like a pinball, a thousand thoughts pinged through Lizzy's brain. Her best friend and worst enemy were finalists. Of course, they were. Why should she expect to be one of the five? Good things didn't happen to people like her. She'd made too many poor decisions, resulting in her constant struggle. She knew from reading the Bible actions have consequences.

Lizzy's stomach churned with the partially consumed taco she'd eaten. *Hurry up,* she wanted to shout to Vice Mayor McGlashan.

"And now, the fifth and final name of the person who will have the opportunity to win the house, is. . ."

The entire room was as silent as a graveyard at

midnight. Lizzy bent forward as the vice mayor spoke. ". . . Elizabeth Greene."

From somewhere in the back of the room came a deep-voiced 'whoop!' Lizzy looked at Abby.

"Mom, that's you," Abby whispered.

"I know." Then Lizzy burst into tears.

The room erupted into joyous mayhem. People embraced, slapped each other on the back, and congratulated the five finalists. Lizzy and Simone made their way through the press of bodies and hugged each other.

Simone had to shout to be heard over the noise. "Can you believe it?"

Lizzy could only nod against her friend's shoulder. She pulled away and looked Simone in the eye. "I'm happy for you." At that moment, Lizzy meant it.

Sometime later when the order was restored, the five were invited to the front of the room to be officially recognized. Lizzy stood in front of the crowd, shifting from one foot to the other. Lizzy didn't know the two men, but one looked like a retired golfer, tan and fit. The other was middle-aged and dressed in a suit. She, Simone, and Mariah were all the same age. Simone wore a dressed-up version of athletic wear. Of course, Mariah looked like a model. Tight black slacks and a white shirt under a denim jacket. Hair and makeup perfect. Even her fingernails matched the color of polish on her toes.

Lizzy wished the floor would open up and swallow her. A wide grin and thumbs up from

Roman was all it took to keep her from bolting out the door. As her name was announced again, Abby jumped up from her seat and ran to Lizzy, causing a collective "ahhhh" from the crowd.

"As you know," Mayor Dorgan said as he took control of the podium. "The final winner will be chosen by lottery. The essays of these fine citizens of Main will be published in our local paper, The Herald, both in print and online. The lottery will be held next week at this same time."

Lizzy stopped listening as the mayor droned on. She focused instead on Roman's steady gaze. What was he thinking? His blue eyes bored into hers, giving her strength to stand there and let everyone look at her. Some judged. 'That's the girl who got pregnant in high school.' Some sympathized, like Sarah and the other church ladies. Mariah's family wondered how Lizzy had been able to put two sentences together, much less write a winning essay.

Lizzy glanced around the room, then back at Roman. He seemed to be saying "I'm proud of you. You deserve to be up there. Well done."

Lizzy straightened her back. She did deserve to be there. She allowed herself to relax.

-*-

After the publicity died down, Roman wove his way through the press of bodies to be near Lizzy. Abby saw him and grabbed his hand, pulling him into their circle.

"My mom is awesome," she exclaimed.

Roman ruffled Abby's hair. "I know."

"What should we do to celebrate, Roman?"

Abby asked.

Roman pretended to think. "Hm. How about ice cream?"

"Yeah!"

He moved in to give Lizzy a quick hug before more well-wishes nudged him out of the way.

Roman and Abby stepped away, letting more people in to congratulate Lizzy. "Let's wait by the door for your mom."

When the crowd thinned, Roman led Abby to where Lizzy spoke with someone he didn't recognize. Lizzy glanced his way, then excused herself from the conversation.

Roman licked his dry lips. "Abby wants to go for ice cream. You okay with that?"

To his relief, Lizzy smiled. "As long as I'm invited too."

Abby filled the silence between them with chatter.

"Can you believe they called Mom's name last? I thought I was gonna barf. How cool was that? I hope we win. We are gonna win, right Mom? Roman, did you see . . ."

Roman tuned out, concentrating instead on the emotions flitting across Lizzy's face. Relief, happiness, trepidation, and something he couldn't put his finger on. He bumped her shoulder with his as they walked out of the ice cream store with their cones.

"Pretty cool, huh?"

"The ice cream?"

"Funny."

Lizzy's smile glowed. "I can't believe I'm a

finalist."

Roman took a bite of his cone. "I can. Your essay was good. I mean, great. It had to have been for it to get picked."

Lizzy's face clouded for a moment. "That awful Mariah better not win."

Abby skipped around in a circle while attempting to keep her ice cream from melting over the edge of the cone. "Why is Mariah awful?"

Lizzy glanced at Roman and raised her eyebrows. "I, well, uh. Remember those girls who said mean things to you because you got a Fit Bit for your birthday?"

"Yeah, but now they're my friends because Dad gave me a phone."

Lizzy cleared her throat. "Well, Mariah used to say mean things to me too."

Abby stopped and looked up at Lizzy. "But Mom, you said I have to forgive my enemies and pray for them. I did, and now those girls are my friends."

Roman's heart swelled with pride for this little girl who wasn't his.

"I know, Bug. I'm still working on the forgiveness thing."

Abby resumed her skipping. "You'll get there, Mom."

Roman laughed, and Lizzy joined in.

Later, after ice cream and a leisurely walk around City Hall Park, Roman returned home with a full heart. Now he needed to figure out what he could do to convince Lizzy he was the One, with a capital O.

1. Ask about her day

    If bad, send an encouraging scripture verse meme

    If good, (nope, go back, delete)

    If bad, take donuts or ice cream

    If good, send encouraging scripture verse meme

Roman dragged his hands through his hair. Would this work? His secret obsession with Hallmark movies should have prepared him for this. With a frustrated sigh, he continued typing.

2. Surprise her with dinner from the Thai place she likes (what is her favorite meal there???)

3. Make her jealous.

Roman shook his head, then deleted number three. Dumb.

3. Take Abby out somewhere for Lizzy to have some 'me time.'

He smiled. Now there was something he knew would have a positive impact.

Drumming his fingers on the table, he wracked his brain for something to add. Flowers? Too obvious. Candy? There needed to be a Source Code for something as complex as romance.

Picking up his phone, he tapped out a quick text to Lizzy.

Congrats again. I'm proud of you.

He waited for the "Delivered" message. No response.

-*-

Sleep refused to give Lizzy a respite from exhaustion. Conflicting emotions pulled her from exhilaration over being one of the essay finalists to confusion over the feelings which had surfaced during Roman's hug.

With a sigh, she turned on the light and padded to the kitchen where the sketchbook lay on the table.

Idly flipping through the pages, Lizzy remembered drawing the tiny boat tossed on angry waves. She was the boat and the cold water still wanted to drown her.

God, what should I do about Roman?

She'd misjudged him badly. Guilt weighed heavy on her heart. There must be a way to make it up to him. Of course, he only wanted to offer her a place to stay, not a 'friends with benefits' situation.

Grrrr.

Roman's hug goodbye after ice cream had felt so, well, right. With her face against his shoulder, she'd experienced rest for the first time in a very long time. She'd breathed in the smell of a newly laundered shirt and the faint wisp of aftershave. It felt like home.

Grabbing some colored pencils from the cloth bag sitting next to the sketch pad, she began to draw.

What appeared resembled a Picasso-like picture, unstructured with faces and objects mismatched. Not from God.

Lizzy closed the book and shuffled to her bedroom, pausing at Abby's door to watch her daughter sleep. How wonderful to be a child with no worries. Vastly different from Lizzy's childhood. Always wondering if Mom would be sober at the end of the day. Or if there would be enough to eat. Or if she'd be teased at school for wearing the same dirty clothes two days in a row.

Lizzy's heart swelled with fierce love. She'd do whatever it took to give Abby the childhood she had missed.

Just then, Lizzy's cell pinged with an incoming text. She headed into her bedroom and read the text from Roman.

Roman: **Congrats again. I'm proud of you.**

Smiling, she lay down and was asleep in minutes.

Chapter 17

Roman dusted, vacuumed, scrubbed both bathrooms, and sanitized the kitchen to within an inch of its life. Mom could suss out bad housekeeping like a drug-sniffing German Shepherd. His parents had decided at the last minute to visit today. Sensing the impending chaos, Millie had disappeared.

A text pinged at three o'clock.

Mom: **We're stopping at the grocery store for a few things**

Roman groaned. He wanted to take them out for dinner, but this text meant Mom would be cooking. Which meant a lot of noise and chaos, something he hadn't experienced since he'd moved out of his parents' home. Solitude calmed him and helped him concentrate on work.

Although lately, Roman wished he had someone to share his day with. That was why he made the hundred-yard trek from his back door to Lizzy's. She didn't seem to mind. In fact, she welcomed his presence. Sometimes he'd clean her kitchen while Lizzy put Abby to bed. He loved seeing her face on those occasions.

She'd grin from ear to ear, as if he'd given her a diamond necklace. Then they'd sit in the living room or on the back porch and talk, usually about nothing in particular.

Soon he heard the double tap of a car horn, his dad's signature greeting. Roman dragged himself to the front door, opened it, and braced himself. He loved his family, but sometimes they could be a bit much.

As expected, Mom was the first one out of the car. She bustled toward him, grabbed his cheeks with both hands, and squeezed.

"My little *ragazzino*, Romano." Mom stepped back and examined him from head to toe. "You are too skinny, Romano. I will fix that."

Roman shook his head. Mom was deep into her Italian *madre* mode. Before Dad could exit the SUV, the back door opened, and two little girls exploded from the vehicle.

"Wait a minute, you too." His oldest sister jumped out and attempted to corral the girls.

"You brought Rose with you?"

Mom shrugged with an expressive Italian shrug. "Of course. She wants to see you too. And your brother is on his way."

Roman smiled at his dad, who rolled his eyes. Dad was a bit eccentric as well, but he understood life around a gaggle of women.

"Don't worry, little brother," Rose said. "We're staying at an Air B&B outside of town. I wouldn't expose you to these two for three days." She grabbed each of the girls by the shoulder. "Say hello to your uncle Roman."

"Hello, Uncle Roman," they recited with a giggle. They were identical twin hurricanes. At least Roman could tell Elise from Leslie.

"Don't stand there and stare," Mom admonished. "Help your father with the bags. I'm going inside to see what kind of place my son lives in." She sniffed, as if she'd already found it lacking.

Roman sighed and walked around to the back of the SUV.

"Holy cow, Dad," Roman exclaimed as his dad raised the rear hatch. "Did you bring the entire kitchen with you?"

Roman counted three boxes of kitchen implements, including a stock pot, cast iron fry pan, and a mixer resembling an outboard motor.

Dad laughed, then pulled Roman in for a hug, slapping him on the back before releasing him.

"You know your mother. She'll cook enough food to stock your freezer for a month."

Yes, Roman did know his mother.

-*-

Lizzy arrived home from work and hung her purse on one of the coat hooks. Abby had chattered all the way home about her dad and how he'd taught her to text.

"As if I needed help. Duh. Everyone knows how to text."

Weariness pulled at Lizzy's shoulders. If only she could crawl under the covers and sleep until things went back to normal.

Not gonna happen, girlfriend.

"Mom, I'm going to call my dad," Abby said,

holding her brand-new phone.

Lizzy reached out her hand. "Let me see it for a minute. I need to get his number."

Abby clutched the phone to her chest before reluctantly placing it in Lizzy's outstretched palm.

"Let me get his info, and then we'll talk later about phone rules."

"Mooom." Abby sighed.

Lizzy used her phone to send a text to Dylan. **This is Lizzy. We need to talk.**

Hopefully, it would get his attention. Meanwhile, Abby bounced up and down beside her. "Are you done?"

With a grim set to her mouth, Lizzy held the phone out but didn't release it. "You can call your dad and that's it."

"Seriously?"

"Yes, seriously. There are rules about cell phone use, texting, and screen time. Until I set some ground rules, that's it."

Abby snatched the phone and spun on her heels. "You're mean. I should go live with my dad."

Lizzy's heart shattered. In one day, Dylan had stolen Abby from her, like he'd stolen her innocence ten plus years ago.

Why was her life being churned up? Lizzy struggled to keep from crying.

She shuffled into the hall and stood outside Abby's closed bedroom door; another sign things had changed. Abby's voice sounded excited, but the words were indistinguishable. Lizzy continued to her bedroom, fell onto the bed, and was instantly asleep.

She woke up to a small hand stroking her cheek.

"Mom?"

Lizzy cracked open her eyes. Abby's face was inches from hers. "I'm hungry, Mom."

Lizzy stretched, then swung her legs over the side of the bed. She gathered Abby in her arms. "I love you, Ladybug."

Abby squirmed. "I love you too, Mom, but I'm starved."

The digital clock on the nightstand read six-thirty. "I'll bet you are. Let's see what we find for dinner."

They headed into the kitchen as Roman appeared outside the back door. He raised his hand to knock.

Abby leaped to the door and opened it. "Hi, Roman. We're going to fix dinner."

Roman stepped into the house. Lizzy swept her glance from his feet to jean-clad legs and blue tee shirt. He looked good. Darn it.

"I'm glad I caught you before you ate," Roman said. "My mom cooked up a huge batch of cioppino and we're getting ready to eat."

"Sounds yummy." Lizzy watched as Roman's face grew pink.

"Please come," he pleaded. His voice dropped to a near whisper. "I love my family, but they're driving me nuts right now."

Lizzy chuckled. What she wouldn't give for a big, noisy family.

"Can I bring something?" Lizzy opened the fridge in search of something she could throw together.

"Not at all. Just come. My mom made a salad, and we have sourdough bread."

Abby leaned into Roman while looking entreatingly at Lizzy. "Can we, Mom? Can we go? Please?"

Lizzy shrugged. "I don't see why not. Can you give me five minutes?"

"Sure. Shall I wait?"

"If you want." Lizzy practically sprinted into the bathroom. She ran a toothbrush over her teeth and pulled her hair into a loose ponytail at the base of her neck. After splashing water on her face, she added a bit of pink lip gloss.

"It'll have to do," she said to her reflection.

Meeting Roman's family might be fun. Or it could be a disaster. Either way, she'd get a great Italian meal out of it.

-*-

Roman chatted with Abby while Lizzy did whatever she was doing.

"You gave your mom a scare, you know," he said, settling himself at the table.

"But it was my *dad*," Abby said, as if it made perfect sense to leave school with a stranger.

"I know you've been taught about 'stranger danger.'"

Abby put her hands on her hips. "I prayed God would let me meet my dad, so, I had to go with him."

Roman hid a smile at the emotion running across Abby's face. She was adorable. But still, to hop into a car with a man who said he was her father was unbelievably dumb. And scary. He shivered a little thinking about an alternative to the happy ending.

Lizzy breezed into the room. "Sorry I took so long. Ready?"

Roman's breath caught. Lizzy was stunning. She'd changed out of her work clothes into a pair of black leggings with a flowery top. Her chestnut hair was pulled back, emphasizing the heart-shape of her face. His gaze settled on shiny pink lips. What would it be like to kiss off the lip gloss? He was about to introduce Lizzy to his family, and he was thinking about kissing her.

Slow down, bubba, his inner geek said.

Roman wet his lips. "Ready?"

They stepped through the door. Lizzy reached behind her to close it. Abby took hold of one of his hands, and with the other, he gently guided Lizzy across the yard. His heart beat a quick tattoo. Would she be overwhelmed by his crazy mother and loud family or would they be quick to embrace Lizzy and Abby.

Before he could form another thought, they were at his back door.

Roman stopped. "Remember, I warned you."

Lizzy smiled up at him and winked. "I got this."

_*_

Roman's hand on the small of Lizzy's back both warmed and caused chills. What would it be like to have his constant care as a part of her life, forever?

Before Lizzy could think through the prospect,

they were stepping through the back door of Roman's house. The babble of voices rising and falling in good-natured argument filled her ears, while the smell of tomato stock sloshed over her senses and made her stomach grumble in anticipation. The television blared in the background, the volume far too high for a home this size. The windows were clouded with steam from the boiling stew simmering on the stove.

Roman raised his voice over the clamor. "Mom, Dad, this is my neighbor, Elizabeth, and her daughter, Abby."

Sudden silence dropped as everyone turned to stare. Time stood still for a moment.

Roman's mother rushed to Lizzy and grasped both her shoulders before leaning in to buss a kiss on either cheek. "*Bella, bella, mi amore,*" she gushed. "My name is Maria, and this is my husband, Lorenzo."

Roman's dad stood with his hand outstretched. "Call me Bud."

Bud clasped his enormous hand over Lizzy's smaller one. "Nice to meet you," Lizzy said, sweeping her eyes over the younger woman and two little girls.

"I'm Rose," the woman said. "Roman's oldest sister. These are my girls, Elise and Leslie."

"Hi. This is my daughter, Abby. She turned ten not too long ago."

Abby pouted. "I prefer to be called Abigail." Lizzy resisted the urge to roll her eyes.

Rose smiled. "Perfect. The girls are seven."

Maria leaned down to Abby's level. "What a

bella chica you are."

Abby blushed, then looked up to Lizzy. "I don't know what it means," she whispered.

Roman laughed. "It means you are a beautiful young lady."

Abby grinned. She looked at Roman's mom and said, "Roman and my mom went on a date, but they aren't going to live together because that would be wrong."

The blood from Lizzy's head swept to her feet then back up again, leaving her with vertigo. The room was silent again before chaos erupted.

"A date!" Maria launched into an Italian monologue while Lizzy ushered her daughter into the bathroom.

"What, Mom?" Abby asked when Lizzy closed and locked the door.

Lizzy took a deep breath and exhaled. "Please do not say another word tonight about Roman and me going out to dinner. It wasn't a date."

Tears filled Abby's eyes. "I don't understand."

Lizzy grabbed her daughter in a fierce hug. "I know you don't, Bug. Things between adults are complicated."

Abby pulled away. "That's what you always say when you don't want to explain something."

"Let's not say anything else, okay?" Lizzy brushed the hair from Abby's face.

They returned to the dining room to find everyone seated at the table.

Lizzy glanced at Roman. "I'm sorry."

Roman stood and pulled out the chair next to

him. "Come sit here."

Roman's brother leaned across the table. "I'm Rory, the other better-looking Rossi son."

"What happened while I was in the bathroom?" she asked out of the side of her mouth.

Roman shrugged. His eyes looked wild as if he was about to bolt for the door. If he abandoned her now, well, she'd follow him and plan to leave the country.

Roman's mom smiled. "Come, sit. Let's eat some cioppino and get acquainted."

The table had been set with his Target plates and silverware. A card table had been set up in the kitchen with places set for the three girls. Abby sat with the twins and started a conversation.

While Roman's dad dished up the steaming cioppino, Rose passed a basket of fragrant sourdough bread. Rory grabbed the wooden salad bowl and helped himself to a heaping pile of lettuce. Maria gave him a look.

"Guests first, Rory. Have I not taught you better?"

Rory's face flamed. "Sorry."

Maria took the salad bowl from him and sent it in Lizzy's direction. "My Romano tells me you live in the little house next door."

Lizzy dished up some salad on her plate. "Yes. But I have to move soon. The lady who owns the house passed away, and her kids want to sell it."

Maria set a steaming bowl of cioppino in front of Lizzy. "But that is terrible. Where will you go?"

"We're working on that, Mom," Roman said.

"But Roman, you must do something." Maria

glanced from Roman to Lizzy. "You have all this room here. Why don't you come home and let your friend stay here?"

Lizzy and Roman exchanged a look. Lizzy thought back to the misunderstanding at the restaurant. She smothered a smile. It hadn't been the first time she'd overreacted to something, and it wouldn't be the last.

The conversation flowed around her, but Lizzy concentrated on enjoying Maria's cooking. She'd never had cioppino before. Crab, shrimp, and some other fish she couldn't identify swam in a savory tomato base. What she wouldn't give to cook like this. But all those ingredients cost money Lizzy didn't have.

"What do you think of the cioppino?" Maria asked.

Lizzy took a spoonful, blew on it, and put it in her mouth. "It's delicious."

Maria beamed. "It is my great-great-grandmother's recipe from Genoa."

Rory scoffed. "Oh, come on, Mom. You know cioppino originated in San Francisco."

Mom's hand flew to her throat. "No, no no! It is *una bugia*."

Roman's dad patted her hand. "Rory is kidding, Ma."

Lizzy smiled as Maria threw Rory 'the look.' Again.

"Mom, Elise is kicking me under the table," Leslie exclaimed. Rose jumped up to referee while Rory leaned over to Roman.

"Your lady is pretty. When you blow it, can I

swoop in with candy and flowers?" He wagged his eyebrows in Lizzy's direction.

Abby's voice broke into their conversation. "Mom, when are you going to go on another date with Roman?"

Maria was quick to respond. "Yes, Roman. When are you and your lovely friend going on another date?"

Lizzy wished a hole would open and she could fall into it. Along with her daughter.

"Mom, this isn't something I want to talk about right now." Roman ran a hand over his head. "Can we please change the subject?"

Maria huffed. "Fine."

Roman remained mostly quiet throughout the meal. Lizzy watched him out of the corner of her eye while Maria and Rose peppered her with questions.

"Where did you grow up?"

"Where do you work?"

"What about your parents?"

"Do you attend church?"

Roman squirmed in his seat and held up a hand. "Mom, Rose, stop. Take a breath and let Lizzy enjoy this delicious meal."

Lizzy sent him a grateful smile.

That worked. Mom beamed. "You are right, *mi figlio.*"

Lizzy nodded and took a few more spoonfuls of the stew. "It is wonderful."

Rory leaned forward. "So, do you prefer to be called Lizzy or Elizabeth?"

"Lizzy."

Rory nodded. "Good to know."

Soon dinner was over, and Rose began to clear the dishes.

"Let me help," Lizzy said, rising from her seat.

"No, I've got this. Could you see about the girls?" Rose nodded toward the kid's table where the threesome was giggling.

"Sure."

When the kid's table had been cleared, Roman announced, "I'll take the trash out." He nodded his head toward Lizzy, then the front door.

"I'll help," Lizzy said.

Mom clasped her hands together under her chin. "So sweet, my little ones." Her eyes filled with tears as a sappy smile filled her face.

Roman rolled his eyes. Grabbing the garbage bag, he hoisted it out of the can and carried it to the front door.

"Don't wait on us for dessert," he said, holding the door for Lizzy to proceed him.

When the door closed behind them, Lizzy whirled to face him. "When I murder my daughter, will you visit me in prison?"

"Not if I get there first."

"What happened in there?"

Roman hoisted the bag of trash into the large garbage can on the side of his house. "I have no idea."

"I don't know what's gotten into Abby lately."

"Abigail," Roman corrected her.

"Right. Actually, I do know what's gotten into her. Ever since her dad showed up, she's been mouthy and whiny." Lizzy looked up at him with moist eyes. "Can you believe she told me she wanted to go live with him?"

Roman pulled her to him. "I'm sure she didn't mean it," he said, rubbing her back. Lizzy sniffled against his chest.

The breeze kicked up, blowing Roman's hair. Lizzy shivered in his arms.

"We should go inside where it's warmer."

Lizzy pulled away. "I suppose."

Lizzy hated to pull out of Roman's embrace. How wonderful it was to be held. But every moment they remained outside gave Roman's mother more fodder for her quest to find out if there was something going on between them.

"I'm sorry about all this," Roman said.

"It isn't your fault. I don't know what to do about Abby. It's as if she's become a different person."

"My family—"

"I love your family. They're awesome."

"But my mom—"

"She's amazing." Lizzy had already fallen in love with Roman's family. They were boisterous and loud and utterly captivating. They'd swept her up in their enthusiasm and love. The contrast between Maria's unconditional love and her own mother's criticism couldn't have been more different.

Was it possible to be in love with a man's family, yet conflicted about the man himself?

They walked slowly to the front door. Roman opened it for Lizzy to proceed him. She glanced around the room with a moment of panic.

"Where's Abby?"

Rose stepped from the kitchen holding a towel. "They're in the bedroom. I believe your daughter is showing my girls her new phone."

Lizzy clenched her jaw. Darn you, Dylan.

Rose motioned to her. "Come on in here. You can help me finish drying." Rose pulled a clean towel from a stack on the counter and tossed it to her.

Lizzy stood next to Rose and grabbed the lid to a pot. Rose bumped her shoulder. "Now I can get to know you without any interruptions."

Lizzy forced herself to relax. "Sure."

"How long have you and Roman known each other?" Rose asked.

"Not long. I moved in a few weeks ago. We met then."

Rose set down the dried pan and squeezed Lizzy into a side hug. "I'm glad you did. He's been lonely for a while. Ever since, well, he was engaged once. His fiancé broke up with him a few months before the wedding. I'm sure he's talked about it."

Lizzy nodded. "He mentioned it."

"He was hurt pretty badly. We never thought they were a good fit, but once Roman gets something in his head, he can be stubborn."

Lizzy silently agreed.

Rose handed Lizzy another pot. "Roman's been different these past few weeks."

"How so?"

Rose paused. "Calmer, I think. You know my brother is a little . . . different."

Lizzy leaned a hip against the counter. Rose wasn't telling her anything she hadn't noticed. Part of Roman's attraction was his quirkiness.

"I'd like to think you are part of the reason he's doing better."

"Me?"

Rose smiled as she took the pot from Lizzy's hands. "It's been a long time since Roman has let anyone new into his life. He's talked about you to Rory, and now I can see why."

Lizzy grew warm.

"And your little girl, well, Roman adores her."

While Lizzy processed this information, Rose abruptly changed the subject.

"Were you married before?"

"Uh, no." Why not tell Roman's sister the whole sordid story? "I was in high school, hanging out with a rough crowd and doing things I'm now ashamed of. I ended up pregnant at sixteen. Abby was born right after my seventeenth birthday. I dropped out of school."

"Oh, wow. That's rough. Is her dad in the picture?"

Lizzy huffed out a laugh. "Yes and no. He ghosted me shortly after I told him I was pregnant. His family moved to Portland, and I lost contact with him. Then last week, he showed up and abducted Abby from school and kept her all day."

"You must have been frantic." Rose shuddered.

Lizzy nodded. "Now he wants to be a part of her life. We still haven't talked about how this is all going to work."

"I'm sorry. I'll be praying for you. What does Roman have to say about all this?"

Lizzy pursed her lips. "He said he'd help me find an attorney so I can keep custody. It's overwhelming." Lizzy hung her drying towel over the stove handle.

"I'm glad you have Roman to lean on. He's my rock. And he'll be yours, too."

Lizzy tried to return the smile Rose gave her, but her mouth remained closed. How could she tell these wonderful people she and Roman were friends and nothing more. It was all too much. The house, having to move, loss of hours at work, Dylan, and now this. Tears pushed their way up from Lizzy's chest and overflowed down her cheeks. She choked back a sob as Rose gathered her in her arms.

"Oh, my dear, what is it? What did I say?"

Lizzy could only cry against Rose's soft tee shirt. After a few moments, Lizzy pulled away. "I'm sorry. There's a lot going on right now."

Rose took hold of Lizzy's shoulders. "It will all work out. You'll see. Roman won't let anyone take your daughter away."

Lizzy wiped her face with the dishtowel. "It isn't the only thing. It's—"

"What did you do to Lizzy?" Roman stepped into the kitchen and swept his gaze over Lizzy's blotchy face. "Gee, Rose, I can't leave you with her for a minute."

Chapter 18

Roman finished talking to his dad and Rory. He stepped into the kitchen to rescue Lizzy from his talkative sister.

"What's going on?" he demanded. "Did you make Lizzy cry?" He pulled Lizzy away from Rose and put his arms around Lizzy protectively.

"Of course not." Rose's retort was quick and sharp.

He looked down at Lizzy for confirmation.

"I'm sorry. I should go home," Lizzy said. "I'm a little tired is all."

Roman glared at his sister. "I'll walk you home. Let's gather up Abby."

After a flurry of goodbyes from his dad, mom, Rory, Rose, and the twins, they made their way to the back door. Before they could make their escape, his mom embraced Lizzy one more time.

"Welcome to our *familiglia, mi figlia*." Maria kissed both of Lizzy's cheeks, then bent down and kissed Abby's forehead. "We will talk tomorrow, you and I. And get to know each other." She clapped her hands together.

Roman slid the door closed behind them.

"They can be a bit much."

"You warned me." Lizzy fell into step next to him.

"Why were you crying?"

He felt Lizzy shrug next to him. "Your sister is nice."

"So, that's why you were crying?" Roman would never understand the workings of the female mind.

"I told her about Dylan and the rest. You know, the house, everything seemed to pile up, and I . . ."

"You cried."

"Exactly."

Too many questions he was dying to ask. But Abby took that moment to ask, "When are you and my mom getting married?"

Lizzy froze. "Abby, what makes you think Roman and I are getting married?"

"It's Abigail."

"Answer the question," Lizzy said with a warning in her voice.

They were almost to Lizzy's back door. Roman asked, "Want me to go in with you?"

"No. I need to have a conversation with my daughter. Alone."

Roman watched as Lizzy took Abby's arm and propelled her into the house. He was glad to not have to witness what would be a stern talk from an angry mother.

-*-

Lizzy marched Abby to the bathroom. "Brush your teeth, get into your PJ's, and wait for me in your room."

Abby made the good choice to keep any words of argument to herself. Her daughter was dancing on Lizzy's last nerve. Not a good place to be.

Lizzy went into her bedroom and changed into a soft pair of sweats and an oversized tee shirt. She'd kicked off her shoes and slipped into a thick pair of socks. After a few deep breaths and more than one prayer, Lizzy straightened her shoulders and marched into her daughter's room.

Abby set her phone on the nightstand when Lizzy stepped through the door. Another good choice. The thought of wrestling the phone from Abby's hand did not sit favorably.

Lizzy sat on the edge of the bed. "Abby, we need to discuss a few things."

"Like when I can go see my dad?" Abby blinked through tear-filled eyes.

Lizzy sighed. "That, and about you leaving school with him. What if he hadn't been your dad? We've talked a dozen times about stranger danger." Lizzy shuddered, thinking about what could have happened. "Why would you hop in his car and accept what he said?"

Abby sniffled. "I don't know. You said you were going to try to find him. I thought you found him and told him where I went to school." She wiped away tears with her fingers.

Lizzy resolved to stay firm, even though Abby's tears nearly had her undone. "You should have called me or had him call me. Anything other than taking off from school without a word."

"Okay."

"I'm going to talk to him about what role he expects to have in your life." What happened to Dylan that he wanted to be a father now after ten years. He'd missed all the hard stuff; colic, the hundreds or thousands of dollars spent on diapers, scrimping to pay for daycare. She could go on and on. The more Lizzy dwelled on the past, the angrier she became.

"Now let's talk about the phone." Lizzy glanced at the shiny new iPhone. Her ten-year-old daughter had the latest version, while Lizzy coaxed her ancient cell phone to continue to work. "You may not take it to school." Abby started to object. "Period. End of discussion."

Abby glared but stayed silent.

"You may not access the internet from it, nor can you engage in social media."

"But, Mom, when can I?"

Lizzy ran a hand through her hair. "I don't know. This is all new territory for me. I have to think about it."

"But what if something happens at school and I need to call you? What if I take the phone in my backpack but don't touch it unless it's an emergency?" Abby clasped her hands together as if in prayer.

"Let me think about it," Lizzy conceded. "Finally, we need to talk about Roman."

"Are you and him getting married?"

Lizzy shook her head. "Roman and I are not getting married."

"But Elise and Leslie and me think it would be

cool. Then we could see each other all the time."

Lizzy frowned. "Sorry, no."

"Are you going to live together?"

"No," Lizzy exclaimed. "We talked about this. Christians aren't supposed to live together without being married."

"But Roman's family is cool. You like him, don't you?"

Lizzy sighed. "It's complicated, Bug."

"You always say that when you don't want to talk about something." Abby huffed in frustration.

"We will talk about it. But not tonight." Exhaustion rested heavily on her shoulders. "Go to sleep and we'll talk tomorrow."

Lizzy leaned over and pushed Abby's hair away from her cheek, then kissed her. "Good night, Ladybug."

Abby turned on her side, arms wrapped around Spot. "Night, Mom."

Lizzy fell into bed shortly after turning off the light to Abby's room. Sleep evaded her as she mulled over the evening with Roman's family.

While they were a bit overwhelming, the love they exuded for each other and her was a warm change from her mother's judgment. A sliver of longing slid into her heart, leaving a crack. What would it be like to be a part of a big, happy family? *His* big, happy family.

Lizzy mentally ticked off Roman's good qualities.

He was gainfully employed.

Owned his house, or at least wasn't renting.

Didn't seem to have any bad habits. That she

knew of.

Was a Christian.

Loved Abby.

Passably good-looking. Lizzy smiled at this. He was cute in a quirky, nerdy kind of way.

He loved her.

Lizzy flopped onto her back. Roman loved her. Or so Simone said. But did he? Lizzy ping-ponged the discussion in her head. The question remained, how did she feel about Roman?

Lizzy turned on her side and clutched a fluffy pillow to her chest.

Dear Lord, I need direction. Would you mind sending me a letter or something, telling me what to do?

-*-

The house was quiet when Roman stepped through the back door. "Where is everybody?"

Rory lounged on the sofa, channel surfing. "Rose took the girls to the Air B&B. Mom and Dad are getting ready for bed."

Roman grabbed a sweatshirt from the hooks hung by the back door and tossed it to his brother. "C'mon, let's sit outside."

Rory groaned as he rolled to a sitting position. "I ate too much."

"Easy to do with Mom's cooking." Roman slid the back door open and stepped out into the crisp Oregon evening. The sun had set, leaving a sliver of gold-lit clouds on the horizon.

The brothers sat on Roman's stiff plastic lawn chairs.

"When you gonna get some decent back yard

furniture?" Rory asked, shifting his bulk to get comfortable.

Roman shrugged. "After I settle down," he said with a ghost of a smile.

"What's up with that, anyway?" Rory asked, leaning forward to rest his forearms on his thighs.

"It's complicated." Roman cringed. Such a cliché.

"Are you or are you not in a relationship with the lovely Lizzy?"

Roman took a deep breath. "Here's the thing. Lizzy and I went out to dinner -"

"Like on a date?"

"Not a date. Two friends having a meal."

Rory grinned, his teeth white in the darkness. "Right."

"Anyway, Lizzy's landlord decided to sell her house. Since her work hours were reduced, she can't find anything to rent within her price range. I offered her to move in here, and I'd find a place to rent."

Rory scratched his head. "I'm confused. Why is this a problem?"

"She thought I was asking her to move in with me. You know, friends with benefits."

Rory leaned back in the chair. "Ah. Not your finest moment."

"Since Dylan is back in Abby's life—"

"Wait, who is Dylan?"

"Dylan is Abby's dad. He appeared the other day, and since then, Abby's been a brat. She seems intent on hooking me and Lizzy up."

Rory grinned. "And that's a problem, why?"

Roman groaned. "When Abby blurted out about the date thing, now Mom is putting two and two together and coming up with wedding invitations."

Rory stood and stretched. "I used to think your life was boring." He patted Roman on the shoulder. "You better figure this out, fast."

Later, after everyone was asleep, Roman lay in the dark, wide awake. Trying to come up with a plan had his brain on overdrive. Tomorrow he'd rein in his mom. Then he'd make sure she and Lizzy had no more contact until Mom and Dad went home. Problem solved.

Millie, stretched out on the bed next to him, purred her agreement.

Chapter 19

Lizzy woke the next morning to the sound of rain hammering on the roof. Most days she didn't mind the rain, but today the gloomy skies mirrored her mood. If only she could pull the covers over her head and go back to sleep. For a month. When all the chaos in her life was past.

With a sigh, Lizzy rolled out of bed and padded into the kitchen to make a huge pot of coffee. While it brewed, she rousted Abby from sleep and urged her into the bathroom to get ready for school.

Returning to the kitchen, Lizzy gazed out the window toward Roman's house. Lights were on, and she could see Maria moving around the kitchen. Her heart filled with warmth, remembering how it had felt to be folded into Roman's family. They'd satisfied the longing she'd had since her dad left and her mom turned to alcohol.

Lizzy poured her first cup of coffee and called to Abby. "Are you ready for breakfast?"

"Not yet."

Lizzy sat at the table and opened her sketch pad, skipping past the storm drawing and the plan for Abby's mural, looking for the drawing of the family in front of the house. She gulped hot liquid, then fanned her mouth from the sudden burn, remembering she'd torn it out and ripped it up.

What she needed was a trip to the beach. She'd check her schedule for the next time she had a day off, then drive to the ocean and clear out the cobwebs and confusion.

Lizzy breezed into work and clocked in at exactly two minutes before eight o'clock. Josiah looked up from a clipboard when she exited the break room.

His eyebrows raised. "You're early."

Lizzy grinned. "Yup. Trying to earn 'Employee of the Month.' If we had such a thing."

Josiah shook his head with a tight smile. Lizzy didn't envy him the responsibility he carried for the profitability of the store. With the cut in employees' hours, it meant Josiah had to work even more.

"Hey, Boss," Lizzy called after him. Josiah stopped and spun around.

"Yes?"

"Can I grab some empty boxes from the storeroom?" Time to stop procrastinating and start packing. Whether she won the house lottery or not, moving out of her cozy bungalow was inevitable.

Halfway through her shift, Lizzy looked up from the customer she was helping and saw Mariah waiting in line. Lizzy's stomach tightened. After Mariah's revelation about the root of her animosity, Lizzy had forgotten all about it. She'd been caught up in her own drama over Dylan, Roman, and being named a finalist in the lottery.

Mariah stepped to the counter after Lizzy's customer completed his transaction. Today she wore brightly colored yoga pants and a fitted workout shirt accentuating her slim figure. Lizzy sucked in her tummy.

"How can I help you?" Lizzy asked, eyeing Mariah's empty hands.

Mariah glanced around, chewing on her bottom lip. "I wondered if I could stop by your house later." Her words sped up. "I would have texted or called but I didn't have your number. There's something I wanted to talk to you about." Mariah held her breath, waiting for Lizzy to answer.

Her sinful side wanted to say, "Not in a million years do I want you in my house." With a sigh, Lizzy remembered the phrase 'What Would Jesus Do.'

"Sure. What time?"

Mariah named a time, and Lizzy agreed. After Mariah left the store, their brief conversation tumbled over and over in Lizzy's brain. What could her childhood archenemy want to talk about?

Just what she needed – more drama.

Lizzy half-listened to her daughter's chatter on the way home from Abby's after-school daycare. Her goal was to go inside, change clothes, and throw on some makeup. Like she was gearing up for battle.

Lizzy pulled to a stop in front of her house. "Help me bring in these boxes, Ladybug."

Abby sprang out of the car and raced to the front door.

"Hey!" Lizzy shouted. Abby was bent over something sitting on the welcome mat. She climbed out of the Honda and strode to the porch.

Abby straightened. "Look, Mom. It's flowers."

Lizzy froze. Someone had left a small flower arrangement outside her front door. The colorful arrangement of orange lilies, red pansies, and miniature sunflowers sat in a wooden box.

"Who's it from?" Abby demanded, grabbing the tiny white envelope tucked into the bouquet.

Lizzy snatched it from her hand. "I'll take it. Let's get the boxes unloaded and take these flowers inside, then we'll look at the card."

Abby rolled her eyes. "Fine."

Lizzy tapped the card against her lips. Receiving flowers was a whole new experience. Who could have sent them? She went through several possibilities.

Abby's dad, Dylan, trying to make up. Mariah. Neither one was likely.

It had to be Roman.

"Hurry up, Mom. Let's go." Abby's strident voice interrupted Lizzy's thoughts. She'd been staring at the flowers sitting on the porch.

Once the door was unlocked and the boxes piled in a corner of the room, Lizzy plunked down on the sofa to open the little card.

"Who's it from?" Abby pressed herself up against Lizzy's arm.

"Give me a moment, Bug." Lizzy used a fingernail to open the flap. She slid the card out.

Sorry for all the drama with my family. Roman

"What's drama?" Abby asked, taking the card from Lizzy's fingers and reading it to herself.

Lizzy smiled. What a sweet gesture. Not necessary. But still…

The doorbell rang and Lizzy realized too late she hadn't changed nor freshened up for Mariah's visit. Her khaki work pants had a smear of grease on one leg. Two drips from the peanut butter and jelly sandwich dotted her work smock.

Lizzy shot to her feet and quickly unbuttoned the smock and tossed it behind the couch as Abby raced to open the door. With one hand Lizzy straightened her ponytail and with the other pulled her shirt down.

"Mariah. Hi. You're early."

Mariah glanced at her Apple watch. "No, I'm right on time." She stepped through the door and glanced around the room.

Lizzy squeezed her lips together to keep from making a snarky comment.

Mariah shifted her purse from one hand to the other. "Your house is really cute."

Was she serious, or was this another set up for an insult lobbed her way? Lizzy straightened her shoulders. This woman would not make her feel inferior. At least she hoped not.

"Do you want some coffee?" Lizzy offered.

"Oh, um, sure." Mariah clutched her designer purse against her chest. "Thanks."

"Sit down and I'll go make a pot." Lizzy spun on her heels and strode into the kitchen. Something had Miss Confidence looking uncomfortable, perched on the edge of the sofa.

Lizzy listened with half an ear as Abby tried to engage Mariah in conversation.

"Are you a friend of my mom's?"

There was a pause. "Yes. At least I hope so."

"I'm Abigail. I'm named after my great-great-grandmother. Did you know she was a dancer?"

"Uh, no. I didn't know."

"She was a chorus line dancer. I'm going to be a dancer when I grow up. Want to see some of my moves?"

Lizzy smiled as she waited for the coffee to brew. Her daughter didn't know a stranger. Abby wasn't afraid of anything, while Lizzy's life was ruled by terror. Fear something would happen to Abby. Or something would happen to her, and she couldn't take care of her daughter. Fear Dylan would take Abby away.

Roman's friendship added a new dimension to her fearful existence by forcing her to Open her heart, which was a whole new terror. Now his parents had drawn her in as well.

"Do you take anything in your coffee?" Lizzy called into the living room.

"Yes, please. Cream and sugar."

Of course, the princess would want to ruin her coffee. Lizzy pulled a carton of milk from the fridge and sniffed it. Yup, still good. She splashed some into a mug and added a hefty spoon of sugar. She carried both mugs into the living room and set them on the coffee table.

"Here you go."

Mariah picked up her mug and gripped it with both hands. She took a tentative sip. "Perfect.

Thank you."

Lizzy let the silence lengthen.

"I guess you're wondering why I'm here," Mariah said.

Lizzy resisted the urge to roll her eyes.

Mariah glanced at Abby, who had finished her dance and was sitting on the floor tapping on her phone.

Mariah took another sip, then set the mug down. "I've been meeting with Pastor Roy." She cleared her throat. "Let me back up. Scott and I broke up."

Stinks to be you, Lizzy thought. Then instantly repented. "Go on."

"Scott didn't want children and I do. So, he dumped me. The thing is, we were living together, and I stopped using birth control." Mariah tightened her hands into fists, then loosened them.

Lizzy remembered Mariah's purchases of pregnancy tests. "I can see how it would be a problem."

"As you can imagine, I was devastated. I've never been dumped."

Lizzy almost laughed. *Sorry, not sorry.*

"I started meeting with Pastor Roy. He made me realize I was living a lifestyle not pleasing to God." Mariah reached for her mug and took another drink. "I guess I was pretty good at playing 'Christian' by going to church. But I'd never really committed my life to Him."

"I get it." Lizzy did. It was one thing to say you were a Christian, and another to fully devote yourself to Jesus.

"Anyway, I realized a lot of things. I realized I've been mean to you. Mostly because I've been jealous."

This time Lizzy did laugh. "Jealous? Of me?" Mariah had to be kidding.

"I know, it sounds silly. But as I told you before, you have this beautiful daughter." She pointed in Abby's direction. "You're artistic. You've made a life for yourself all on your own. I'm still dependent on my parents." Mariah shrugged. "What I want to say is I'm sorry. I hope you can forgive me."

Lizzy gulped her coffee and waited for the burn to go away while she considered the other woman's words. She knew enough about forgiveness to know she couldn't withhold it from another without causing grief to the Holy Spirit. But to forgive all the slights, insults, and bullying for the past thousand years was a hard pill to swallow.

Mariah must have sensed her hesitation. "It's not like I want us to be best friends or anything."

Uh, no. Never going to happen.

"I don't know what to say," Lizzy said. She looked at Abby, then back at Mariah with an exaggerated sigh. "I forgive you."

Mariah visibly relaxed. "I know I don't deserve it. But thank you." She stood and picked up her purse. "Oh, and by the way, I hope you win the house lottery."

Lizzy stood. "What I don't get is why you entered at all. You have a place to live."

Mariah frowned. "Not anymore. Now that Scott and I are no longer a couple, I've moved back in with my parents."

"But you didn't know what would happen when you entered the contest," Lizzy protested.

Mariah chewed on her lip before answering. "I've only shared this with Pastor Roy, so I hope you can keep a confidence." She waited for Lizzy's nod. "The reason I wanted the house is so I could take in foster kids. My parents don't approve of a single woman being a foster parent. I investigated a program called Safe Families. It's for parents who need short-term care for their kids without putting them in the system."

"I don't understand."

Mariah shifted her purse from one shoulder to the other. "For instance, if a mother is required by the courts to go to six weeks of detox, she can utilize Safe Families instead of putting the kids in foster care. It enables her to still be able to have her kids visit without having to get court approval. You can check it out at Safe-Families.org."

Lizzy couldn't form words. It was as if Cruella Deville suddenly decided she loved Dalmatian puppies.

"Well, anyway. I better go. Thanks for letting me come over."

Chapter 20

Roman paced from one end of his living room to the other while checking his cell phone for a text from Lizzy. She should have gotten the flowers by now. Why hadn't she texted him? Was it too much to expect a simple 'thank you?' What if she was mad at his lame attempt to woo her. He waited for his inner geek to comment. But for once, it was silent.

Rory burst through the front door. "Warning! Mom is on the rampage."

Before Roman could answer, Mom hurried in on Rory's heels with Dad trailing behind.

"Look what I brought," Mom said waiving a stack of magazines. She fanned them out on the coffee table. "Bride's Magazine, Modern Bride, Brides of the Pacific Northwest." She beamed like a proud grandma.

Rory quirked an eyebrow at Roman. "Wow. I'm speechless."

"Where is that *bella signorina* of yours?"

Rose and her twins swept into the house, adding more chaos.

"Uncle Roman, look what we got!" exclaimed

Elise. Or it could have been Leslie.

She held up some sort of toy.

"Great," Roman replied. He put a hand to his head.

The girls headed into the kitchen with a flurry of excited giggles. A minute later he heard the water running.

Rory sent him a warning look before disappearing down the hall toward Roman's office.

Roman licked his lips forming the words he needed to say. "Mom, Dad, sit down."

Dad sat on the sofa, scooting Millie from her favorite spot. She yawned and stretched, then sauntered into the kitchen.

"What is it, my Romano?" Mom asked, perching on the edge of a chair.

Roman paced in front of his parents. "Mom, you need to back up the train."

"Train?"

. Roman sighed. "Mom, Lizzy and I are not in a relationship. We're friends. That's it. Friends."

"But Roman—"

Roman sat on the sofa and reached for his mother's hands. "Mom, when I'm ready to be in a relationship again, I'll tell you. If it's with Lizzy . . ." he shrugged.

"I tried to tell her, son," his dad said. "You know how much your mom wants you to be happy."

Mom looked like she was about to cry.

"I'm sorry, Mom. Lizzy is wonderful and I care about her. But I don't know if she feels the same way."

"But Roman—"

"No buts, Mom. I need to do this on my own, okay? Please respect me on this. I care a lot for Lizzy, and I hope she cares for me. Until I find out how she feels, I can't have you assuming things." He swept his hand toward the magazines spread on the coffee table.

Mom kept her gaze on their clasped hands. "The love you feel for her shines from your eyes, Roman. And I think I see the same reflected in Lizzy's eyes."

Roman pressed his lips together. He hoped his mother was right.

Mom pulled her hands away and wiped her eyes. "After Shayna broke your heart, I thought you'd never find someone else. Your Lizzy would be perfect for you."

Roman agreed with his mom. But he'd need to stick to his plan to woo her. Without his mom's help.

"I'm going to fix dinner." Mom stood and straightened her shoulders before marching into the kitchen.

Roman turned and headed into his bedroom for some solitude. He swept a sweaty hand down the leg of his jeans, then dialed Lizzy's number.

She picked up on the third ring with a breathless, "Hello?"

"Hey. It's Roman. Did you get the flowers?"

"Oh, yeah. Thanks."

Not the reaction he'd hoped for.

"You're welcome. Say, my family is driving me crazy. Want to escape with me and grab some dinner?"

"Sure. Sounds great. What about Abby?"

"Bring her over. She can hang out with the twins."

"You will never believe what happened to me," Lizzy said.

"You mean in addition to having flowers delivered to your front door?"

"Well, yes. But it was nice. What I have to tell you borders on crazy."

Roman couldn't wait to hear what Lizzy had to say. "I'll send Rory over to get Abby and I'll follow. Whatever you do, don't come over here or my mom will have you in her clutches."

"So noted."

Thirty minutes later, he and Lizzy were seated at a small restaurant in downtown Main. New owners updated the original building to resemble an Italian bistro. Roman pulled a chair out for Lizzy at one of the tall round tables.

"Is this okay?" he asked.

"Yeah, fine."

Roman felt Lizzy's palpable tension as she nibbled at a fingernail, then flipped her hair over her shoulder and back again. Whatever she would share must have upset her.

The server brought them water in a clear glass bottle.

"Do you want to wait until after we order before you spill the beans?" Roman asked.

Lizzy nodded, studying the menu with a frown. "Sure."

Roman's stomach did a summersault. Lizzy's one-word answers had him picturing several scenarios, all of them bad. Maybe Abby's dad had shown up again. Or there was a hitch in the lottery for the house. Or she had to move out sooner than she expected.

"Do you know what you want?" Roman asked, hoping to end his internal misery.

"I'll have the Spaghetti Carbonara." Lizzy closed the menu with a decisive snap and laid it on the table.

"I'll have the same," Roman told the server.

Once their orders for salad dressing were completed and the waiter hurried away, Roman folded his hands on the table in front of him.

"What happened?"

Lizzy's eyebrows rose and fell as she shook her head. "Mariah came into the store today."

"The mean girl?" Roman remembered his confrontation with her in the gym.

"Yeah. She asked to come over to the house."

Roman nodded his encouragement.

"She came over and told me she was sorry for all the times she'd been cruel and asked me to forgive her."

"Wow." No way could he have seen that coming.

"She and her boyfriend were living together, and he dumped her because she wants kids, and he didn't."

Roman brushed his hair back. "Didn't I see them in church?"

"That isn't even the best part. Mariah's been meeting with our Pastor, and she gave her life to Christ. She felt guilty over being mean, and she came over to apologize."

Their salads arrived. Roman waited for the server to leave then reached across the table for Lizzy's hand. "Let's say grace."

He prayed a quick prayer, then as they dug into their salads, he asked. "Did you? Forgive her?"

Lizzy stabbed a piece of lettuce with more force than was necessary. "What could I do? I had to forgive her." She shrugged.

"I'm proud of you. It must have been hard."

"That's not all," Lizzy said, leaning toward him. Roman listened as she told him about Mariah's desire to help kids who needed a temporary home with their parents who were incarcerated or in rehab.

Roman set his fork down. "That's amazing."

"I know," Lizzy said. "Now I'm conflicted. I kind of want her to win the house."

Roman's mind whirled with this new information. Not only was Lizzy the most generous person he'd ever met, now she was willing to give up her dream of owning the home, so kids could have a safe place to go. He was desperate to find a solution to Lizzy's housing problem because he was desperately in love with her.

-*-

Lizzy watched as several emotions skittered across Roman's face. The realization hit his was a face she knew as well as her own. It was as if she knew what he was thinking. Her heart surged when he'd said, 'I'm proud of you.' Words she didn't remember hearing in her twenty-seven years.

Gazing into Roman's blue eyes, Lizzy realized

she was falling in love with him. Scratch that. She'd fallen in love and hadn't wanted to admit it. After Dylan's abandonment, she'd closed her heart to concentrate on raising Abby. But God had shown through His word and her sketches Roman was the one.

Her emotions rocked with this new revelation. Roman hadn't actually said he loved her. He'd only shown it by his actions. If he didn't feel the same, her heart would be shattered. Sweat tickled her underarms as she watched Roman from under her eyelashes. She'd have to figure out a way to see if his feelings matched hers.

Roman took her home and dropped her at the front door of the house. "Want me to bring Abby home?"

A plan began to form in Lizzy's head. "No, it's okay. I'll come over and get her."

"But my mom—"

"It's fine. Drive us around the corner to your place. I'll get out there."

Roman shook his head but did as she asked.

Inside Roman's house, Lizzy slipped off her sweater and hung it on a hook by the door. Maria jumped to her feet and grabbed Lizzy in a warm hug. Abby ran from the kitchen and hugged her legs.

"We had homemade macaroni and cheese. It was awesome." Abby's mouth still showed evidence of her meal.

"I can see that." Lizzy ruffled her daughter's hair.

After kissing both cheeks, she said, "I am glad

you are back. Look what I found today." Maria swept a hand over the magazines displayed on the coffee table.

"Wow," Lizzy responded.

Rory stood. "If there's gonna be a bunch of girl talk, I'm leaving." He headed into the kitchen.

"I'll go with you," Abby said. "Mom, can Rory give me a snack?"

"Sure, Bug. But nothing sweet, okay?"

"Okay." Abby followed Roman's brother into the kitchen while Roman stood in the entry, frozen.

"Roman, I would like a cup of coffee," Lizzy said. "Would you mind making some of the amazing stuff you buy online?"

"Uh, sure." Roman's movements were jerky as he stepped into the kitchen behind his brother. Soon Lizzy heard the beans being ground and smelled the fragrance of her favorite brew.

Lizzy sank to the floor in front of the coffee table as Maria returned to the couch. Bud wore noise-canceling headphones and seemed to be watching something on his iPad.

"Where are Rose and the girls?" Lizzy asked.

"They're back at the Air B & B. Packing. We're leaving tomorrow."

"I'm sorry to hear. Well, since our time is short, let's take a look at those magazines. Is someone in your family getting married soon?"

Maria's face suffused with color. "No, no. But I think it is fun to look at magazines, yes?"

"Yes. I've never been married. When I do eventually get married, I want all the stuff. White dress, flowers, three-tiered cake. You know, everything."

Maria beamed. "Yes. Let us hope you find that special someone for you and your little girl."

Lizzy and Roman's mom dug into the bridal magazines. Maria dogeared several pages as they thumbed through the photos. Roman returned to the living room holding two mugs of coffee.

"Thanks," Lizzy said, smiling up at him. "Coffee for you, Maria?"

Roman's mom shook her head. "No, no. Coffee at night keeps me awake."

"Not me. Roman and I often share a cup or two in the evenings. He's probably the only one I know who dares have caffeine at night."

Roman perched on the edge of the sofa and eyed Lizzy over the rim of his cup. His expression held a mixture of confusion and frustration. Lizzy resisted the urge to pat his leg and tell him everything would be all right.

Lizzy finished the last of her coffee and stood. "I better get my daughter home. It's a school night."

Maria nudged Bud and motioned for him to remove the headphones. They stood in unison and came around to embrace her.

Maria took both of Lizzy's hands in hers. "I am *eccitato* to meet you and to know you are a friend for my Romano."

Lizzy grabbed her in a hug. "I'm happy I got to meet you." Her throat closed with unshed tears. She loved this woman already.

-*-

Roman couldn't find words as he watched Lizzy interact with his mom. What was happening?

Why was Lizzy allowing Mom to sweep her into all this wedding talk? He shook his head and drained his cup.

Rory plopped onto the sofa next to his mom. "Got everything arranged for the nonexistent wedding?"

Maria sniffed. "I am honoring Roman's boundaries. Lizzy and I merely looked at magazines."

Roman let himself relax for the first time that evening. "I appreciate it, Mom."

Rory shrugged. "Whatever."

Dad lumbered to his feet and glanced around the room at them. "I'm going to bed."

After his dad disappeared down the hall, Mom focused his laser gaze on Roman. "My dear son. You need to make sure you tell Lizzy how you feel before she gets a notion and moves on."

The tension was back, tightening Roman's shoulders and making his stomach churn.

Roman cringed as Mom stepped closer. When she was in full-on Italian Mama mode, she was a force to be reckoned with. Rory sank onto the sofa with a grin, clearly ready to enjoy the show.

"Romano, if you let the *signorina* get away, I will disown you. You better tell this girl how you feel, and I mean pronto." Mom shook her finger under Roman's nose. "It is obvious you're in love with her, and my Italian mama's sixth sense says she feels the same."

Roman glanced at Rory to see him grinning at him.

"I think I need to move a bit more slowly,

Mama. I'm not sure Lizzy—"

Mom's chest heaved with fury. "*Primero*, you go tomorrow, and you buy the biggest ring you can find. *Segundo*, you go to her house, and you get down on one knee and you tell her you can't live without her."

Roman glanced at Rory, who was struggling not to laugh. Mom turned on him and pointed. "Rory, you be quiet." That scared him enough to resume a straight face.

Mom turned back to Roman. "*Capisci?*"

Roman hung his head. "Yes, Mom, I understand."

Mom stalked down the hall to the guest bedroom. Roman swept a hand across his forehead in an exaggerated gesture before dropping onto the sofa.

"Nice going, Ro," said Rory with a grin.

"Thanks for having my back, bro," Roman said sarcastically.

"Any time. Any time."

Roman escaped to the sanctuary of his bedroom to process the evening. Mom was like a hurricane, flattening everything in its path. But not in a bad way. She did have a point. He'd lost his heart to Lizzy. If Mom was right, and Lizzy did feel the same way, was it too soon to bust out a ring and a proposal?

The memory of Shayna's betrayal still stung. He'd done and said all the right things, from the proposal to the wedding plans to the honeymoon trip. When it shattered like crystal, he'd struggled with depression over her rejection. What if Lizzy thought he wasn't good enough. What if she wanted something he wasn't able to give her.

Millie nuzzled his hand, begging for a tummy rub. Roman absently stroked her soft fur, talking to God about what he should do.

The next morning Roman waved goodbye to his family as they pulled away from his house with thrown kisses. He took his mom's advice and rode his bike into the quaint downtown section of Main. The jewelry store was tucked between a bar and a thrift shop.

He stepped into the store, shaking off the cold from his ride, and was immediately greeted by a gray-haired matronly-looking woman.

"How can I help you today?" Her glasses hung on a heavy gold chain.

"I'm – I'm, um, looking for an engagement ring."

The woman beamed up at him. "Wonderful. I'm Martha and I'll be happy to help you." She led him to a glass case along one side of the store. "First, tell me a little about your lady so I'll know what to show you."

Roman closed his eyes for a moment, picturing Lizzy. "She's not too tall. Maybe five-four." He saw her constantly drooping ponytail. "She's kind of messy."

Martha chuckled. "Nothing too formal."

"Right. She has small hands."

Martha showed Roman several styles and different types of gems. "Some women prefer something less traditional. The latest fashion is to have something other than a diamond."

Roman concentrated on Lizzy's style. Perhaps she would like something trendy. Or not. After becoming nearly cross-eyed with choices, Roman still hadn't decided.

Martha removed her glasses. "I may have something which will work. It came in last week. I haven't had a chance to put it on display." She locked the cabinet and disappeared through a door in the back of the store.

Roman wandered to the front and stared out the window. Rain had begun to fall, and his bike was soaked. He'd be soaked as well on the ride home.

Way to go, genius, his inner geek said. *You should have driven.*

Martha returned and called Roman back to the engagement ring display. She pulled out a black velvet mat and set the ring on it. "This is rose gold. It's become more traditional in the past couple of years. White gold means friendship and yellow gold means fidelity. Rose gold has a romantic quality to it, especially for an engagement ring."

Roman picked up the ring and turned it this way and that. The almost round cut diamond was held by four prongs with tiny diamonds on all four sides near the band. The band itself was plain rose gold. Roman's breath caught. This was the one. He smiled.

"I'll take it."

Martha beamed. "Let me get a box."

Roman rode his bike home in the downpour, not minding the soaking. Nothing could dampen his excitement over finding the perfect ring. All he needed now was the courage to do a proper proposal.

-*-

"Today's the day, Bug," Lizzy said as she gathered Abby's hair into a ponytail.

Abby bounced up and down. "When can we go, Mom?"

"Be still for two seconds. The lottery isn't until seven. We'll leave around six-thirty or so, okay?"

Lizzy finished with Abby's now lop-sided pony and dropped her arms. "Let's get you to school."

"Will Roman be there tonight too?"

"The whole town will be there, Bug." Lizzy hadn't seen Roman since his parents and siblings returned home. She bit her lips, wondering if he was avoiding her. Anyway, she'd see him tonight. Excitement bubbled in her tummy over the outcome of the house lottery. It would be super cool if she won.

The hours at work crawled by with excruciating slowness. When she was finally finished with her shift, it was like being released from prison. With her shorter hours, Lizzy could dash home and freshen up before picking Abby up from after-school daycare.

As she walked through the front door, her phone buzzed with a text.

Simone: **What are you going to wear?**

Lizzy: **IDK. You?**

Simone: shrugging emoji

Lizzy searched through her closet, rejecting

outfit after outfit. She finally settled on a sea green maxi dress with a black sweater over it. The rain stopped, so she put on a pair of low-heeled sandals that had seen better days. She hoped no one would notice the scuffed soles.

After adding a light dusting of neutral eye shadow, she pulled her hair from its scrunchie and ran a brush through the tangles. There was enough time to use the curling iron to make some fat curls before picking up Abby.

Satisfied with her look, Lizzy drove to the school, then made a quick turn into the McDonald's drive-through.

"Really? McDonald's?" Abby squealed with excitement over the rare treat.

They couldn't afford it, but Lizzy was too nervous to cook, much less eat.

At home, Lizzy used the time to brush Abby's hair and form a French braid down her back. Abby picked out a purple dress and black leggings.

Abby spun in a circle while Lizzy complimented her daughter's outfit. "You look beautiful, Ladybug." She pulled Abby into a hug. "Tonight, we'll find out who is the big winner."

Abby rested her hands on Lizzy's cheeks. "I hope it's us."

"Me too, Bug. Me too."

Chapter 21

Roman brushed the dust from the shoulders of his one sports jacket. The last time he'd worn it was a distant memory. Paired with a pair of dark slacks and a white shirt, he should be suitably dressed for the announcement of the house lottery winner.

He cracked open the black box and took another look at the ring nestled there before tucking it into his pocket. Nerves bounced like jumping beans in his stomach. Forget about eating. He'd do it later, after the announcement. Hopefully in celebration of Lizzy's win. In a nice quiet place where no one could watch.

He pulled out his phone and sent a text to Lizzy.

Want a ride?

Her answer came quickly.

Sure. Thanks.

Roman**: Be there in 10.**

He took one last glance in the mirror. Satisfied there was enough product in his hair to keep it off his face, he strode to the kitchen. Grabbing his wallet and keys, he headed into the garage, then backtracked into the house to get his cell phone.

I know, I know, he said to his inner geek before it could speak.

Lizzy and Abby opened the front door as Roman pulled up to the front of her house. Lizzy adjusted her glasses before turning to lock the door. Abby bounced to the car and climbed into the back seat.

"Hi, Roman."

Before he could answer, Lizzy opened the passenger door and sank into the seat in a cloud of fragrance.

"You look nice," Roman said.

Lizzy smoothed down her dress with one hand. "You think this is okay for tonight?"

"It's more than okay." Roman patted the pocket of his jacket, too aware of the small box there. "Are you ready to win?" he asked, pulling away from the house.

Lizzy exhaled with a *whoosh.* "I think so."

"My mom and dad want a text as soon as we know the results. Will your mom be there tonight?"

Lizzy's mouth turned down. "No. She has to work."

"I'm sorry about that."

"Yeah, me too. I gave her plenty of time to change shifts with someone. She doesn't think I'm going to win anyway. It's probably why she didn't try very hard."

"My dad won't be there either," Abby piped up from the back seat.

Roman and Lizzy exchanged glances.

Everyone was silent on the way to the

community center. Even Abby must have felt the tension. For once, she didn't fill the silence with chatter.

The community center buzzed with excited conversation. A table had been set up at the front of the room for the five potential winners. A metal basket resembling a bingo cage sat at one end. Spectators stood in groups of four or five, smiling and drinking coffee. Roman grimaced. He promised himself he wouldn't grab a cup of the awful stuff, so he'd have something to do with his hands.

Roman glanced around the room and nodded to a few people he recognized from church. "Looks like the whole town is here," he commented.

Lizzy rubbed her upper arms then hugged them to her chest. "I'm so nervous I could throw up."

Roman placed a hand on her shoulder. "You'll be fine. This will all be over in less than an hour."

"Do you mind sitting with Abby?" Lizzy asked.

"It's Abigail"

"Not now, Bug," Lizzy warned. "Go with Roman and mind your manners."

Abby huffed, then took Roman's hand. "C'mon. Let's go find a seat."

He allowed himself to be pulled toward the front row. "I'll be praying," Roman said over his shoulder.

-*-

Lizzy spied Simone talking to her fiancé, Adam. She made her way through the crowd as friends from church and the community wished her luck.

"Simone! Finally. It took me a minute to get to you," Lizzy exclaimed.

The two women hugged while Adam grinned. "I hope this doesn't affect your friendship if one of you is the winner."

Lizzy hoped the same thing. Of course, she'd be happy if her best friend won. Maybe Simone would let her stay at the house while Lizzy looked for a new place to live.

"I'll be right back," Adam said, squeezing Simone's hand. "I see someone I need to talk to." He threaded through the mass of people toward a man in a business suit.

Simone rolled her eyes. "That's my man. Always networking. Anyway, how are you?"

"I'm nervous," Lizzy answered. "I wish it was over."

Before Simone could respond, Mariah joined them.

"Hi, ladies." She greeted them with a tentative smile.

Simone glared at her with narrowed eyes.

"Oh, hi," Lizzy said. *Awkward.*

"I wanted to say good luck to both of you," Mariah said.

"Huh," huffed Simone.

"Thanks, Mariah. You too." Lizzy smiled.

"Okay, well, Mayor Dorgan wants us at the table in the front." Mariah turned and headed toward the front of the room.

"What was that all about," Simone hissed. "Why were you being nice to her?"

"I'll tell you after," Lizzy said, grabbing her friend's arm and dragging her along.

When the five finalists were seated at the head table, Mayor Dorgan stood and banged his gavel on the podium stationed at the front of the room.

"Attention everyone. Please find a seat and let's get this party started."

Murmuring and shuffling gradually came to a halt. Mayor Dorgan spoke into the microphone. "Let me explain how this is going to work. There are five numbered balls in the cage. Each of our essay winners will be given a number from one to five. Once completed, our City Manager will twirl the cage and when it stops, one ball will roll out. He or she will be our winner."

There was some murmuring and whispering from the crowd.

"First, let me congratulate again the excellent writing of these five contestants. We are blessed to have such talent amongst our community."

The mayor droned on. Lizzy wiped her sweaty hands on her thighs. She could hardly hear beyond the pounding in her head. Mariah smiled at her from across the table, while Simone grabbed her hand and squeezed.

While Mayor Dorgan finished up his speech, the City Manager handed each of them a folded piece of paper. Lizzy disentangled her hand from Simone's and opened her paper with shaking hands. She'd been given the number four.

Simone turned hers a little in Lizzy's direction. Simone was number one. Lizzy glanced over to Mariah, who mouthed the number three.

Mayor Dorgan reminded the crowd of the lottery rules. "As you know, the winner must live in the house for at least a year. All back property taxes must be paid. There are some cosmetic improvements to be done both outside and inside."

There was more, but Lizzy stopped listening as she glanced around the community center. People stood in the back, along the sides, and a few filled the aisles. Every seat was taken. She saw Simone's family and Mariah's family. Other than Abby and Roman, she had no one there to cheer her on. Her mom couldn't be bothered. If she and Roman were together, she'd bet her next paycheck his whole family would be in attendance.

With a sigh, she turned her attention back to the mayor.

"And now, without any further delay, let's do this!" He stepped away from the podium and gave a nod to the City Manager, who spun the basket with a flourish.

"Oh, Lord, help me," Lizzy whispered. If her number four was called, she'd own a house. She'd never have to worry about living in her car with Abby. There'd never be any threat of eviction or having her home sold out from under her like her current situation.

Lizzy's thoughts spun like the five white balls in the cage. She looked across the room to see Roman's eyes focused on her. She smiled. Her heart had been closed for such a long time, she hadn't wanted to let him get close in case he abandoned her like Abby's dad. But she knew now she loved Roman and could see herself spending the rest of her life with him.

Lizzy decided as the cage slowed its revolutions. No matter how this turned out, the minute she could get up from the table, she would tell him how she felt.

One of the balls rolled down the chute as the cage stopped. The City Manager grabbed the ball before anyone could see which number was written on it. He focused his attention on it, then raised it high like a trophy.

"The winner is … Number Three!"

Mariah gasped, then burst into tears.

"I don't believe it," Simone said with a grimace.

Lizzy stood and leaned across the table. "Congratulations, Mariah. I am happy for you."

Mariah's family mobbed her with hugs and kisses. Simone's mom and dad threaded their way through the crowd to commiserate.

Mayor Dorgan thanked everyone for coming and tried to make a closing speech, but no one listened. He couldn't be heard over the commotion anyway.

Lizzy turned to find Roman and Abby a few steps away. Her stomach jumped when she saw the sympathy in his eyes. Abby moved in for a hug.

"I'm sorry, Mom. I really wanted you to win."

"It's okay, Ladybug. God's got this." Lizzy looked up at Roman, who moved closer.

"I have something …" Lizzy said.

"I have something …" Roman said.

They both laughed.

"You first." They said at the same time.

Lizzy licked her dry lips. "I want to say something. I hope you're okay with it." She had a moment of indecision as she looked down at Abby's expectant face. Lizzy had always put Abby first, and now she was thinking about herself. What if this went wrong? If she and Roman got together, would Abby want to go live with her dad?

Lizzy had a sudden urge to dash outside and run all the way home.

Roman pulled her into a hug. "Whatever you're going to say, it's okay."

Lizzy leaned into him, savoring the feeling of being held. He smelled of spice and soap. "What I want to say is…" the words stuck in her throat. "Well—"

Roman pushed away, holding Lizzy's shoulders. She looked up at him and saw the emotions running over his face.

Lizzy took a deep breath. "I love you." There. She'd said it and the world hadn't come to an end.

Roman looked stunned. "Really?"

Lizzy's eyes filled with tears as she smiled at him. "Yes."

"That's …" Roman grabbed her in a bear hug and swung her around.

Abby squealed and threw her arms around them. "Does this mean you and Roman can get married now?"

Lizzy noticed the crowd closest to them had gone silent as Roman pulled away. He reached into his jacket pocket and pulled out a black box. While everyone around them watched, he knelt on one knee and opened the box.

Holding it aloft, he said, "Elizabeth Greene, will you marry me?"

The onlookers gave a collective sigh as Lizzy burst into tears. "Yes!"

Roman stood and removed the ring, sliding it onto Lizzy's finger.

"Let me see!" Abby said, pulling on Lizzy's arm.

Lizzy had never seen anything more perfect. The diamond sparkled in the fluorescent lights of the community center.

Roman pulled her close, then gently kissed her. Lizzy felt every nerve ending tingle from her head to the tips of her toes. At that moment, nothing else existed except Roman's lips on hers.

Epilogue:

Lizzy turned this way and that, examining herself in the full-length mirror tacked to the closet door.

"You look amazing," Mariah said, straightening Lizzy's veil.

Simone wiped a tear from her eye. "I can't believe you're getting married before me."

Lizzy smiled. "It did happen fast, didn't it?" She reached for two small gift bags on the tall dresser. "I have a little something for you ladies." Lizzy handed a bag to each of them. While they dug through the tissue, Lizzy continued. "Simone, you've been my best friend for as long as I can remember. Thank you for staying with me through all my crazy ups and downs. I love you like a sister."

Simone reached in and hugged Lizzy.

"I love you too, Lizzy."

"Mariah, I never thought we could be friends. I've envied you since you got your first bra. Thank you for reaching out and taking a chance. I can't thank you enough for letting me stay with you for the past few months. I know you'll fill this house with lots of kids who need a temporary home."

Mariah dabbed at her eyes. "Don't make me cry. I'll ruin my makeup."

Typical Mariah. But now Lizzy understood the other woman's insecurities. Deep inside they were much the same.

Abby burst into the room in her pink lace gown. "Look at me! I'm a princess." She whirled around as the women laughed.

"Come on, let's get a move on," Simone said. "You don't want to be late for your wedding."

Simone and Mariah gathered up the train of Lizzy's dress as they made their way through the living room and out the front door. It had rained earlier in the morning, leaving the air crisp and clear. Roman had arranged a limo, and it sat idling in front of the house. A driver wearing a jaunty cap jumped out of the car and opened the passenger door.

He tipped his hat and bowed. "Good afternoon, ladies."

Abby giggled as the women climbed in. She bounced from one seat of the luxurious interior to the other. "I've never been in a limo before. This is cool."

Lizzy agreed. As much as she enjoyed the short ride to the church, her heart was already at the altar, saying her vows and marrying her best friend.

They arrived at the church and Simone's mom ushered them into a side room where they would wait for the ceremony to begin. She fussed around Lizzy, fluffing her gown and straightening her veil.

"Your mama is in her seat," Danielle said. "I better dash. It's my turn now."

Simone handed Lizzy the bouquet of yellow roses. Lizzy had chosen yellow because it represented friendship. She'd been blessed with Simone, her best friend from childhood, and two new friends, Mariah and Roman.

"Okay, sweetie, this is it," Simone said, bending down and kissing Abby's head. "You're the best flower girl ever."

Abby grinned, then picked up her basket and headed for the door to the church.

"You ready, girlfriend?" Simone asked.

Lizzy took a deep breath. "Yes." She was ready. She'd finally opened her heart to love. Roman had come along at exactly the right time. God was faithful to show her a new future with an amazing man.

Nothing could steal her joy today. Not even the fact after a couple of days spent with Lizzy's mom, Abby would spend the rest of the week with Dylan. They hadn't finished how joint custody would work, but at least he hadn't flaked out.

Mariah sent Lizzy an air kiss as she exited the room. The processional music continued its slow beat. Simone grabbed Lizzy in one last hug as she followed moments later.

Lizzy made her way to the door of the church. The wedding march grew louder as she stepped from the doorway to begin the long walk down the aisle to where her love waited.

-*-

Roman was sure he would either pass out or

throw up as he waited for Lizzy to appear in the doorway of the church. Abby had successfully fulfilled her duty by tossing yellow rose petals down the center aisle. Mariah and Simone had made their excruciatingly slow ascent and now stood on his right.

He glanced at Rory, who gave him a toothy grin. His cousin, Eric stood to Rory's left.

Finally, the music changed. Lizzy stood in the doorway in her wedding finery. Roman sucked in a breath as if he'd been punched in the solar plexus. Lizzy's hair tumbled around her shoulders in large curls beneath the gauzy veil. How had he managed to capture the heart of this gorgeous creature?

Roman watched her take a few steps toward the front. She had no one to walk her down the aisle. She must be terrified of tripping in the floor-dusting dress. He had a sudden urge to run to Lizzy's side, holding her arm to keep her from falling.

How weird would it be? People would stare, that's for sure.

Do it, his inner geek said.

Huh? Was his inner geek trying to make him look bad?

Do it, Romeo, it repeated.

Roman inhaled as if he was going underwater, then strode down the aisle. He stopped in front of Lizzy, smiled, then turned and took her arm.

"Let's do this together," he whispered.

THE END

About the author

Do you like great stories that won't make you cringe?

Do you want to read about women who overcome life's challenges, without sex, violence, and politics?

Then you've come to the right place!

Jane writes books for women who need answers to the "why" question in the context of suffering and loss.

When she's not hunched over her computer, she can be found traveling the United States in her Motor Home. Follow her on <u>Amazon</u>